I0592333

James Lackington

Memoirs of the First Forty-Five Years of the Life of James Lackington

James Lackington

Memoirs of the First Forty-Five Years of the Life of James Lackington

ISBN/EAN: 9783337094935

Printed in Europe, USA, Canada, Australia, Japan

Cover: Foto ©Andreas Hilbeck / pixelio.de

More available books at **www.hansebooks.com**

MEMOIRS

OF

The First FORTY-FIVE YEARS

OF

The LIFE

OF

JAMES LACKINGTON,

The present Bookseller in Chiswell-street, Moorfields, London.

Written by Himself.

In FORTY-SIX LETTERS to a FRIEND.

With a TRIPLE DEDICATION.

1. To the PUBLIC.
2. To RESPECTABLE } BOOKSELLERS.
3. To SORDID } BOOKSELLERS.

A NEW EDITION,

Corrected, and much enlarged; interspersed with many *original humourous* Stories, and *droll* Anecdotes.

" No youth did I in education waste;
" Happily I'd an intuitive *Taste*:
" Writing ne'er cramp'd the sinews of my thumb,
" No barb'rous birch did ever brush my b——.
" My guts ne'er suffer'd from a college cook,
" My name ne'er enter'd in a buttery book.
" Grammar in vain the sons of Priscian teach;
" Good parts are better than eight parts of speech.
" Since these declin'd, those undeclin'd they call;
" I thank my stars, that I declin'd them all.
" To Greek or Latin tongues without pretence,
" I trust to Mother Wit and Father Sense.
" Nature's my guide; all pedantry I scorn;
" Pains I abhor, I was an Author born."

" ———such the vanity of great and small,
" Contempt goes round, and all men laugh at all."

LONDON:

Printed for the AUTHOR, No. 46 and 47, Chiswell-Street; and sold by all other Booksellers.

MDCCXCII.

[Price 5s. in Boards.]

A TRIPLE DEDICATION:

1. TO THE PUBLIC.

"In things indiff'rent Reason bids us chuse,
"Whether the whim's a monkey or a muse."
CHURCHILL.

WORTHY PATRONS,

WERE I to address you in the accustomed declamatory strain which has long been adopted as the *universal language* of dedications, viz. FLATTERY, I should not only merit your contempt, for thus endeavouring to impose upon your understandings, but also render myself ridiculously conspicuous, by a feeble attempt to perform that; for which, as well by nature as long established habit, I am totally disqualified.

On the other hand, I should esteem myself equally meriting your censure, as being guilty of a flagrant species of ingratitude, were I to omit availing myself of so favourable an op-

 portunity

portunity as now preſents itſelf of expreſſing the reſpect and veneration I entertain for you, reſulting from the very extenſive and ample encouragement with which you have crowned my indefatigable exertions to obtain your patronage, by largely contributing to the diffuſion of ſcience and rational entertainment, on ſuch moderate terms as were heretofore unknown.

Permit me to indulge the pleaſing hope, that when I aſſert my mind is deeply impreſſed with the moſt grateful ſenſe of the obligation, I ſhall be honoured with credit. If this opinion be well founded, to enlarge on the ſubject were ſuperfluous—if otherwiſe, the ſtrongeſt arguments, the moſt ſplendid and forcible language could convey, would not enſure conviction; I therefore deſiſt, fully perſuaded that the moſt ſatisfactory demonſtration I can poſſibly exhibit of the ſincerity of this declaration, will be, an inviolable adherence to that uniform line of

conduct

conduct which has already secured your approbation to a degree eminent as unprecedented, and which is indeed daily rendered more evident, by a progressive increase in the number and extent of your commands; trusting, that so long as you find my practice invariably correspondent to those professions so frequently exhibited to your notice (from which to deviate would render me unworthy your protection) you will, in defiance of all malignant opposition, firmly persevere in the liberal support of him whose primary ambition it is, and during life shall be, to distinguish himself as,

WORTHY PATRONS,

Your much obliged,

Ever grateful,

And devoted humble servant,

Chiswell-Street,
October 1791.

JAMES LACKINGTON.

2. To that part of the numerous body of BOOKSELLERS of Great Britain and Ireland, whoſe conduct JUSTLY claims the additional title of RESPECTABLE;

Whoſe candour and liberality he has in numerous inſtances experienced, and feels a ſenſible pleaſure in thus publicly acknowledging.

And laſtly (though not leaſt in *Fame*)

3. To thoſe ſordid and malevolent BOOKSELLERS, whether they reſplendent dwell in ſtately manſions, or in wretched huts of dark and grovelling obſcurity;

—"I'll give every one a ſmart laſh in my way."—

To whoſe aſſiduous and unwearied labours to injure his reputation with their brethren and the public, he is in a conſiderable degree indebted for the confidence repoſed in him, and the ſucceſs he has been honoured with, productive of his preſent proſperity,

THESE MEMOIRS

are, with all due diſcrimination of the reſpective merits of each,

Inſcribed by

THE AUTHOR.

PREFACE.

"To print, or not to print?—that is the queſtion:
"Whether 'tis better in a trunk to bury
"The quirks and crochets of outrageous fancy,
"Or ſend a well-wrote copy to the preſs,
"And, by diſcloſing, end them?———
——— ——— ——— ———
"For who would bear th' impatient thirſt of fame,
"The pride of conſcious merit, and 'bove all,
"The tedious importunity of friends——
——— ——— ——— ———
"To groan and ſweat under a load of wit?
——— ——— ——— ———
"The Critics do make cowards of us all." JAGO.

CUSTOM, it has been repeatedly obſerved by many of my worthy (and ſome perhaps *unworthy)* predeceſſors in authorſhip, has rendered a preface almoſt indiſpenſibly neceſſary; while others again have as frequently remarked, that "*cuſtom is the law of fools.*" Thoſe conſiderations induced me to heſitate whether I ſhould uſher my performance into the world with a preface, and thus hazard

hazard being claſſed with the adherents to that law, or by omitting it, eſcape the opprobrium, for "*who ſhall decide when doctors diſagree?*" Now though I would not take upon me to decide in every point in which doctors diſagree, yet after giving the preſent ſubject that mature conſideration which ſo important a concern required, I thought myſelf fully competent to decide, if not to general ſatisfaction, at leaſt ſo as fully to ſatisfy one particular perſon, for whom I profeſs to have a very great regard, though perhaps few are to be found who would be equally condeſcending to him; who that perſon is I do not wiſh publicly to declare, as (being a very modeſt man) it might offend him, I ſhall only ſay, the more you read the memoirs contained in the following pages, the better you will become acquainted with him. I ground my deciſion on theſe arguments: I concluded, as moſt of my brethren of the quill do of their labours, that my

per-

performance poſſeſſed ſo much intrinſic merit, as would occaſion it to be univerſally admired by all good judges, as a prodigious effort of human genius, and that this approbation muſt naturally excite the envy of ſome authors, who had not met with that high applauſe they deemed themſelves entitled to, and incline them to ſearch for imperfections in my work, and though I was perſuaded of the impoſſibility of their finding any, yet being thus foiled, they might catch at the want of a preface, and conſtrue *that* into an omiſſion, ſo that in order to diſarm them, I reſolved to have one, eſpecially as thoſe who deem prefaces unneceſſary may, if they chooſe, decline reading it, whilſt thoſe on the other ſide of the queſtion, if there was none, might be diſappointed, and have cauſe for complaint; but to be ſerious (if I can).

Almoſt every author on producing the effuſions of his pen (and his brain if he has any)

any) thinks it prudent to introduce himſelf by a kind of *Prologue,* as it may be called, ſtating his reaſons with due preciſion for intruding himſelf on his readers (whether true or otherwiſe, is not always material to enquire) beſpeaking their candour towards his weakneſſes and imperfections (which by the bye, few authors are ſo ſenſible of as their readers) and not unfrequently endeavouring to ſoothe thoſe GOLIAHS in literature, ycleped *critics,* (with whom not many little Davids are found hardy enough to contend) hoping thus to coax them into good humour; or, perhaps, if his vanity preponderates, he throws the gauntlet of defiance, with a view of terrifying them either to hold their peace, or to do juſtice to thoſe mighty abilities *he* is confident he poſſeſſes in a degree eminently ſuperior to moſt of his brethren.

For my own part, I diſclaim adopting either of theſe modes: convinced, that in the first case, every reader, whatever the author may plead, will, (and indeed ought) to judge for himself; and with regard to professed critics, were I so disposed (which I am not) neither my natural or acquired abilities enable me to *bully* those who must be very ill qualified for their task, if they were thus to be intimidated from declaring their real sentiments; and, on the other hand, to affect a degree of humility, and by flattery to aim at warping their minds, is, in my opinion, paying them a very bad compliment.

So much for others—now for myself:

Never should I have ventured to appear in this habit before the public, had not the following motives urged me thereto:

Many friends have frequently expressed a desire of obtaining from myself such particulars as they could rely on, of my passage through life, and many enemies (for such I have in common with other men, from the monarch down to the poor cobler) have been induſtrious in propagating whatever reports they thought would beſt tend to impede my farther progreſs; among the reſt, the editors of a periodical publication now on the decline (whether deſervedly or not, let others determine) thought proper to exhibit me as they have done many much more eminent and diſtinguiſhed characters, in a literary portrait, containing a few outlines it is true, but with ſome features which they muſt have known to be falſe.

After having been repeatedly *threatened* by a very particular friend and others, that if I declined drawing up a narrative, they were determined to do it for me, the firſt mentioned gentleman prevailed on me (as the moſt likely mode to bring it to a period) to devote now and then a ſpare hour in minuting down ſome of the moſt material occurrences of my life, and to ſend them to him in an epiſtolary form, intending to digeſt

the

the whole into a regular narrative for publication; that gentleman, however, on perusal, was of opinion, that it would be additionally acceptable to the curious part of the public, if exhibited to them in the plain and simple manner in which these letters were written, as thus tending to display such traits and features of a somewhat original character, and give a more perfect idea of "I, great I, the little hero of each tale," than any other mode that could have been adopted; especially, as many *intelligent* persons were confident I could not write at all, while others *kindly* attributed to me what I never wrote.

——————"Then think,
"That he who thus is forc'd to speak,
"Unless commanded, would have dy'd in silence".

If among the multitude of memoirs under which the press has groaned, and with which it still continues to be tortured, the following sheets should afford some degree of *of entertainment*, as a relaxation from more *grave and solid studies*, to an inquisitive and *candid reader* (those of an opposite description are not to be pleased with the ablest performance) and he should deem it not the worst, nor the most expensive among the numerous tribe, I shall esteem myself amply rewarded; had I, however, been disposed to be more attentive to entertainment, and less to veracity, I might, to many, have rendered it much more agreeable, though less satisfactory to myself, as I believe the observation long since made to be just, that few books are so ill written, but that something may be gleaned from their perusal.

Should the insignificance of *my* life induce any person better qualified to present the world with *his*, big with interesting events, my disposing of several large editions of that performance will afford me more *solid* satisfaction as a *bookseller*, than any success or emolument which can possibly arise from this, my first, and most probably last, essay as an *author*.

If unfortunately any of my kind readers should find the book so *horrid dull* and *stupid*, that they cannot get through it, or if they do, and wish not to travel the same road again, I here declare my perfect readiness to supply them with abundance of books, much more learned, much more entertaining, much more witty, much more —— whatever they please, they never shall want books while L. is able to assist them; and whether they prefer one of his writing, or that of any other author, he protests he will not be in the smallest degree offended: let every author make the same declaration if he can.

Should my memoirs be attended with no other benefit to society, they will at least tend to shew what may be effected by a persevering habit of industry, and an upright conscientious demeanour in trade towards the public, and probably inspire some-one, of perhaps superior abilities, with a laudable ambition, to emerge from obscurity, by a proper application of those talents with which Providence has favoured him, to his own credit and emolument, as well as the benefit of the community. To such an one I ever have, and ever shall wish every possible success, as it has uniformly been my opinion, that whatever is thus acquired, is more honourable to the parties than the possession of wealth obtained without any intrinsic merit or exertion, and which is too frequently consumed with rapidity in the pursuit of vice and dissipation.

One word to my old *friends* the booksellers under *number three* of my dedication. This publication it is to be expected will tend to excite some degree of mirth in them. Conscious that I have often been the cause (however unintentional on my part) of exciting less pleasing sensations in them, I will readily allow them full scope; however, according to the well known adage, "Let

"them

them laugh who [illegible] I hope they will indulge in the same propensity to laughing, if not at them, at least *with* them. As a proof of my friendly disposition, I shall here add a piece of advice which I do not hesitate to pronounce will, if attended to, entitle them to promotion in my *first* class of booksellers, and equally prove beneficial to them: a constant perseverance in the mode of conduct they have hitherto pursued; and those who have children will, I hope, see the propriety of inculcating the same doctrine to them for their future benefit: as I do flatter myself my advice will prove equally productive of benefit to great numbers of the community at large as to booksellers.

If they observe any person by industry and application endeavouring to obtain an honest livelihood in that line for which his talents or disposition have qualified him, let them not attempt by dark unhandsome insinuations and false aspersions, to injure him, as, if he happens to be a man of a becoming spirit, such conduct will only tend to increase his exertions, and render him still more cautious to obtain a good character; in so doing their weapons will recoil on themselves, and they will have the mortification to see him flourish, whilst they become objects of contempt in the eyes of the public, and will of course be avoided by them.

But I forget myself, from debating whether a preface was really necessary or not. If I proceed thus, I shall produce one as long as my book, as indeed some of my seniors in authorship have done before me, though not altogether consistent with propriety.

I will therefore conclude with a wish that my readers may enjoy the feast with the same good humour with which I have prepared it; they will meet with some *solid* though not much *coarse* food, and the major part, I hope, light and easy of digestion; those with keen appetites will partake of each dish, while others more delicate may select such dishes as are more light, and better adapted to their palates; they are all genuine British fare, one dish of French constitution *ragout* excepted. But lest they should be at a loss to know what the entertainment consists of, I beg leave to inform them that it contains forty-six dishes of various sizes, which (if they calculate the expence of their *admission tickets*) they will find does not amount to *three halfpence* per dish; and what I hope they will consider as *immensely* valuable (in compliance with the precedent of a modern author, eminent in the culinary science,) a striking likeness of their *Cook* into the bargain.

I have also prepared a bill of fare; turn over this leaf, and you will find it. Ladies and Gentlemen, pray be seated; you are heartily welcome, and much good may it do you.

CONTENTS.

CONTENTS.

LETTER

LETTER VI.

LETTER VII.

LETTER VIII.

LETTER IX.

LETTER X.

LETTER XI.

LETTER XII.

LETTER

LETTER

LETTER XX.

LETTER XXI.

LETTER XXII.

LETTER XXIII.

LETTER XXIV.

LETTER XXV.

LETTER XXVI.

LETTER XXVII.

LETTER XXVIII.

LETTER XXIX.

LETTER XXXV.

LETTER XXXVI.

LETTER XL.

LETTER XLI.

LETTER XLII.

LETTER XLIII.

LETTER XLIV.

LETTER XLV.

LETTER XLVI.

PREFACE

TO THE

SECOND EDITION.

"'Tis nothing new, I'm ſure you know,
"For thoſe who write, their works to ſhow;
"And if they're prais'd, and render'd vain,
"'Tis ten to one they write again
"And then they read it o'er with care,
"Correcting here, and adding there."

Mrs. Savage.

THE former edition of my Memoirs was no ſooner publiſhed, than my old envious friends, mentioned in the third claſs of my dedication, found out that it was "d—n'd ſtuff! d—n'd low!" the production of a cobler, and only fit to amuſe that honourable fraternity, or to line their garrets and ſtalls: and many gentlemen, who are my cuſtomers, have informed me, that when they aſked for them at ſeveral ſhops, they recei-

 ved

PREFACE

TO THE

SECOND EDITION.

"'Tis nothing new, I'm ſure you know,
"For thoſe who write, their works to ſhow;
"And if they're prais'd, and render'd vain,
"'Tis ten to one they write again:
"And then they read it o'er with care,
"Correcting here, and adding there."

Mrs. Savage.

THE former edition of my Memoirs was no ſooner publiſhed, than my old envious friends, mentioned in the third claſs of my dedication, found out that it was "d—n'd ſtuff! d—n'd low!" the production of a *cobler*, and only fit to amuſe that honourable fraternity, or to line their garrets and ſtalls: and many gentlemen, who are my cuſtomers, have informed me, that when they aſked for them at ſeveral ſhops, they received for an anſwer, that they had already too much waſte paper, and would not increaſe it by keeping Lackington's Memoirs: and ſome kindly added, "You need not be in a haſte to purchaſe, as in the courſe of the Christmas holidays, Mr. Birch in Cornhill will wrap up all his mince-pies with them, and diſtribute them through the town for the public good." But the rapid ſale of this Life ſoon cauſed them to alter their ſtories: and I was very much ſurpriſed to hear that ſeveral of thoſe gentlemen, who had ſcarce done exclaiming, "Vile traſh! beneath all criticiſm!" &c. began to praiſe the compoſition; and on looking into the Engliſh Review, I found that the editors had filled ſeven pages in reviewing thoſe Memoirs, and had beſtowed much praiſe on the author. I was then ready to conclude, that their generous and manly impartiality had, in a miraculous manner, effected the converſion of others. But I was ſoon convinced, that

mean-

meanness can never be exchanged for generosity; and that those that had been "unclean were unclean still;" or, as Churchhill says,

> "That envy, which was woven in the frame
> "At first, will to the last remain the same.
> "Reason may drown, may die, but envy's rage,
> "Improves with time, and gathers strength from age."

It seems that several of those liberal-minded men, being prodigiously mortified at the encreasing sale of my Life, applied to different authors in order to get one of them to father my book: but those authors, either from principle, or from knowing that my manuscript was kept in my shop for the inspection of the public, or for some other motive, refused to adopt the poor bantling: and not only so, but laughed at, and exposed the mean contrivance, to the very great disappointment of those *kind and honest-hearted friends of mine,*

That

That I might not be justly charged with ingratitude, I take this opportunity of thanking my friends, customers, and the public for their candid reception of my volume; the sale of which, and the encomiums I have received on the subject, both by letter and otherwise, have far exceeded my most sanguine and self-flattering expectations; I very sensibly feel the obligation. Their generosity has overwhelmed me; I am overpaid, and remain their debtor.

> "A truce with jesting; what I here impart
> "Is the warm overflowings of a grateful heart;
> "Come good, come bad, while life or mem'ry last,
> "My mind shall treasure up your favours past."

But, lest I should be over vain, I must at the same time declare, that I have received scurrilous abusive letters from several of Mr. Wesley's people, merely because I have exposed their ridiculous principles and absurd practices; but more particularly, for having

pulled

pulled off the hypocritical veil from some of those sanctified deceivers which are among them.

The numerous letters of approbation which I have received from rational intelligent gentlemen, convinces me that I have not wronged the cause of manly and rational christianity, nor was it ever my intention so to do.

I here also present my compliments and sincere thanks to my impartial friends, under the second class of my dedication, for the friendly disposition they have shewn, in freely distributing my Memoirs among their customers, and they may be assured, that I will not let slip any opportunity of making them proper returns for all their favours.

I cannot conclude this Preface without saying something about this second edition.

When I put the first edition to the press, I really intended to print but a small number; so that when I was prevailed on, by

some

ſome of my friends, to print double the number which I at firſt propoſed, I had not the leaſt idea of ever being able to ſell the whole; and of courſe had not any intention of printing a ſecond edition. But the rapid ſale of the work, and the many letters which I am continually receiving from Gentlemen, in various parts of Great Britain and Ireland, who are pleaſed to honour me with their approbation and thanks, encouraged me to read the whole over with more attention, to correct ſuch typographical errors as had eſcaped my obſervation, and to improve the language in numberleſs places.

In executing this plan, I perceived that I had omitted to introduce many things which would have been an improvement to the work; and while inſerting them, others occurred to my memory, ſo that moſt parts of the work is now very much enlarged. But although theſe additions have greatly increaſed the expences of printing and paper, yet I have not added any thing to the price.

To ſuch as aſk why theſe additions had not been printed ſeperately, to the end that ſuch as purchaſed the firſt edition, might have had them without purchaſing the whole work over again? I anſwer, had it been practicable, I would have done that; but thoſe additions being ſo many, and ſo various, rendered that method ridiculous, as every one who will take the trouble to compare the two editions, muſt readily acknowledge; nor can the purchaſers of the former edition complain with reſpect to the price, it being equal in ſize to moſt new publications which are ſold at Six Shillings. And although ſome may think that the prefixed head is of no value, I can aſſure them, that I am of a very different opinion, *at leaſt of the original*; and I have the pleaſure to add, that a very great number of my cuſtomers have been highly pleaſed to have ſo ſtriking a likeneſs of their old bookſeller. Nor am I the firſt bookſeller who has publiſhed his

head;

head; Mr. Nicolson (commonly called Maps,) bookseller at Cambridge, two years since, had his head finely engraven; it is a good likeness, and is sold at 10s. 6d. Francis Kirkman, partner with Richard Hend (last century) prefixed his portrait to a book, entitled, "The Wits, or Sport upon Sport." This Francis Kirkman also published Memoirs of his own Life, and probably led the way to John Dunton. See Granger's Biographical History of England, vol. iv.

I could make many other apologies——

"—— But why should I distrust,
"My judges are as merciful as just:
"I know them well, have oft their friendship try'd,
"And their protection is my boast——my pride.

CUNNINHAM.

Occasioned by reading

THE LIFE of MR. JAMES LACKINGTON.

Addressed to the ingenious AUTHOR,

By an UNKNOWN FRIEND.

SINCE your Pen, Friend Unknown, such improvement conveys,
'Tis but justice to you that this Tribute repays;
For when in the Bosom mild Gratitude burns,
'Tis a pleasing relief which the Feeling returns:
For as dear as the Light to the thoughts of the Blind,
Is the Pen, or the Voice, that enlightens the Mind;
And the more, as from Nature and Genius untaught
Your various adventures and humour are brought,
Which display all the farce of the Methodist Plan,
The shame of Religion, of Reason, and Man;
While no Libertine Motives their Secrets dispense,
But Propriety joins hand-in-hand with good Sense.

Oh!

Oh! with thee, could the Crowd view each ſanctified ſcene,
Where the Hypocrite oft wears Simplicity's mien;
Where youth, ſecond-childhood, and weakneſs of Sex,
Are objects they ever prefer to perplex;
Like thee, they'd contemn, or indignantly leave,
Whom Folly, and Knav'ry, combine to deceive;
And whoſe Newgate-Converſions blaſphemouſly paint
The Wretch moſt *deprav'd*, the moſt *excellent* Saint.
Go on; and diſcover each latent deſign,
And your rivals expoſe, who 'gainſt Learning combine:
O'er ſuch craft ſhall fair conduct, like thine, ſtill prevail,
And an envy'd ſucceſs lay them low in the Scale.
But as Time is too ſhort all your ſteps to retrace,
Let your LIFE ſpeak the reſt, and ſucceed in their place:
How Books mend the manners; and now ſo abound,
Where Rudeneſs and Ignorance lately were found.
But plain Truth, for itſelf, it muſt ſtill be confeſt,
Is the faithfulleſt advocate—therefore the beſt:
So I riſe from the Feaſt with a ſatisfied mind,
That the ſame every Taſte, and each Temper, may find.
Still, to drop all compariſon, Mental's the fare,
That needs only good-taſte to invite us to ſhare;
Entertainment and Knowledge, the objects in view;
Then receive, as the Donor, the Praiſe that is due.

C. H——S.

BURY ST. EDMUND'S.

THE

LIFE

OF

J. LACKINGTON,

BOOKSELLER.

LETTER I.

"Others with wishful eyes on Glory look,
"When they have got their picture toward a book,
"Or pompous title, like a gaudy Sign
"Meant to betray dull sots to wretched wine,
"If at his title L—— had dropt his quill,
"L—— might have past for a great genius still.
"But L——, alas! (excuse him if you can)
"Is now a Scribbler, who was once a man.

DEAR FRIEND,

YOU, have often requested me to devote what few leisure moments I could spare, in minuting down some of the principal occurrences of my life, with a view, sooner or later, of exhibiting the account to the public eye; who, as you were pleaſed to ſay, could not but be ſomewhat curious to learn ſome well-authenticated particulars of a man, well known to have riſen from an obſcure origin to a degree of notice, and to a participation of the favor of the Public, in a particular line of buſineſs, I may without vanity ſay, hitherto unprecedented. This will appear more conſpicuous if you conſider, that I was not only poor, but laboured under every other diſadvantage.

Ever willing to pay a becoming deference to the judgment of a perſon of your acknowledged merits, and whom I have the felicity of numbering among my firmeſt friends, yet being leſs anxious to appear as an adventurer among the numerous tribe of authors, than to continue a conſiderable vender of the produce of their labours, I have continually delayed complying with your kind wiſhes.—By the bye, does the publication of a Catalogue of Books entitle the compiler to the name of *Author?* If it does, many Bookſellers

ſellers have long had a claim to that diſtinction, by the annual publication of their Catalogues, and myſelf, as *author* of a very voluminous one every ſix months. The reaſon for my aſking this queſtion is; I laſt year obſerved, that a certain bookſeller publiſhed his firſt Catalogue with this introduction:——"As this is the firſt Catalogue ever the AUTHOR made, and is done in great haſte, he hopes inaccuracies will be treated with lenity."

But to return from this digreſſion. I ſhould probably have ſtill delayed compiling my narrative, if the editors of a certain periodical publication, who monthly labor to be witty, had not deemed me of ſufficient conſequence to introduce into their work, what they are pleaſed to call a *Portrait* of me! and though it was by them intended as a caricatura, yet I am perſuaded it will appear to thoſe who beſt know me, as a daubing more characteriſtic of the heavy bruſh of a manufacturer of ſigns, than the delicate pencil of a true portrait-painter; and on that account I ſhould moſt certainly have conſidered it as unworthy notice, had they not daubed me with falſe features. This at once determined my wavering reſolution, and I am now fully reſolved to minute down ſuch particulars of my paſſage through life, as, though not adorned with an elegance of ſtile, will, I aſſure you, poſſeſs what to you, I flatter myſelf, will be a greater recommendation, viz. a ſtrict adherence to truth. And though no doubt you will meet with ſome occurrences in which you may find cauſe for cenſure, yet I hope others will preſent themſelves, which your candour will induce you to commend. Should you be able to afford the whole a patient peruſal, and think the account meriting the public eye, I ſhall cheerfully ſubmit to your deciſion, convinced that you will not,

> " With mean complacence e'er betray your truſt,
> " Nor be ſo civil as to prove unjuſt."

John Dunton, a brother *Bibliopole*, long ſince exhibited a whole volume of dulneſs, which he called his " Life and *errors*." The latter

latter term I believe might be a very proper appendage to the title page of the innumerable lives which have been, and which will be published: For what man will dare to say of himself, his life has not been loaded with errors? That mine has been such, I readily acknowledge; and should this narrative be published, many perhaps may deem that act another (possibly the greatest) error. To those I shall only observe, that "to err is human, to forgive divine."

As an additional stimulus, I can assure you as an absolute fact, that several gentlemen have at different periods (one very lately) intimated to me their intentions of engaging in the task, if I any longer declined it.

Of my first-mentioned *kind Biographers* I shall take my leave, with a couplet, many years since written by an eminent poet, and not inapplicable to the present case.

> "Let B— charge low Grub-Street on my quill,
> "And write whate'er he please, except MY WILL.

And of you, for the preſent, after informing you, my next ſhall contain a faithful account of particulars relative to the early part of my life, with aſſuring you that I am,

Dear Friend,

Your ever obliged.

LETTER

LETTER II.

" Why ſhould my birth keep down my mounting Spirit?
" Are not all creatures ſubject unto time;
" To time, who doth abuſe the world,
" And fills it full of hotch-podge baſtardy?
" There's legions now of beggars on the Earth,
" That their original did ſpring from Kings;
" And many monarchs now, whoſe fathers were
" The riff-raff of their age; for time and fortune
" Wears out a noble train to beggary;
" And from the dunghill millions do advance
" To ſtate; and mark, in this admiring world
" This is the courſe, which in the name of fate
" Is ſeen as often as it whirls about;
" The river Thames that by our door doth run,
" His firſt beginning is but ſmall and ſhallow,
" Yet keeping on his courſe grows to a ſea.

SHAKESPEAR's Cromwell.

DEAR FRIEND,

IN my laſt I hinted that I ſhould confine myſelf to a plain narrative of facts, unembelliſhed with the meretricious aid of lofty figures, or repreſentations of things which never had exiſtence, but in the brain of the author. I ſhall therefore not trouble you with a hiſtory of predictions which foretold the future greatneſs of your humble ſervant, nor with a minute account of the aſpects of the planets at the very auſpicious and important criſis when firſt I inhaled the air of this buſtling orb; for, extraordinary as it may appear, it has never yet occurred to me, that any of the adepts in the aſtrological ſcience have made a calculation of my nativity; 'tis probable this high honor is by the planets deſtined to adorn the ſublime lucubrations of the very ingenious Mr. SIBLEY, in the next edition of his ſtup—endous work! And here, for the honor of the craft let me remark, that this moſt ſublime genius, has with myſelf, to boaſt (and who would not boaſt of their genealogy in having a prince for their anceſtor?) in being a Son of the renowned PRINCE CRISPIN.

A volume has been written with the title of "The Honor of the Taylors; or the Hiſtory of Sir JOHN HAWKWOOD." But were any learned writer to undertake— The honor of the Shoemakers, or the Hiſtory of ——, how inſignificant a figure would the

the poor Taylors make, when compared with the honorable craft!

> " Coblers from Crispin boast their Public Spirit,
> " And all are upright downright men of merit."

Should I live to see as many editions of my Memoirs published, as there have been of the Pilgrim's Progress, I may be induced to present the world with a Folio on that important subject.

But to begin——

Were I inclined to pride myself in genealogical descent, I might here boast that the family were originally settled at White Lackington, in Somersetshire, which obtained its name from one of my famous ancestors, and give you a long detail of their grandeur, &c. but having as little leisure as inclination to boast of what if true would add nothing to *my* merits, I shall for the present only say, that I was born at Wellington in Somersetshire, on the 31st of August, (old style) 1746. My father George Lackington, was a Journeyman

neyman Shoemaker, who had incurred the diſpleaſure of my grandfather for marrying my mother, whoſe maiden name was Joan Trott. She was the daughter of a poor weaver in Wellington; a good honeſt man, whoſe end was remarkable, though not very fortunate; in the road between Taunton and Wellington, he was found drowned in a ditch, where the water ſcarcely covered his face: He was, 'tis conjectured,

"—— Drunk when he died."

This happened ſome years before the marriage of my Father and Mother.

My grandfather George Lackington had been a Gentleman Farmer at Langford, a village two miles from Wellington, and acquired a pretty conſiderable property. But my father's mother dying when my father was but about thirteen years of age, my grandfather, who had two daughters, bound my father apprentice to a Mr. Hordly, a maſter ſhoemaker in Wellington, with an intention of ſetting him up in that buſineſs at the expiration

piration of his time. But my father worked a year or two as a journeyman, and then diſpleaſed his father by marrying a woman without a ſhilling, of a mean family, and who ſupported herſelf by ſpinning of wool into yarn, ſo that my mother was delivered of your friend and humble ſervant, her firſt-born, and hope of the family, in my grandmother Trott's poor cottage; and that good old woman carried me privately to church, unknown to my father who was (nominally) a Quaker, that being the religion of his anceſtors.

About the year 1750, my father having three or four children, and my mother proving an excellent wife, my grandfather's reſentment had nearly ſubſided, ſo that he ſupplied him with money to open a ſhop for *himſelf.* But that which was intended to be of very great ſervice to him and his family, eventually proved extremely unfortunate to himſelf and them; for as ſoon as he found he was more at eaſe in his circumſtances, he contracted a fatal habit of drinking, and of

courſe

courſe his buſineſs was neglected; ſo that after ſeveral fruitleſs attempts of my grandfather to keep him in trade, he was, partly by a very large family, but more by his habitual drunkenneſs, reduced to his old ſtate of a journeyman ſhoemaker: Yet ſo infatuated was he with the love of liquor, that the endearing ties of huſband and father could not reſtrain him: by which baneful habit himſelf and family were involved in the extremeſt poverty.

" To mortal men great loads allotted be;
" But of all packs, no pack like poverty."

HERRICK.

So that neither myſelf, my Brothers, or Siſters are indebted to a Father ſcarcely for any thing that can endear his memory, or cauſe us to reflect on him with pleaſure.

" Children, the blind effects of love and chance
" Bear from their birth the impreſſion of a Slave.

DRYDEN.

My father and mother might have ſaid with Middleton,

" How adverſe runs the deſtiny of ſome creatures!
" Some only can get riches and no children,
" We only can get children and no riches;
" Then 'tis the prudent part to check our will,
" And, till our ſtate riſe, make our blood ſtand ſtill.

But

But to our mother we are indebted for every thing. "She was a woman take her for all in all, I ſhall not look upon her like again." Never did I know or hear of a woman who worked and lived ſo hard as ſhe did to ſupport Eleven children: and were I to relate the particulars, it would not gain credit. I ſhall only obſerve, that for many years together, ſhe worked generally nineteen or twenty hours out of every twenty-four; even when very near her time, ſometimes at one hour ſhe was ſeen walking backwards and forwards by her Spinning-wheel, and her midwife ſent for the next.

Out of love to her family ſhe totally abſtained from every kind of Liquor, water excepted, her food was chiefly broth, (little better than water and oatmeal) turnips, potatoes, cabbage, carrots, &c. her children fared ſomething better, but not much, as you may well ſuppoſe. When I reflect on the aſtoniſhing hardſhips and ſufferings of ſo worthy a woman, and her helpleſs infants, I find myſelf ready to curſe the huſband and father

that

that could thus involve them in ſuch a deplorable ſcene of miſery and diſtreſs. It is dreadful to add, that his habitual drunkenneſs ſhortened his days nearly one half, and that about twenty years ſince he died, unregretted by his own children; nay more, while nature ſhed tears over his grave, reaſon was thankful that the cauſe of their poverty and miſery was taken out of the way. Read this, ye inhuman parents, and ſhudder! Was a law made to baniſh all ſuch fathers, would it not be a juſt, nay even a mild law?

Here, ſir, permit me to drop ſo gloomy a ſubject, and again ſubſcribe myſelf

Yours, &c.

LETTER

LETTER III.

"Some venial frailties you may well forgive."
FRANCIS's Horace.

DEAR FRIEND,

AS I was the eldeſt, and my father for the firſt few years a careful hard-working man, I fared ſomething better than my brothers and ſiſters. I was put for two or three years to a day-ſchool kept by an old woman; and well remember how proud I uſed to be to ſee ſeveral ancient dames lift up their hands and eyes with aſtoniſhment, while I repeated by memory ſeveral chapters out of the New Teſtament, concluding me from this ſpecimen to be a prodigy of Science. But my career of learning was ſoon at an end, when my mother became ſo poor that ſhe could not afford the mighty ſum of two-pence per week for my ſchooling. Beſides I was obliged to ſupply the place of a nurſe to ſeveral of my brothers and ſiſters. The conſequence of which

was,

was, that what little I had learned was presently forgot; instead of learning to read, &c. it very early became my chief delight to excel in all kinds of boyish mischiefs; and I soon arrived to be the captain and leader of all the boys in the neighbourhood, so that if any old woman's lanthorn was kicked out of her hand, or drawn up a sign-post, or if any thing was fastened to her tail, or if her door was nailed up, I was sure to be accused as the author, whether I really were so or not.

But one of my tricks had nearly proved fatal to me. I had observed that *yawning* was infectious; and with a determination to have some sport, I collected several boys together one market-day evening, and instructed them to go amongst the butchers; whither I accompanied them. We placed ourselves at proper distances, and at a signal given, all began to yawn as wide as we could: which immediately had the desired effect; the whole butcher row was set a yawning; on which I and my companions burst

burſt out into a hearty laugh, and took to our heels. The trick pleaſed us ſo well, that two or three weeks after, we attempted to renew it. But one of the butchers, who was half drunk, perceiving our intention, ſnatched up his cleaver and threw it at me, which knocked off my hat without doing me any harm.

I was about ten years of age, when a man began to cry *apple-pies* about the ſtreets, I took great notice of his methods of ſelling his pies, and thought I could do it much better than him. I communicated to a neighbouring baker my thoughts on the ſubject in ſuch a manner as gave him a very good opinion of my abilities for a pie-merchant, and he prevailed on my father to let me live with him. My manner of crying pies, and my activity in ſelling them, ſoon made me the favorite of all ſuch as purchaſed halfpenny apple-pies, and halfpenny plumb-puddings, ſo that in a few weeks the old pie-merchant ſhut up his ſhop. I lived with this Baker about twelve or fifteen months, in which time I ſold ſuch large quantities of pies, puddings, cakes, &c. that he often declared to his friends, in my hearing, that I had been the means of extricating him from the embarrassing circumstances in which he was known to be involved prior to my entering his service.

During the time I continued with this Baker, many complaints were repeatedly made against me for the childish follies I had been guilty of, such as throwing snow-balls, frightening people by flinging serpents and crackers into their houses, &c. I also happened one day to overturn my master's son, a child about four years old, whom I had been driving in a wheel-barrow. Dreading the consequences, I immediately flew from my master's house, and (it being evening) went to a glazier's, and procured a parcel of broken glass; I also provided myself with a pocketful of peas; and thus equipped made fine diversion for myself and my unlucky companions, by going to a number of houses, one after another, discharging a handful of peas at the windows, and throw-

ing

ing down another handful of glaſs in the ſtreet at the ſame inſtant, which made ſuch a noiſe as very much frightened many people, who had no doubt of their windows being broken into a thouſand pieces. This adventure, together with throwing the child out of the wheel-barrow, produced ſuch a clamour againſt me amongſt the old women, that I would not return to my maſter, and not knowing what elſe to do, I went home to my father, who, you may eaſily conceive could not afford to keep me idle, ſo I was ſoon ſet down by his ſide to learn his own trade; and I continued with him ſeveral years, working when he worked, and while he was keeping *Saint Monday*, I was with boys of my own age fighting, cudgel-playing, wreſtling, &c. &c.

I am,

Dear Friend,

Yours, &c.

LETTER IV.

"Who gather round, and wonder at the tale
"Of horrid apparition, tall and ghaſtly,
"That walks at dead of night, or takes his ſtand,
"O'er ſome new-open'd grave: and (ſtrange to tell!)
"Evaniſhes at crowing of the cock."

BLAIR's Grave.

DEAR FRIEND,

I Muſt not forget an odd adventure that happened when I was about twelve years of age, as it tends to ſhew in part my dauntleſs diſpoſition, which diſcovered itſelf on many occaſions in the very early part of my life.

I had one day walked with my father to Holywell lake, a village two miles from Wellington, where meeting with ſome good ale, he could not find in his heart to part from it until late at night. When we were returning home by the way of Rockwell-Green, (commonly called *Rogue Green*, from a gang of robbers and houſe-breakers who formerly lived there) having juſt paſſed the bridge,

bridge, we were met by ſeveral men and women, who appeared to be very much frightened, being in great agitation. They informed us that they were returning back to Rogue-Green, in order to ſleep there that night, having been prevented from going home to Wellington by a dreadful Apparition, which they had all ſeen in the hollow way, about a quarter of a mile diſtant; adding, that a perſon having been murdered there formerly, the ghoſt had walked ever ſince; that they had never before paid much attention to the well-known report; but now they were obliged to credit it, having had ocular demonſtration. My father had drank too large a quantity of ale to be much afraid of any thing, and I (who could not let ſlip ſuch an opportunity of ſhewing my courage) ſeconded matters for the poor terrified people to return with us; and as I offered to lead the van, they were prevailed on to make the attempt once more; but ſaid, that it was rather preſumptuous, and hoped that no dreadful conſequence would

 enſue

enſue, as all the company, they truſted were honeſt-hearted, and intended no harm to any perſon: they moreover added, that "God certainly was above the Devil." I then advanced, and kept before the company about fifty yards,

> "Whiſtling aloud to bear my courage up."

But when we had walked about a quarter of a mile, I ſaw at ſome diſtance before us in the hedge, the dreadful apparition that had ſo terrified our company. Here it is! (ſaid I) "Lord have mercy upon us!" replied ſome of the company, making a full ſtop; and would have gone back, but ſhame prevented them. I ſtill kept my diſtance before, and called out to them to follow me, aſſuring them that I was determined to ſee what it was. They then fell one behind another, and advanced in ſingle files. As I proceeded I too was ſeized with a timid apprehenſion, but durſt not own it; ſtill keeping on before, although I perceived my hair to heave my hat from my head, and my teeth

teeth to chatter in my mouth. In fact I was greatly agitated at what I ſaw; the object much reſembled the human figure as to ſhape, but the ſize was prodigious. However I had promiſed to ſee what it was, and for that purpoſe I obſtinately ventured on about thirty yards from the place where I firſt had ſight of it. I then perceived that it was only a very ſhort tree, whoſe limbs had been newly cut off, the doing of which had made it much reſemble a giant. I then called to the company, and informed them, with a hearty laugh, that they had been frightened at the ſtump of a tree.

This ſtory cauſed excellent diverſion for a long time afterwards in Wellington, and I was mentioned as an hero.

The pleaſure and ſatisfaction I received from the diſcovery, and the honour I acquired for the courage I poſſeſſed in making it, has, I believe, had much influence on me ever after; as I cannot recollect that in any one inſtance I have ever obſerved the leaſt fear of apparitions, ſpirits, &c. ſince.

> " What education did at firſt receive,
> " Our ripen'd age confirms us to believe."
>
> POMFRET.

Not that I have always ſteadily diſbelieved what has been related of ſuch appearances, a few accounts of which ſeem ſo well authenticated, as at leaſt to make me doubt whether there might not exiſt in the ſcale of beings ſome of a more aërial ſubſtance than mankind, who may poſſeſs both the inclination and the power of aſſuming our ſhape, and may perhaps take as much delight in teazing the human ſpecies, as too many of our ſpecies do in teazing and even tormenting thoſe of the brute creation.

> " Some aſtral forms I muſt invoke by pray'r;
> " Fram'd all of pureſt atoms of the air:
> " In airy chariots they together ride,
> " And ſip the dew, as thro' the clouds they glide;
> " Vain ſpirits, You, that ſhunning heav'n's high noon,
> " Swarm here beneath the concave of the moon,
> " Hence to the taſk aſſign'd you here below!
> " Upon the ocean make loud tempeſts blow;

" Into

" Into the wombs of hollow clouds repair,
" And crafh out thunder from the bladder'd air;
" From pointed fun-beams take the mifts they drew,
" And fcatter them again in pearly dew:
" And of the bigger drops they drain below,
" Some mould in hail, and others fift in fnow."

DRYDEN.

While I am on this fubject, I cannot refift the temptation of relating a truly ridiculous affair that happened about this time at Taunton.

In the workhoufe belonging to the parifh of St. James, there lived a young woman who was an idiot. This poor creature had a great averfion to fleeping in a bed, and at bed-time would often run away to a field in the neighbourhood called the Priory, where fhe flept in the cowfheds.

In order to break her of this bad cuftom, two men agreed to try if they could not frighten her out of it. And one night, when they knew that fhe was there, they took a white fheet with them, and coming to the place, one of the men concealed him-

felf

ſelf to ſee the event, while the other wrapped himſelf up in the ſheet, and walked backwards and forwards cloſe before the cowſhed in which ſhe was laid. It was ſome time before Molly paid any attention to the apparition; but at laſt up ſhe got. "Aha! (ſaid ſhe) a white devil!" and by her manner of expreſſing herſelf ſhe thought it was very ſtrange to ſee a *white* devil. And ſoon after ſhe exclaimed, "A black devil, too! a black devil, too!" With that the man who had the ſheet on, looked over his ſhoulder, and ſaw (or imagined he ſaw) a perſon all over black behind him; the ſight of which made him take to his heels. Molly then clapped her hands as faſt as ſhe could, crying out at the ſame time, "Run, black devil, and catch white devil! Run, black devil, and catch white devil!" and was highly diverted. But this proved a ſerious adventure to the white devil, as he expired within a few minutes after he had reached his own houſe; and from that time poor Molly was left alone to ſleep in peace.

About

About ten years after the above affair, at Wivelſcombe, nine miles from Taunton, a gentleman farmer's houſe was alarmed every night between twelve and one o'clock. The chamber doors were thrown open, the bed-clothes pulled off the beds, and the kitchen furniture thrown with violence about the kitchen, to the great terror of the family, inſomuch that the ſervants gave their maſter and miſtreſs warning to leave their places, and ſome of them actually quitted their ſervice. This dreadful affair had laſted about ſix weeks, when a young gentleman who was there on a viſit, being in bed one night, at the uſual hour he heard his chamber door thrown open, and a very odd noiſe about his room. He was at firſt frightened, but the noiſe continuing a long time, he became calm, and laid ſtill, revolving in his mind what he had beſt do. When on a ſudden he heard the ſpirit creep under his bed, which was immediately lifted up, &c. This convinced him that there was ſome ſubſtance in the ſpirit; on which he leaped

uot

out of bed, ſecured the door, and with his oaken ſtaff belaboured the ghoſt under the bed as hard as he could, until he heard a female voice imploring mercy. On that he opened his chamber door, and called aloud for a light. The family all got up as faſt as poſſible, and came to his room. He then informed them that he had got the ſpirit under the bed; on hearing which, moſt of them were terribly frightened, and would have run off faſter than they came, but he aſſured them, they had nothing to fear: then out he dragged the half-murdered ſpirit from its ſcene of action. But how great was their ſurpriſe and ſhame, when they diſcovered that this tormenting devil was no other than one of their ſervant girls about ſixteen years of age, who had been confined to her bed ſeveral months by illneſs.

This ghoſt was no ſooner laid, than two others alarmed the neighbourhood; one of which for a long time ſhook a houſe every night, and terribly diſtreſſed the family; at length

length they all refolved one night to go over the whole houfe in a body, and fee what it was that fo agitated the building. They examined every room, but in vain, as no caufe could be difcovered. So they very ferioufly as well as unanimoufly concluded, that it muft be *the devil.*

But about a fortnight after this, one of the family being out late in the garden, faw a great boy get in at the window of an old houfe next door (part of which was in ruins) and foon after the houfe began to fhake as ufual, on which the family went out of their own habitation, and entered the old houfe where the boy was feen to get in; yet for a long time they could not difcover any perfon, and were juft turning to come out again, when one of the company obferved the boy fufpended above their heads, ftriding over the end of a large beam that ran acrofs both houfes.

It was then apparent that the violent agitation of the adjoining houfe was occafioned

by

by nothing more than his leaping up and down on the unſupported end of this beam.

Another apparition had for a long time ſtolen many geeſe, turkeys, &c. and altho' it had been ſeen by many, yet nobody would venture to go near it, until at length one perſon a little wiſer than the reſt of his neighbours, ſeeing the famous apparition all over white ſtealing his fowls, was determined to be fully ſatisfied what kind of ſpirit it could be that had ſo great a predilection for poultry. He accordingly went round the yard, and as the apparition was coming over the wall, he knocked it down. This terrible ghoſt then proved to be a neighbouring woman, who had put on her ſhroud, in order to deter any perſons ſhould they by chance ſee her, from coming near her. Thus, though ſhe had for a long time ſucceſsfully practiſed this ingenious way of procuring poultry, the old fox was caught at laſt.

This

This is ſo prolific a ſubject, that I could fill many pages with relations of dreadful ſpectres, which for a while have reigned with tyrannic ſway over weak minds, and at length when calm Reaſon was ſuffered to aſſume its power, have been diſcovered to be no more objects of terror than thoſe I have here noticed. But doubtleſs many ſuch inſtances muſt have occurred to you.

It has indeed often aſtoniſhed me, that in this enlightened age, there ſhould yet remain numbers, not in the country only, but even in the metropolis, who ſuffer themſelves to be made miſerable by vain fears of preternatural occurrences, which generally owe their origin to the knavery of ſome ill-diſpoſed perſon, who has a ſiniſter purpoſe to anſwer thereby, or to the fooliſh deſire of alarming the minds of weak people: a practice ſometimes (though intended as *fun)* productive of very ſerious conſequences. Now and then, indeed, theſe terrors are owing to accidental and ridiculous cauſes. As an

inſtance,

inſtance, I ſhall give you the account of a terrible alarm which ſome years ſince took place in an Hoſpital of this city, as related to me by a gentleman, who at the time reſided in the houſe, for the purpoſe of completing his medical education, and on whoſe veracity I can confidently rely.

For ſeveral nights ſucceſſively a noiſe had been heard in the lower part of the building, like the continual tapping againſt a window, which led the night nurſes *wiſely* to conclude it muſt certainly be occaſioned by the Spirit of one of the bodies depoſited in the dead-houſe endeavouring to eſcape; the ſound ſeeming to proceed from that particular quarter. The dread of theſe *ſagacious ladies* at laſt became ſuch, as totally to prevent their going from ward to ward to do their duty, and determined my friend to attempt to lay this perturbed ſpirit; which however he apprehended would more ſpeedily, as well as effectually be performed by the aſſiſtance of a good cudgel, than by exorciſms; he therefore inſtead of conſulting the Chaplain,

gave

gave orders the next night as ſoon as the uſual *dreadful ſound* was heard, to give him notice. This you may ſuppoſe they did not neglect doing, though at the ſame time they were ſhocked at his temerity, and apprehenſive for the conſequences. Impreſſed with an idea of the alarm being occaſioned by ſome ſervant or patient in the houſe, he immediately ſallied forth, with a candle in one hand, and a good tough twig in the other, accompained by two of the men ſervants of the Hoſpital, accoutred in the ſame manner, reſolved that if detected, the party ſhould meet with an ample reward. The dead-houſe was paſſed; the noiſe continued; though it evidently proceeded from a window at ſome diſtance in the area. When the cavalcade came near the ſcene of action, the window ſuddenly and violently broke, without any thing being ſeen. This my friend confeſſed, for a moment occaſioned his making a halt; but as nothing viſible had eſcaped through the area, it occurred to him ſomething might have made an entrance that way; accordingly he proceeded to the internal part of the building, and on opening the door, the apparition immediately not only appeared, but disappeared, and that so instantaneously as not to afford time to apply the remedy intended. And what think you, was this dreadful spirit? That you may exercise your ingenuity at guessing, I will here conclude with,

Dear Friend,

Yours, &c.

LETTER

LETTER V.

" ——— Were thy education ne'er fo mean,
" Having thy limbs, a thoufand fair courfes
" Offer themfelves to thy election.

BEN JOHNSON'S Every Man in his Humour.

" Laugh if you are wife."

MARTIAL.

DEAR FRIEND,

A CAT.——An odd beginning of a Letter, by the bye—but here highly *important* and proper, as tending to relieve you from the anxious thoughts which (no doubt) muft have filled your mind on the fubject of the concluding part of my former letter. I muft give you one laughable inftance more, which lately happened. Mr. Higley, the bookfeller famous for felling odd volumes or broken fets of books, lived next door to a public-houfe in Ruffell-court, Drury-lane; this public-houfe was feparated from his habitation only by a flight wainfcot partition, through which Mr. Higley caufed an hole to be cut, and a ſlider put over it, ſo that when he wanted any beer, he always drew back the ſlider and had it handed to him through this convenient aperture.

The night after Mr. Higley's death, which happened a few months ſince, the man who was left to take care of the corps, about twelve o'clock hearing the landlord and his family going up ſtairs to their beds, on a ſudden drew back the ſlider and halloo'd through the hole, " Bring me a pint of beer." This order the landlord and his family heard, and were terribly alarmed, as they really thought it had proceeded from the ghoſt of their neighbour Higley; the poor maid let fall the warming-pan, which came tumbling down the ſtairs; the landlady being within the reach of her huſband's legs, caught faſt hold of them, which in his fright he miſtook for poor Higley. But the man burſting into a hearty laugh, reſtored the ſpirits of our hoſt and his family.

Having

Having now, I dare ſay, had enough of *Ghoſteſſes*, I will proceed with my narration.

During the time that I lived with the Baker, my name became ſo celebrated for ſelling a large number of pies, puddings, &c. that for ſeveral years following, application was made to my father, for him to permit me to ſell Almanacks a few market days before and after Chriſtmas. In this employ I took great delight, the country people being highly pleaſed with me, and purchaſing a great number of my Almanacks, which excited envy in the itinerant venders of Moore, Wing, Poor Robin, &c. to ſuch a degree, that my father often expreſſed his anxiety leſt they ſhould ſome way or other do me a miſchief. But I had not the leaſt concern, for poſſeſſing a light pair of heels, I always kept at a proper diſtance.

O, my friend, little did I imagine at that time, that I ſhould ever excite the ſame poor mean ſpirit in many of the bookſellers of London and other places! but,

"*Envy* at laſt crawls forth, from hell's dire throng,
"Of all the direfull'ſt! her black locks hung long,
"Attir'd with curling ſerpents; her pale ſkin
"Was almoſt drop'd from her ſharp bones within,
"And at her breaſt ſtuck vipers, which did prey
"Upon her panting heart both night and day,
"Sucking black blood from thence: which to repair,
"Both day and night they left freſh poiſons there.
"Her garments were deep-ſtain'd with human gore,
"And torn by her own hands, in which ſhe bore
"A knotted whip and bowl, which to the brim,
"Did green gall, and the juice of wormwood ſwim;
"With which when ſhe was drunk, ſhe furious grew,
"And laſh'd herſelf: thus from th' accurſed crew,
"Envy, the worſt of fiends, herſelf preſents,
"Envy, good only when ſhe herſelf torments."

COWLEY.

"—— The true condition of Envy is,
"*Dolor alienæ felicitatis*; to have
"Our eyes continually fix'd upon another
"Man's proſperity, that is, his chief happineſs,
"And to grieve at that."

I was fourteen years and a half old when I went with my father to work at Taunton, ſeven miles from Wellington. We had been there about a fortnight, when my father informed our maſter, George Bowden, that he would

would return to Wellington again. Mr. Bowden was then pleaſed to inform my father that he had taken a liking to me, and propoſed taking me apprentice; I ſeconded Mr. Bowden's motion (having a better proſpect in continuing with Mr. Bowden than in returning to Wellington with my father) as he offered to take me without any premium, and to find me in every thing. My father accepted his offer, and I was immediately bound apprentice for ſeven years to Mr. George and Mrs. Mary Bowden, as honeſt and worthy a couple as ever carried on a trade.

> "Religious, punctual, frugal, and ſo forth;
> "Their word would paſs for more than they were worth."
>
> POPE.

They carefully attended to their ſhop ſix days in the week, and on the ſeventh went with their family twice to an anabaptiſt meeting; where little attention was paid to ſpeculative doctrines; but where ſound morality was conſtantly inculcated.

"For modes of faith let graceleſs zealots fight,
"His can't be wrong whoſe life is in the right."

But in this, as in many other places of worſhip, it was performed in a dull ſpiritleſs manner; ſo that the excellent morality taught there was not ſo much attended to as it would have been had it been enforced, or re-enforced by the captivating powers of oratory.

I well remember, that although I conſtantly attended this place, it was a year or two before I took the leaſt notice of the ſermon, which was read; nor had I any idea that I had the leaſt concern in what the miniſter was (as 'tis called) preaching about. For,

"Who a cold, dull, lifeleſs drawling keeps,
"One half his audience laughs, whilſt t'other ſleeps.

* * * * * *

"Sermons, like plays, ſome pleaſe us at the ear,
"But never will a ſerious reading bear;
"Some in the cloſet edify enough,
"That from the pulpit ſeem'd but ſorry ſtuff,

"'Tis

" 'Tis thus there are who by ill reading ſpoil
" Young's pointed ſenſe, or Atterbury's ſtyle!
" While others, by the force of eloquence,
" Make that ſeem fine, which ſcarce is common ſenſe.
" But ſome will preach without the leaſt pretence
" To virtue, learning, art, or eloquence.
" Why not? you cry: they plainly ſee, no doubt—
" A prieſt may grow *right reverend* without."

Art of Preaching.

I am,

Dear Friend,

Yours, &c.

LETTER

LETTER VI.

" Youth is the ſtock whence grafted ſuperſtition
" Shoots with unbounded vigor."

MILLER's Mahomet.

" —— All muſt lament that he's under ſuch banners,
" As evil community ſpoils our good manners."

SIMPKIN.

DEAR FRIEND,

AT the time that I was bound apprentice, my maſter had two ſons, the eldeſt about ſeventeen years old, the youngeſt fourteen. The eldeſt had juſt been baptized, and introduced as a member of the arianiſtical dipping community where my maſter and his family attended. The boy was a very ſober induſtrious youth, and gave his father and mother much pleaſure. The youngeſt was alſo a good lad. Thus every thing continued well for ſome time after I had been added to the family. Both of the boys had very good natural parts, and had learned

learned to read, write, keep accounts, &c. But they had been at ſchools where no variety of books had been introduced, ſo that all they had read was the Bible. My maſter's whole library conſiſted of a ſchool-ſize Bible, Watts's Pſalms and Hymns, Foot's Tract on Baptiſm, Culpepper's Herbal, the Hiſtory of the Gentle Craft, an old imperfect volume of Receipts in Phyſic, Surgery, &c. and the Ready Reckoner. The ideas of the family were as circumſcribed as their library. My maſter called attention to buſineſs and working hard, "*minding the main chance.*" On Sundays all went to meeting; my Maſter on that day ſaid a ſhort grace before dinner, and the boys read a few chapters in the Bible, took a walk for an hour or two, then read a chapter or two more.

"What right, what true, what fit we juſtly call,
"And this was all our care—for this is all."

We then ſupped, and went early to bed, perfectly ſatisfied with having done their duty;

duty; and each having a quiet confcience, foon fell into the arms of

"Nature's foft nurfe! fweet fleep."

I cannot here omit mentioning a very fingular cuftom of my mafter's: Every morning, at all feafons of the year, and in all weathers, he rofe about three o'clock, took a walk by the river-fide round French-ware-fields, ftopt at an alehoufe that was early open to drink half a pint of ale, came back before fix o'clock, then called up his people to work, and went to bed again about feven.

Thus was the good man's family jogging eafily and quietly on, no one doubting but he fhould go to heaven when he died, and every one hoping it would be a good while firft.

"A man fhould be religious, not fuperftitious."

But, alas! the dreadful crifis was at hand that put an end to the happinefs and peace of this little family. I had been an apprentice about

about twelve or fifteen months, when my maſter's eldeſt ſon George happened to go and hear a ſermon by one of Mr. Weſley's preachers, who had left the plough-tail to preach the *pure* and *unadulterated* Goſpel of Chriſt. By this ſermon the fallow ground of poor George's heart was ploughed up, he was now perſuaded that the innocent and good life he had led would only ſink him deeper into hell: in ſhort he found out that he had never been converted, and of courſe was in a ſtate of damnation, without benefit of Clergy. But he did not long continue in this damnable ſtate, but ſoon became one of

"——— The ſanctified band,
"Who all holy myſteries well underſtand."

SIMPKIN.

He perſuaded himſelf that he had paſſed through the *New Birth*, and was quite ſure that his name was regiſtered in the Book of Life, and (to the great grief of his parents) he was in reality become *a new creature*.

"'Twas

" 'Twas methodiſtic grace that made him toſs and tumble,
" Which in his entrails did like jollup rumble."

Ovid's Epiſt. Burleſqued.

George had no ſooner made things ſure for himſelf, than he began to extend his concern to his father, mother, brother, and me; and very kindly gave us to underſtand, that he was ſure we were in a very deplorable ſtate, "without hope, and without God in the world," being under the curſe of the Law. In the long winter nights, as we ſat at work together, he proved (in his way) that every man had original ſin enough to damn a thouſand ſouls; and a deal was ſaid on that ſubject: Quotations were made from ſome *deep* author who had aſſerted, that there were "infants in hell but a ſpan long;" and that "hell was paved with infant ſculls" &c. As to Morality, George aſſured us it was of no avail; that as for good works, they were only ſplendid ſins; and that in the beſt good work that any creature could perform, there was ſin enough to ſink the doer to the nethermoſt hell; that it was *faith* alone

alone that did every thing, without a grain of morality; but that no man could have one particle of this myſterious faith, before he was juſtified; and that *juſtification* was a ſudden operation on the ſoul, by which the moſt execrable wretch that ever lived might inſtantaneouſly be aſſured of all his ſins being pardoned; that his body from that very moment became the living temple of the Holy Ghoſt; that he had fellowſhip with the Father, Son, and Holy Spirit; and, that Spirit was to be their conſtant and infallible guide:

"Whate'er men ſpeak by this new light,
"Still they were ſure to be in the right.
"This dark-lanthorn of the Spirit,
"Which none ſee by but thoſe that bear it;
"A light that falls down from on high,
"For ſpiritual trades to cozen by;
"An ignis fatuus, that bewitches
"And leads men into pools and ditches,
"This light inſpires and plays upon
"The noiſe of Saint, like bagpipe drone,
"And ſpeaks through hollow empty ſoul,
"As through a trunk, or whiſpering hole,
"Such language as no mortal ear
"But ſpiritu'l eaves-droppers can hear."

My

My maſter very ſeldom heard any of theſe converſations, but my good miſtreſs would ſit down for hours together, with her Bible in her lap, from which ſhe would read ſuch ſcriptures as proved the neceſſity of living a good life, performing good works, &c. ſhe alſo did her beſt to confute the tenets of Original ſin, Imputed righteouſneſs, doctrine of the Trinity, &c. &c. Unfortunately the good woman had no great talents for controverſy; however, George had a very tenacious memory, and employed all his thoughts on theſe ſubjects, ſo that John his younger brother, and I alſo (two competent judges no doubt) thought that he had the beſt of the arguments on theſe edifying ſubjects, and about five months after George's converſion, John went to hear thoſe only true Ambaſſadors from Heaven,

> " Who ſtroll and teach from town to town
> " The good old Cauſe: which ſome believe
> " To be the devil that tempted Eve
> " With knowledge, and do ſtill invite
> " The world to miſchief with new light."
>
> BUTLER.

Theſe

Theſe devil-dodgers happened to be ſo very *powerful* (that is very *noiſy*,) that they ſoon ſent John home, crying out, he ſhould be damn'd! he ſhould be damn'd for ever!

But John ſoon got out of the damnable ſtate, and aſſured us that all his ſins were forgiven, merely by believing that he had paſſed from death into life, and had union and communion with God. He now became as merry as before he had been ſorrowful, and ſung in Mr. Weſley's ſtrain,

"Not a doubt ſhall ariſe
"To darken the ſkies,
"Nor hide for a moment my God from my Eyes."

John ſung to me, and ſaid to me a deal in this wonderful ſtrain, of which I did not comprehend one ſyllable.

"——— His words were looſe
"As heaps of ſand, and ſcatter'd wide from ſenſe.
"So high he mounted in his airy throne,
"That when the wind had got into his head,
"It turn'd his brains to frenzy.

But theſe extraordinary accounts and diſcourſes, together with the controverſies between the mother and the ſons, made me think they knew many matters of which I was totally ignorant. This created in me a deſire for knowledge, that I might know who was right and who was wrong. But to my great mortification, I could not read. I knew moſt of the letters, and a few eaſy words, and I ſet about learning with all my might. My miſtreſs would ſometimes inſtruct me; and having three halfpence per week allowed me by my mother, this money I gave to John (my maſter's youngeſt ſon) and for every three-halfpence he taught me to ſpell one hour; this was done in the dark, as we were not allowed a candle after we were ſent up ſtairs to bed.

I ſoon made a little progreſs in reading; in the mean time I alſo went to the Methodiſt meeting. There, as "enthuſiaſm is the child or melancholy," I caught the infection. The firſt that I heard was one Thomas Bryant,

Bryant, known in Taunton by the name of *the damnation preacher*; (he had juſt left off cobbling *ſoles* of another kind.) His ſermon frightened me moſt terribly. I ſoon after went to hear an old Scotchman, and he aſſured his congregation, that they would be damn'd, and double damn'd, and treble damn'd, and damn'd for ever, if they died without what he called *faith*.

This marvellous doctrine and noiſy rant and enthuſiaſm ſoon worked on my paſſions, and made me believe myſelf to be really in the damnable condition that they repreſented; and in this miſerable ſtate I continued for about a month, being all that time unable to work myſelf up to the proper key.

At laſt, by ſinging and repeating enthuſiaſtic amorous hymns, and ignorantly applying particular texts of ſcripture, I got my imagination to the proper pitch, and thus was I born again in an inſtant, became a very great favourite of heaven, had angels to attend all my ſteps, and was as familiar with the Father, Son, and Holy Ghost, as any old woman in Mr. Wesley's connection; which, by the bye, is saying a great deal.

I am,

Dear Sir,

Yours.

LETTER

LETTER VII.

" No ſleep, no peace, no reſt
" Their wand'ring and afflicted minds poſſeſs'd;
" Upon their ſouls and eyes
" Hell and eternal horror lies,
" Unuſual ſhapes and images,
" Dark pictures and reſemblances
" Of things to come, and of the worlds below,
" O'er their diſtemper'd fancies go:
" Sometimes they curſe, ſometimes they pray unto
" The gods above, the gods beneath;
" No ſleep, but waking now was ſiſter unto death.

Bp. Sprat.

DEAR FRIEND,

IT is perhaps worth remarking, that what the methodiſts call conviction of ſin, being awakened, &c. is often a moſt dreadful ſtate, and has the very ſame effect on ſuch as have lived a very innocent life as it has upon the moſt notorious offenders; this conviction (as they call it) is brought about by the preachers heaping all the curſes in the Bible on the heads of the moſt virtuous as well as moſt vicious; for, ſay they, he who keepeth the whole law and offendeth but in one point, is as much in a ſtate of damnation, as he that hath broken every one of the commandments, or committed robbery, murder, &c. ſo that they pour out every awful denunciation found in the Bible, and many not found there, againſt all who have not the methodiſtical faith: this they call ſhaking the people over the mouth of hell.

Thus are many who before poſſeſſed " conſciences void of offence towards God and mankind" tricked out of their peace of mind, by the ignorant application of texts of ſcripture. Their fears being once ſo dreadfully alarmed, they often become inſupportable to themſelves and all around them; many in this ſtate have put a period to their exiſtence, others run mad, &c.

If the above terror of conſcience was only to take place in knaves and raſcals, there would be no reaſon for blaming the methodiſts on that head; " the wretch deſerves the hell he feels." A terrible inſtance of this kind

kind happened near London-bridge about two years ſince: A perſon in a lucrative branch of buſineſs had put unbounded confidence in his head ſhopman, and well rewarded him for his ſuppoſed faithfulneſs. One morning, this man not coming down ſtairs ſo ſoon as uſual, the ſervant maid went up to call him, and found him hanging up to the bed-poſt; ſhe had the preſence of mind to cut him down, but he being nearly dead, it was ſome days before he perfectly recovered. On his maſter coming to town he was informed what had happened to his favorite ſhopman; he heard the relation with the utmoſt aſtoniſhment, and took great pains to diſcover the cauſe of ſo fatal a reſolution, but to no purpoſe. However he endeavoured to reconcile this unhappy man to life, was very tender towards him, and gave him more encouragement than ever; but the more the maſter did to encourage and make him happy, the more the poor wretch appeared to be dejected; in this unhappy ſtate of mind he lived about ſix months, when one morning not appearing at his uſual time, the ſervant maid went to ſee if he was well, and found him very weak in bed ; a day or two after, his maſter came to town, and being told of his ſituation, went up to ſee him, and finding him in bed, and apparently very ill, propoſed ſending for a phyſician, but the poor devil refuſed to take any thing, and rejected every aſſiſtance, ſaying his time was nearly come. Soon after this the ſervant informed her maſter that he would not have the bed made, and that ſhe had juſt obſerved ſome blood on one corner of the ſheet. The maſter then went up ſtairs again, and by lifting up the bed-clothes found that he had ſtabbed himſelf in ſeveral places, and that in this ſtate he had lain three or four days, and on the ſurgeon's appearance, he refuſed to have the wounds inſpected, and the ſurgeon being of opinion that is was too late to render him any kind of ſervice, they let him lie ſtill. The maſter ſoon after this preſſed him much to know the myſterious cauſe of ſo much miſery, and ſo unnatural an end. The

dying

dying wretch exclaimed, "a wounded conſcience, who can bear." The maſter then endeavoured to comfort him, and aſſured him that his conſcience ought not to wound him, "I know you (continued he) to be a good man, and the beſt of ſervants." Hold! hold! exclaimed the wretch, your words are daggers to my ſoul! I am a villain, I have robbed you of hundreds, and have long ſuffered the tortures of the damned for being thus aconcealed villain, every act of kindneſs ſhewn to me by you has been long like vultures tearing my vitals. Go, ſir, leave me, the ſight of you cauſes me to ſuffer excruciating tortures; he then ſhrunk under the bed-clothes, and the ſame night expired in a ſtate of mind unhappy beyond all deſcription.

Terrible as the above relation is, I aſſure you that I have not heightened it: when an ungrateful villain is puniſhed by his own reflections, we acknowledge it to be but juſt. In Morton's Hiſtory of apparitions are ſeveral ſhocking ſtories of perſons, who by their abandoned

abandoned practices, brought on themselves all the horrors of a guilty conscience.

"O treacherous conscience; while she seems to sleep
"On rose and myrtle, lull'd with syren song;
"While she seems nodding o'er her charge to drop
"On headlong appetite the slacken'd rein,
"And gives up to licence unrecall'd,
"Unmarked; see from behind her secret stand,
"The sly informer minutes every fault,
"And her dread diary with horror fills.
"A watchful foe! the formidable spy,
"List'ning, o'erhears the whispers of our camp:
"Our dawning purposes of heart explores
"And steals our embryos of iniquity.
"As all rapacious usurers conceal,
"Their doomsday-book from all consuming heirs,
"Thus with indulgence most severe she treats,
"Writes down our whole history, which death shall read,
"In ev'ry pale delinquent's private ear.

Night Thoughts.

But the case is otherwise amongst the methodists, they work on the fears of the most virtuous; youth and innocence fall victims daily before their threats of hell and damnation, and the poor feeble minded, instead of being comforted and encouraged are often by by them sunk into an irrecoverable state of gloomy despondence and horrible despair.

It is true that many of their hearers are not only methodistically convinced, or alarmed, but are also *hocus pocusly* converted; but with thousands that is not the case, even with those who join their society, where so much of divine love, assurance, and extasies are talked of, where enthusiastic, rapturous, intoxicating hymns are sung, and besides the unhappy mortals in their own community, thousands there are who have lost their peace of mind by occasionally hearing their sermons.

And even those among them who have arrived to the highest pitch of enthusiasm, and who at times talk of their foretaste of heaven, and of their full assurance of sins forgiven, and of talking to the Deity as familiarly as they will to one another; (all which, and much more, I have heard a thousand times) yet even those very pretended favorites of heaven are (if we be-

lieve

lieve themſelves) miſerable for the greateſt part of their time, having doubts, fears, horrors of mind, &c. continually haunting them wherever they are. Between twenty and thirty years ſince, ſome thouſands of them in London took it into their heads that the world would be at an end on ſuch a night, and for ſome days previous to this fatal night, nothing was attended to but faſting and praying, and when it came, they made a watch-night of it, and ſpent it in prayer, &c. expecting every moment to be the laſt; and it is remarkable, that thouſands who were not methodiſts gave credit to this ridiculous prophecy, and were terribly alarmed; but the next morning they were aſhamed to look at one another, and many durſt not appear in their ſhops for ſometime afterwards. But others of them ſaid that God had heard the prayers of the righteous, and ſo ſpared the world a little longer. Some years after that Mr. Weſley alarmed his people all over England, with the tail of a comet; great numbers were dreadfully ap-

prehenſive

prehenſive leſt this comet ſhould ſcorch the earth to a cinder; but the ſaints by prayer made the comet keep a proper diſtance.

Charnock, of the laſt century, in his diſcourſe on Providence, has proved (in his way) that the univerſe was created and kept agoing for the ſake of the elect, and that as ſoon as their number is complete, the whole will be deſtroyed.

The fanatics in every age have found their account in making their followers believe the end of the world was at hand. In ſome of the wills and deeds, by which eſtates have been given to monaſteries, &c. in France, they have expreſſed their belief of the world's being nearly at an end, as a reaſon for making ſuch liberal donations to the church. But it is happy for us that in England ſuch wills would be ſet aſide. A caſe of this nature occured while Lord Northington was at the head of the law department. Reilly the preacher, had wheedled, or frightened, an old woman (Mrs. Norton) out of a deed

of

of gift of fifty pounds per year, but after the old woman's panic and fear of damnation was over, ſhe had recourſe to Chancery, and his Lordſhip annulled the deed of gift. His Lordſhip's remarks on ſuch kinds of impoſition are very curious, and worth your reading. See Collectanea Juridica, vol. 1. p. 458.

In fact, the very beſt of the methodiſts are like children, elated or depreſſed by mere trifles; and many who joined them while young and ignorant, quit their ſociety as they attain to years of diſcretion, or as their judgment is better informed.

I am,

Dear Friend,

Yours, &c.

LETTER

LETTER VIII.

" Religion's lustre is by native innocence
" Divinely fair, pure, and simple from all arts;
" You daub and dress her like a common mistress,
" The harlot of your fancies; and by adding
" False beauties, which she wants not, make the world
" Suspect her angel face is foul within."

ROWE's Tamerlane.

DEAR FRIEND,

THE enthusiastic notions which I had imbibed, and the desire I had to be talking about religious mysteries, &c. answered one valuable purpose; as it caused me to embrace every opportunity to learn to read, so that I could soon read the easy parts of the Bible, Mr. Wesley's Hymns, &c. and every leisure minute was so employed.

In the winter I was obliged to attend my work from six in the morning until ten at night. In the summer half year, I only worked as long as we could see without candle; but notwithstanding the close attention

I was

I was obliged to pay to my trade, yet for a long time I read ten chapters in the Bible every day; I alſo read and learned many hymns, and as ſoon as I could procure ſome of Mr. Weſley's Tracts, Sermons, &c. I read them alſo; many of them I peruſed in *Cloacina's* Temple, (the place where my Lord Cheſterfield adviſed his ſon to read the claſſics, but I did not apply them after reading to the farther uſe that his Lordſhip hints at.)

I had ſuch good eyes, that I often read by the light of the Moon, as my maſter would never permit me to take a candle into my room, and that prohibition I looked upon as a kind of perſecution, but I always comforted myſelf with the thoughts of my being a dear child of God; and as ſuch, that it was impoſſible for me to eſcape perſecution from the children of the devil, which epithets I very *piouſly* applied to my good maſter and miſtreſs. And ſo ignorantly and imprudently zealous (being a real methodiſt) was I for

the

the good of their *precious* ſouls, as ſometimes to give them broad hints of it, and of the dangerous ſtate they were in. Their pious good old miniſter, the Reverend Mr. Harriſon, I called " *a blind leader of the blind*;" and I more than once aſſured my miſtreſs, that both he and his whole flock were in a ſtate of damnation, being " ſtrangers to the hope of Iſrael, and without God in the world." My good miſtreſs wiſely thought that a good ſtick was the beſt way of arguing with ſuch an ignorant infatuated boy as I was, and had often recourſe to it; but I took care to give her a deal of trouble; for whenever I was ordered in my turn to read in the Bible, I always ſelected ſuch chapters as I thought militated againſt Arians, Socinians, &c. and ſuch verſes as I deemed favourable to the doctrine of Original Sin, Juſtification by Faith, imputed Righteouſneſs, the doctrine of the Trinity, &c. On ſuch parts I always placed a particular emphaſis, which puzzled and teazed the old lady a good deal.

Among other places I thought (having so been taught by the methodists) that the sixteenth chapter of Ezekiel very much favoured the doctrines of original sin, imputed righteousness, &c. that chapter I often selected and read to her, and she as often read the eighteenth chapter of the same prophecy, for the sake of the parable of the Father's eating *sour grapes.*

Whenever I read in St. Paul's Epistles on justification by faith alone, my good mistress would read in the Epistle of St. James, such passages as say that a man is not justified by faith alone, but by faith and works, which often embarrassed me not a little. However I comforted myself with the conceit of having more texts of Scripture on my side of the question than she had on her side. As to St. James, I was almost ready to conclude, that he was not quite orthodox, and so at last I did not much mind what he said.

" —— False

"——False opinions rooted in the mind,
"Hoodwink the soul and keep our reason blind.
"In controverted points can reason sway,
"When passion or conceit hurries us away?"

Hitherto I had not frequented the methodist meetings by the consent or knowledge of my master and mistress; nor had my zeal been so great as to make me openly violate their commands. But as my zeal increased much faster than my knowledge, I soon disregarded their orders, and without hesitation ran away to hear a methodistical sermon as often as I could find opportunity. One Sunday morning at eight o'clock my mistress seeing her sons set off, and knowing that they were gone to a methodist meeting, determined to prevent me from doing the same by locking the door, which she accordingly did; on which in a superstitious mood, I opened the Bible for direction what to do (ignorant methodists often practise the same superstitious method) and the first words I read were these, "He has given his angels charge concerning thee, lest at any time thou shouldest dash thy foot against a stone." This was enough for me; so without a moment's hesitation, I ran up two pair of stairs to my own room, and out of the window I leaped, to the great terror of my poor mistress. I got up immediately, and ran about two or three hundred yards, towards the meeting-house; but alas! I could run no farther; my feet and ancles were most intolerably bruised, so that I was obliged to be carried back and put to bed; and it was more than a month before I recovered the use of my limbs. I was ignorant enough to think that the Lord had not used me very well, and resolved not to put so much trust in him for the future.

This my rash adventure made a great noise in the town, and was talked of many miles round. Some few admired my amazing strength of faith, but the major part pitied me, as a poor ignorant, deluded and infatuated boy; which did not at all please,

Dear Friend,

Yours, &c.

LETTER IX.

"One makes the rugged paths ſo ſmooth and even,
"None but an ill-bred man can miſs of heaven.
"Another quits his ſtockings, breeches, ſhirt,
"Becauſe he fancies virtue dwells in dirt:
"While all concur to take away the ſtreſs,
"From weightier points, and lay it on the leſs."

STILLINGFLEET on Converſation.

"'Gad I've a thriving traffic in my eye,
"Near the mad manſions of Moorfields I'll bawl;
"Friends, fathers, mothers, ſiſters, ſons and all,
"Shut up your ſhops, and liſten to my call.

FOOTE.

DEAR FRIEND,

IN the fourth year of my apprenticeſhip, my maſter died; now although he was a good huſband, a good father, and a good maſter, &c. yet as he had not the methodiſtical faith, and could not pronounce the *Shibboleth* of that ſect, I *piouſly* feared that he was gone to hell.

My miſtreſs thought that his death was haſtened by his uneaſy reflections on the bad

bad behaviour of his ſons, after they commenced methodiſts, as before they were *converted* each was dutiful and attended to his trade, but after they became *ſaints* they attended ſo much to their ſpiritual concerns that they acted as though they ſuppoſed they were to be fed and cloathed by miracles, like Mr. Huntingdon, who informs us in his book called " The Bank of Faith," that the Lord ſent him a pair of breeches, that a dog brought him mutton to eat, fiſh died at night in a pond on purpoſe to be eaten by him in the morning; money, and in ſhort every thing he could deſire he obtained by prayer. Thus as Foote ſays,

" With labour, toil, all ſecond means diſpenſe,
" And live a rent-charge upon providence.

To give you a better idea of methodiſtical ignorance and neglect of ordinary means of living, &c. I will relate one inſtance more. Mary Hubbard (an old woman of Mr. Weſley's ſociety) would often waſh her linen, hang it out to dry, and go away to work in the fields, or to

Taunton

Taunton market, four miles from her houſe; and when blamed, ſhe would anſwer "that the Lord watched over her, and all that ſhe had, and that he would prevent any perſon from ſtealing her two old ſmocks, or if he permitted them to be ſtolen, he would ſend her two new in their ſtead." And I ſeriouſly aſſure you, ſir, that there are many thouſand Mary Hubbards amongſt the methodiſts.

As I had been bound to my miſtreſs as well as my maſter, I was of courſe an apprentice ſtill. But after my maſter's death I obtained more liberty of conſcience (as I called it) ſo that I not only went to hear the methodiſt ſermons, but was alſo admitted into their ſociety; and I believe they never had a more devout enthuſiaſtical member; for ſeveral years I regularly attended every ſermon and all their private meetings.

As you are probably unacquainted with the nature of theſe *private meetings*, a ſhort account of them may perhaps afford you ſome amuſement.

The late Mr. Weſley inſtituted amongſt his people, beſides the public preachings, ſeveral kinds of private meetings; and as the *prayer-meeting* is the leaſt private of any of them, I will firſt take notice of that.

To the prayer-meetings, which were in general held in private houſes, they often invited people who were not of their ſociety. An hymn was firſt ſung, then they all knelt, and the firſt perſon who felt a motion, made an extemporary prayer; when he had done another began, and ſo on, for about two hours.

But it ſo happened ſometimes, that one of the brethren began to pray without having *the gift* of prayer (as they call it), and then he often ſtuck faſt, like ſome of the young orators at Coach-maker's Hall, &c. Prayer-meetings were held in ſuch high eſteem amongſt them that they aſſerted, more were "*born again*," and more "*made free* from all the remains of ſin," or in other words of their own, "made *perfect* as God is perfect," in

theſe

theſe kinds of meeting, than at public preaching, &c. Thus, as Pomfret ſays,

"The ſpirits heated will ſtrange things produce."

But it is impoſſible for you, my friend, to form any juſt idea of theſe aſſemblies, except you had been preſent at them: one wheedles and coaxes the Divine Being, in his addreſſes; another is amorous and luſcious; and a third ſo rude and commanding, he will even tell the Deity that he muſt be *a liar* if he does not grant all they aſk. In this manner will they work up one another's imaginations until they may actually be ſaid to be in a ſtate of intoxication, and whilſt in this intoxicated ſtate, it often happens that ſome of them recollect a text of ſcripture, ſuch as, "thy ſins are forgiven thee," or "go and ſin no more," &c. and then they declare themſelves to be born again, or to be ſanctified, &c.

They have another kind of private meeting after the public preaching on Sunday evenings, in which the preacher meets all the

the members of the ſociety, who ſtay behind after the general congregation is diſmiſſed. To this ſociety the preacher gave ſuch advice as he deemed better ſuited to a godly few than to a promiſcuous multitude of "*outward court* worſhippers."

Their *Love-feaſt* is alſo a private meeting of as many members of the community as pleaſe to attend; and they generally come from all parts, within ſeveral miles of the place where love-feaſts are held.

When all are met they alternately ſing and pray; and ſuch amongſt them as think that their *experience* (as they call it) is remarkable, ſtand up in their place and relate all the tranſactions between God, the devil, and their ſouls. At ſuch ſeaſons as this I have heard many of them declare they had juſt received the pardon of all their ſins while Brother ſuch-a-one was in prayer; another would then get up and aſſert that he was juſt at that inſtant made perfectly free from ſin.

At

At theſe times the Spirit is ſuppoſed to be very powerfully at work amongſt them; and ſuch an *uniſon* of ſighing and *groaning* ſucceeds, that you would think they had all loſt their ſenſes. In this frantic ſtate, many apply to themſelves ſuch texts of ſcripture as happen to come into their heads.

In the Love-feaſt they have *buns* to eat, which are mutually broken between each brother and ſiſter, and they have alſo *water* to drink, which they hand from one to another. Theſe meetings begin about ſeven o'clock, and laſt until nine, or ten.

In London, Briſtol, and other large places, they have ſome *private* meetings, unknown to the community at large. Theſe meetings conſiſt of all married men at one time, young and unmarried men at another time: the married women by themſelves, and the ſingle women by themſelves; and to each of theſe claſſes Mr. Weſley went, and gave ſuch advice or exhortations as he thought ſuitable to their ſituation in life, ſeldom fail-

ing

ing to ſpeak much in praiſe of celibacy, to the *Maids* and *Bachelors* under his paſtoral care. I will in my next give you an account of their watch-nights, claſs-meetings, bands, and other particulars.

I am,

Dear Friend,

Yours, &c.

LETTER

LETTER X.

"——————— Here Gamaliel ſage
" Trains up his babes of grace, inſtructed well
" In all the —— diſcipline of prayer;
" To point the holy leer: by juſt degrees
" To cloſe the twinkling eyes, expand the palms,
" To expoſe the whites, and with the ſightleſs balls
" To glare upon the crowd: to riſe, to ſink
" The docile voice; now murm'ring ſoft and ſlow,
" With inward accent calm, and then again,
" In foaming floods of rapt'rous eloquence
" Let looſe the ſtorm, and thunder thro' the noſe
" The threatened vengeance."

SOMERVILLE.

DEAR FRIEND,

THE *Watch-night* begins about ſeven o'clock. They ſing hymns, pray, preach, ſing, and pray again; then exhort, ſing and pray alternately, until twelve o'clock. The hymns which they ſing on thoſe nights, were wrote for ſuch occaſions, and abound with gloomy ideas, which are increaſed by the time of night; and it muſt be remarked, that the major part of thoſe who

who attend theſe nocturnal meetings having faſted the whole of the day (according to Mr. Weſley's orders) are in a very proper ſtate of mind to entertain the moſt extravagant whims or enthuſiaſtic notions that can poſſibly enter the heads of any viſionaries. So that ſuch nights are often very prolific, as numbers are ſaid to be born again, and become the temples of the Holy Ghoſt on watch-nights, which makes thoſe nights eſteemed by them.

Mr. Weſley, in every place where his people were numerous, had divided them into *claſſes*, conſiſting of twelve or fourteen brothers or ſiſters. Sometimes men and women met together in the ſame *claſs* (as they called it) and other claſſes conſiſted of all men or all women. Each of theſe claſſes had one in it who was called the *leader*. In ſuch claſſes where men and women meet together, the leader was always a brother: and ſo of courſe when the claſs conſiſted of men alone. But in in the women's claſſes a ſiſter was always the leader.

When they met together, the leader firſt gave out an hymn, which they all ſang; after the hymn they all knelt, and their leader made an extemporary prayer; after which they were ſeated, and when the leader had informed them of the ſtate of his own mind, he enquired of all preſent, one after another, how they found the ſtate of their ſouls. Some he found were full of faith and *aſſurance*, others had dreadful doubts and fears; ſome had horrid temptations; others complained of a lukewarm ſtate, &c. In theſe meetings, ſome of the members ſpoke of themſelves, as though they were as pure as angels are in heaven, but with the generality of them, it was far otherwiſe, and nothing was more common among them than to hear the major part exclaiming againſt themſelves, and declaring that they were the moſt vile and abandoned wretches on this ſide hell, that they wondered why the earth did not open

and

and ſwallow them up alive. But they generally added, that "the blood of Chriſt cleanſes from all ſin," and that "where ſin abounded there would grace much more abound." Indeed it was eaſy to remark that the reaſon why they painted themſelves in ſuch odious colours, was only to boaſt of an aſtoniſhing quantity of grace that God had beſtowed on them, in thus pardoning all their abominations and numbering them with the houſehold of faith, who ought to have been ſhut up in the nethermoſt hell. To each of theſe the leader gave a word of comfort, or of correction in the beſt manner he was able. They then ſang and prayed again. This laſted about one hour. And every one in Mr. Weſley's connexion did, or was expected to meet, each in his own claſs once in a week. In theſe claſſes each made a weekly contribution towards the general ſupport of the preachers, &c. Such as were very poor contributed a penny per week, others two-pence, and ſome who could afford it ſixpence. This money was entered in a book kept for that purpoſe,

purpoſe, and one in every claſs called the ſteward, had the care of the caſh.

I now come to ſpeak of the *Bands*, which conſiſted only of *juſtified* perſons; that is ſuch as had received the *aſſurance* of their ſins being pardoned. In the claſſes, both the *awakened* (as they call them) and the juſtified, and even thoſe that were made *perfect* met all together, as did the married and the ſingle, and often men and women. But none were admitted into any *band* but ſuch as were at leaſt in a juſtified ſtate, and the married of each ſex met by themſelves, and the ſingle by themſelves. About ten was the number generally put in one band; all theſe muſt belong to and meet in ſome claſs, once a week, when not hindered by ſickneſs, &c. and they were alſo to meet weekly in their band. When met, they firſt ſung, then made a ſhort prayer; that done, the *band-leader* informed them of the ſtate of his mind during the laſt week, &c. He then made inquiry into the ſtate of all preſent, and each related what had paſſed ſince they laſt met; as what viſitations they had received from God, what temptations from the devil, the fleſh, &c. And it is a maxim amongſt them that expoſing to one another what the devil has particularly tempted them to commit, will make the old fellow more careful how he tempts, when he knows that all his ſecrets will be told the next meeting. In the claſſes they only confeſſed in general terms, that they have been tempted by the world, the fleſh and the devil. But in the bands they confeſſed the particular ſins which they had been tempted to commit, or had actually committed.

The laſt time I met in band was in London, where an old man (near ſeventy years of age) informed us that he had for ſeveral weeks together laboured under a very grievous temptation of the devil, who all this time had been conſtantly tempting him to commit adultery; he farther informed us, that having let too much of his houſe to lodg-

ers,

gers, they were obliged to put the maid's bed in the room where he and his wife ſlept; and that one morning he had ſeen the maid lying aſleep, nearly or quite uncovered, and he again aſſured us that ever ſince that time the devil had been every day tempting him to do that which was nought with the maid. I could not help thinking the old gentleman was right in charging it on *the devil*, as there was little reaſon to think it was any temptation of *the fleſh*. Permit me to add, that this *old buck* had a wife about half his own age. I have been informed that ſome young men of the brotherhood, have at times diſguiſed themſelves in women's clothes, and have ſo got into the women's bands; it may be very curious to hear the confeſſions of the holy ſiſters. By this time I ſuppoſe you have had enough of *band-meetings*.

Mr. Weſley inſtituted another kind of private meeting for the higheſt order of his people, called the *ſelect bands*; to which none were admitted but ſuch as were ſanctified, or made *perfect* in love, and freed from all the remains of ſin. But as I never profeſſed *perfection*, I was not permitted to enter into this holy of holies. But I have known a great number of theſe perfect ſaints, of both ſexes; and I alſo lived in the ſame houſe a whole year with one of theſe intire holy ſiſters. A few days before I came to live in Chiſwell-Street, one of theſe perfect ſiſters was detected in ſtealing coals out of the ſhed of one of the ſanctified brothers, but ſhe, like the old fellow above mentioned, ſaid it was the devil that tempted her to do it.

Four times every year new *tickets* are diſtributed to all Mr. Weſley's people throughout the three kingdoms. Their ticket is a very ſmall ſlip of paper, with a text of ſcripture on it, which is exchanged every quarter for ſome other text. Such as are only in a *claſs*, have a different text from ſuch as are in a *band*, ſo that no one can be admitted into a general meeting of the bands, appointed by any of the preachers when he intends to give them an exhortation, nor into any particular

band,

band, by a common ſociety ticket. On the common tickets are ſuch texts as theſe: "Now is the accepted time."—"Awake thou that ſleepeſt," and ſuch like. But thoſe for the *bands* are in a higher ſtrain; as, "Be ye perfect as your heavenly father is perfect."—"Go on unto perfection."—"Ye are children of the light."—"Your bodies are temples of the Holy Ghoſt;" and other texts of a ſimilar tendency. For theſe tickets, each poor perſon paid one ſhilling, ſuch as were rich paid more; indeed the money ſeemed to be the principal end of iſſuing tickets, at leaſt in country places, the members in the community being ſo well known to each other, that they ſcarce ever ſhewed their tickets in order to gain admittance. I forgot to inform you that prayer-meetings, claſs-meetings, band-meetings, &c. were in general held in private houſes, belonging to ſome of the brethren.

I am, dear Friend,

Yours, &c.

LETTER XI.

" Stiff in opinions, always in the wrong;
" Was every thing by ſtarts and nothing long."

* * * * * *

" Then all for women, panting, rhiming, drinking,
" Beſides ten thouſand freaks that died in thinking."

DEAR FRIEND,

YOU now ſee what ſort of a ſociety I was got into. In country places particularly, they conſiſt of farmers, huſbandmen, ſhoemakers, woolcombers, weavers, their wives, &c. I have heard Mr. Weſley remark that more women are converted than men; and I believe that by far the greateſt part of his people are females; and not a few of them ſour, diſappointed old maids, with ſome others of a leſs prudiſh diſpoſition.

Lavater in his eſſay on phyſiognomy ſays, " Women ſink into the moſt incurable melancholy, as they alſo riſe to the moſt enraptured

raptured heights." In another place he ſays, "By the irritability of their nerves, their incapability for deep inquiry and firm deciſion, they may eaſily from their extreme ſenſibility, become the moſt irreclaimable, the moſt rapturous enthuſiaſts."

There are thouſands in this ſociety who will never read any thing beſides the Bible, and books publiſhed by Mr. Weſley. For ſeveral years I read very little elſe, nor would I go (at leaſt very ſeldom) to any other place of worſhip; ſo that inſtead of hearing the ſenſible and learned miniſters of Taunton, I would often go four, five, or ſix miles, to ſome country village, to hear an inſpired huſbandman, ſhoemaker, blackſmith, or woolcomber; and frequently in froſt and ſnow have I roſe a little after midnight (not knowing what time of night it was) and have wandered about the town until five o'clock, when the preaching began; where I have often heard a ſermon preached to not more than ten or a dozen people. But ſuch of us as did attend at this early hour, uſed afterwards to congratulate each other on the great privilege we enjoyed, then off we went to our work, ſhivering with cold.

I was firſt converted to methodiſm when I was about ſixteen years of age, from that time until I was twenty-one I was a very ſincere enthuſiaſt, and every ſpare hour I enjoyed I dedicated to the ſtudy of the Bible, reading methodiſtical books, learning hymns, hearing ſermons, meeting in ſocieties, &c. My memory was very tenacious, ſo that every thing I read I made my own. I could have repeated ſeveral volumes of hymns; when I heard a ſermon, I could have preached it again, and nearly in the ſame words; my Bible had hundreds of leaves folded down, and thouſands of marks againſt ſuch texts as I thought favoured the doctrines (or whims) which I had imbibed. So that I ſtood forth as the champion of methodiſm wherever I came.

But alas! my godly ſtrict life at length ſuffered interruption. I will give you a farther

farther account of the methodifts when I come to the time when I finally left their fociety.

The election for two members of Parliament was ftrongly contefted at Taunton, juft as I attained my twenty-firft year; and being now of age, the fix or feven months, which I had to ferve of my apprenticefhip were purchafed of my miftrefs by fome friends of two of the contending candidates; fo that I was at once fet free in the midft of a fcene of riot and diffipation.

> " Prefent Example gets within our guard,
> " And acts with double force, by few repell'd."
>
> YOUNG.

> " Nor fhame, nor honour could prevail,
> " To keep me thus from turning tail."

As I had a vote, and was alfo poffeffed of a few ideas above thofe of my rank and fituation, my company was courted by fome who were in a much higher fphere; and (probably what they partly intended) in fuch company I foon forgot my godly or methodiftical con-

nections,

nections, and ran into the opposite extreme: so that for several months most of my spare hours were devoted to the

> "Young-ey'd God of Wine! Parent of joys!
> "Frolic and full of thee, while the cold sons
> "Of temperance, the fools of thought and care,
> "Lay stretch'd in sober slumbers."
>
> MALLET's Eurydice.

Here I had nearly sunk for ever into meanness, obscurity and vice; for when the election was over, I had no longer open houses to eat and drink in at free cost.

However I did not sink quite so low as the commonalty of journeymen shoemakers, but in general worked very hard, and spent my money in better company.

Notwithstanding, at times I was very uneasy, and although I had not been at any methodistical meeting during the time that I had lived this dissipated life, yet my mind was not freed intirely from the superstitious fears I had there imbibed; so that whenever any person asked me, what would become of

me

me (that had lived ſuch a holy life) if I ſhould die in the ſtate of *backſliding* from "the good old way?" I always acknowledged that I ſhould be eternally damn'd, were that to be the caſe. But I muſt confeſs that I was not much afraid of dying in ſuch a ſtate, as I was too much prepoſſeſſed with the methodiſtical notions of *free grace*, that would not let me finally be loſt, preſuming that I muſt wait as it were for a *ſecond call* to repentance, juſtification, &c. which I had been taught to believe might take place inſtantaneouſly, and put the devil to flight in a hurry, and ſo matters would be all right again.

I often privately took the Bible to bed with me, and in the long ſummer mornings read for hours together in bed, but this did not in the leaſt influence my conduct. As you know great events often ariſe from little cauſes, I am now going to relate a circumſtance, trivial in itſelf, though productive of a more conſiderable change in my ſituation, than any I had yet experienced.

I was

I was twenty-one years of age the 11th of September 1767, the election was over the latter end of March 1768. It was in this year that my new master's wife insisted on my purchasing milk of a milk-maid who was a customer at the shop; which command I refused to comply with, as I had a smart little milk-maid of my own. But as my mistress *wore the breeches*, my master was obliged, by his wife's order, to inform me that I must comply with her mandate, or get another master. I left him without hesitation; and the same afternoon went to Wellington, took leave of my father and mother, and informed them of my intention to go to Bristol. After two or three days, I returned back to Taunton, where I stayed a day or two more. In which time I became enamoured with, or infatuated by, the beautiful *Nancy Trott*: and although I saw the impropriety of the measure, yet I could not resist the fair tempter, who prevailed with me to permit her to accompany me in my journey.

" Reason

"Reafon was given to curb our headftrong will,
"And yet but fhews a weak phyfician's fkill;
"Gives nothing while the raging fit does laft,
"But ftays to cure it when the worft is paft.
"Reafon's a ftaff for age, when Nature's gone;
"But Youth is ftrong enough to walk alone."

DRYDEN's Con. of Gran.

We refted a week in Bridgewater, where I worked and got money to convey us to Exbridge, feventeen miles on this fide Briftol; and there I faw my conduct in fuch a point of view as made me refolve to leave her.

"In well-feign'd accidents, now they hail my ear,
"My life, my love, my charmer, or my dear."
"As if thefe founds, thefe joylefs founds could prove
"The fmalleft particle of genuine love.
"O! purchas'd love, retail'd through half the town.
"Where each may fhare on paying half-a-crown;
"Where every air of tendernefs is art,
"And not one word the language of the heart;
"Where all is mockery of Cupid's reign,
"End in remorfe, in wretchednefs and pain.

Art of living in London.

My finances amounted to three fhillings and one penny, out of which I gave her half-a-crown,

crown, and with the remaining ſevenpence, without informing her of my purpoſe, I ſet off for Briſtol; where I arrived in a few hours, and got work the ſame evening.

A few days after, I went to the inn where the Taunton carrier put up, to enquire after *Miſs Trott*, as I wanted to know if ſhe had returned ſafe to Taunton. I was informed that ſhe was in Briſtol nearly as ſoon as I was. Knowing but little of the world, and ſtill leſs of women of her deſcription, I was quite unhappy on her account, for fear that being in a ſtrange place ſhe might be in want and diſtreſs; which thought induced me to offer to ſeveral of my countrymen five ſhillings to the firſt who ſhould bring me an account where I might find her; but I did not ſee her until ſeveral weeks after that.

The Taunton Carrier gave me a letter from my good Miſtreſs Bowden (who by marrying again had changed her name to Dingle). The contents of this letter very much ſurpriſed me. It informed me that a day or two before I fell out with my laſt miſtreſs (which was the trifling cauſe of my leaving Taunton) *Betty Tucker*, a common laſs, had ſworn a child to me; that the pariſh officers had been to my maſter's ſhop within an hour after I had left it to go to Wellington, and that they had been at Wellington juſt as I had left that place, and afterwards hearing that I was in Bridgewater they had purſued me thither. But the morning on which they arrived, I had ſet off for Exbridge; and believing that I had intentionally fled before them, they had given over the chaſe for the preſent.

Reflecting on this affair, although my conduct was very far from entitling me to entertain ſuch a ſuppoſition, yet I was then weak enough to imagine, that being a particular favourite of heaven a kind of miracle had been wrought to ſave me from a priſon, or from marrying a woman I could not bear the idea of living with a ſingle week; and as I had not any knowledge of her being

with

with child (not having ſeen her for three months before) I had not taken any meaſure to avoid the conſequence, but put myſelf in the way of the officers: for, as I have juſt told you, after I had taken leave of my father and mother, I went back to Taunton, and walked about publicly one whole day, and part of another.

This girl was delivered about two months afterwards of a ſtill-born child, ſo that I was never troubled for expences. Methinks you are ready to ſay with Pomfret,

"'Tis eaſy to deſcend into the ſnare,
"By the pernicious conduct of the Fair:
"But ſafely to return from their abode
"Requires the wit, the prudence of a God."

I am,

Dear Friend,

Yours, &c.

LETTER

LETTER XII.

" ——————— Learn to ſcan
" The various foibles of imperfect man."

Art of Living in London.

DEAR FRIEND,

THE ſubject of my laſt recalls to my mind a ridiculous affair, which excited much mirth in that part of the country.

During the Election at Taunton, a gentleman one day came in a poſt-chaiſe to the White-hart Inn, kept by Mr. Baldwin, and after having refreſhed himſelf, ſtrolled into the yard, and ſeeing the hoſtler, aſked him if he could inform him where they took in the *news?* The hoſtler underſtanding him in a literal ſenſe, directed him to a bookſeller's ſhop on the oppoſite ſide of the way; this ſhop was kept by Miſs A—d—n, a beautiful young lady of irreproachable character, and one whoſe fine underſtanding and poliſhed taſte did honour to the profeſſion; which profeſſion ſhe only adopted for an amuſement, as ſhe poſſeſſed an independent fortune.

Our gentleman on entering the ſhop, enquired of the ſhopmaid for her miſtreſs, but the maid being uſed to ſerve in the ſhop, and knowing that her miſtreſs had ſome ladies with her, informed the gentleman that ſhe could help him to any thing that he wanted. But on his ſaying he had ſome private buſineſs with her miſtreſs, he was ſhewed into a back parlour, and the miſtreſs being informed a gentleman wanted to ſpeak to her, ſhe went directly to him. The moment ſhe entered the room, he claſped her in his arms, called her a divine creature, &c. This ſo alarmed Miſs A—d—n, that ſhe ſcreamed aloud; on hearing of which, the ladies, preceded by the houſemaid and ſhopmaid repaired to the parlour, where they found Miſs A—d—n almoſt in fits. The gentleman thinking that it was only a trick to raiſe her price, took but little notice, on which one of the maids ran out and called in ſeveral of the neighbours, who on coming into the parlour, ſaw with aſtoniſhment our Sir Harry Wildair taking improper liberties with Miſs

A—d—n,

A—d—n, and desired him to desist. But he desired them not to attempt to put tricks on travellers, and ordered them to leave the room. Instead of obeying his injunctions they in a resolute tone ordered our spark to go instantly about his business. However he still kept his ground, until the mayor of the town, who happened to live just by, was called in. Mr. Mayor demanded to know why he took such freedom with the lady? Our gentleman, seeing that the affair began to look very serious, now became calm, and informed the company that having an inclination for a frolic, he had enquired for a bad house, and had been directed there; adding that if there had been any mistake, he was very sorry for it, and would beg the lady's pardon. On hearing this, the company was more surprized than before, and demanded of the gentleman, who had informed him that that house was a bawdy-house? He, without hesitation replied, the hostler at the White Hart. Upon this the hostler was sent for, and on his being asked, if he had directed that gentleman, to Miſs A—d—n's as to a bawdy-houſe? The poor fellow, with marks of terror and ſurpriſe anſwered, No. The Gentlemen never aſked me for a bawdy-houſe, he only aſked me for a houſe where they took in the news. So that the hoſtler's underſtanding him in a literal ſenſe, cauſed all the confuſion. The affair however had got ſo much air that our ſpark was glad to leave the town immediately.

A very ſtrange unaccountable circumſtance happened in this Inn, about the ſame time; one of thoſe occurrences that puzzle the philoſopher, and ſtrengthen ſuperſtition in weak minds. Three or four gentlemen of the neighbourhood were drinking wine in one of the rooms, when the landlord of the Inn (as it appeared to them) walked into the room, and coming up to the table, around which they were ſeated, they addreſſed him with Mr. Baldwin, how do you do? ſit down and take a glaſs of wine with us; but inſtead of doing as requeſted, the ſuppoſed Innkeeper

keeper walked out of the room, without making any reply; which not only ſurprized, but offended the company, who rung the bell violently, and on the waiter's appearance, they ordered him to ſend in his maſter. The waiter informed them that his maſter was not at home. The gentlemen replied that he was at home a few minutes ſince, and therefore they inſiſted on ſeeing him; but the man aſſured them they were miſtaken, as his maſter was in Briſtol, and had been there ſeveral days. They then ordered the waiter to ſend in Mrs. Baldwin, who immediately appearing, the gentlemen aſked her where Mr. Baldwin was, and ſhe informed them as the waiter had already done, that he was in Briſtol, and had been there ſeveral days, on which the gentlemen grew very angry, and ſwore that Mr. Baldwin had juſt before come into the room, and on their requeſting him to partake of their wine, had inſulted them by going out of the room, without deigning to give them an anſwer. Mrs. Baldwin, then drew out of her pocket a letter ſhe had that morning received from Mr. Baldwin, by which it was apparent, that he really was in Bristol. The story was then told round the neighbourhood, and all the old women concluded that Mr. Baldwin must certainly be dead, and that he died at the very instant that the gentlemen saw him come into the room; but Mr. Baldwin returning two days after, rendered it necessary for them to vary their story; they then asserted that it was a token, or some warning of his death, and had no doubt but it would very soon happen. It was generally thought that Mr. Baldwin was weak enough to pay such attention to the story and the inference, as to hurt his health, as he really died within a year after, and the old women were not a little pleased at the event, as it tended to justify the truth of their prediction.

A more ridiculous affair happened about ten years since, at the two Bells, opposite Whitechapel Church. The landlord was sitting one night with some jovial company, one of whom happening to say that he prayed to God, that ſuch a thing ſhould not come to paſs, the landlord replied in a good humoured manner, your prayers will neither do good or harm; upon which the other ſaid a deal to perſuade the hoſt that his prayers would do great things; but the more he ſaid in praiſe of his prayers, the more the landlord laughed at, and ridiculed him. The man at laſt inſiſted that he could pray the landlord to death in two months time, and offered to bet him a crown bowl of punch to the truth of it, which the landlord accepting, the wager was laid, and almoſt every night after this, the man came to the houſe, and conſtantly laughed at the landlord, and aſſured him that he would loſe his wager; and however ſtrange it may appear, our hoſt did die within the time, and his widow paid the wager. I think there cannot remain a doubt but that the ridiculous talk of the fellow actually affected the landlord's mind, and haſtened his death, and the following inſtances tend alſo to ſhew how eaſily the lives of ſome are ſhortened.

Joſeph Scales, Eſq. about five years ſince, in turning ſhort one day in one of the ſtreets of London, met a man whom he had not ſeen for ſome time, and innocently addreſſed him with, Ha ! what are you alive yet ! which had ſuch an effect on the poor man that he died a few hours after.

Being at Briſtol about four years ſince, I enquired after a worthy leatherſeller whom I had formerly known, and was informed that he was lately dead, and that his death was ſuppoſed to have been haſtened by a famous fortuneteller, who having caſt his nativity, declared that he would die within ſix months, which affected his mind ſo as to accompliſh the prediction. The ſtory of the late Dr. Pitcairn, of Edinburgh, and the collier is well known.

I have ſet down the above inſtances, in order to ſhew how eaſy it is to trifle away the lives of our fellow creatures, and ſurely ſuch who wantonly do it, muſt afterwards have very gloomy reflections.

I am, dear Friend,

Yours, &c.

LETTER XIII.

" I had a Friend that lov'd me:
" I was his Soul: he liv'd not but in me.
" We were ſo cloſe link'd in each other's breaſt,
" The rivets were not found that join'd us firſt.

DRYDEN's All for Love.

DEAR FRIEND,

IN my laſt I mentioned my arrival at Briſtol, where I took a lodging in a ſtreet, called (I think) Queen-Street, in Caſtle-ſtreet, at the houſe of a Mr. *James*; a much more decent reſidence, than commonly falls to the lot of journeymen ſhoemakers.

In this houſe I found a Mr. John Jones, a genteel young man, juſt turned of twenty-one years of age: He was alſo a ſon of *Criſpin*, and made women's ſtuff ſhoes; which he ſold by the dozen to warehouſes. This Mr. Jones and I were ſoon very intimate; we kept ourſelves neatly dreſſed, and in general worked

worked hard, ſpending our money chiefly in the company of women. As,

> " All men have follies, which they blindly trace,
> " Thro' the dark turnings of a dubious maze.
> " But happy thoſe, who by a prudent care,
> " Retreat betimes from the fallacious ſnare."
>
> POMFRET.

We followed this courſe about four months. During this time Mr. Jones once perſuaded me to go with him to the Playhouſe, where we ſaw Shakeſpear's fine comedy of " As you like it." This was a feaſt indeed to me, who had never before ſeen nor even read any theatrical production. 'Tis impoſſible for me to deſcribe my ſenſations on the occaſion. Between the play and the entertainment (which was the Mayor of Garrat) Mr. Edward Shuter performed a ſhort piece called " The drunken man." This was the only time that I ever ſaw that extraordinary genius, but he made ſuch an impreſſion on my mind, that it is impoſſible I ever ſhould forget him. I believe it is not generally known, and as few would ever have ſuſpected,

that

that this child of Momus was alſo a child of grace.

Since the publication of the firſt edition of theſe memoirs, I have read " The memoirs of Mr. Tate Wilkinſon," patentee of the Theatres Royal of York and Hull, and was much ſurprized to learn that the famous Ned Shuter was a *gracious ſoul.* I will give you a paſſage or two out of Mr. Wilkinſon's memoirs, vol. iii. page 27, &c. " My imitation of Whitefield was beyond compare. Mr. Foote was ſtruck by ſtepping in by chance, and once hearing Whitefield; the mixture of whoſe abſurdity, whim, conſequence and extravagance, pleaſed his fancy, and entertained him highly, as Whitefield was that day dealing out damnation, fire and brimſtone, as cheerfully as if they were ſo many bleſſings. What pity it is that our fears only, and not our reaſon, will bring conviction; but reaſon handed by unaffected pure piety and religion would be a day of woe to methodiſm."

" Mr.

" Mr. Foote was only a ſpy at Whitefield's academy, while I (ſays Mr. Wilkinſon) had been a zealot for ſome ſeaſons before my encounter at Covent-Garden with Mr. Foote, my attendance had been conſtant with my friend Shuter, and as he actually was one of the new-born, and paid large ſums to Whitefield, I was always permitted to ſtay with him, for he really was bewildered in his brains, more by his wiſhing to acquire imaginary grace, than by all his drinking, and whenever he was warm with the bottle, and with only a friend or two, like Maw-worm, he could not mind his ſhop, becauſe he thought it a ſin, and wiſhed to go a-preaching; for Shuter like Maw-worm believed he had a call. I have gone with Shuter at ſix in the morning of a Sunday to Tottenham-Court-Road, then before ten to Mr. Weſley's in Long-Acre; at eleven again to Tottenham-Court-Road Tabernacle, dined near Bedlam (a very proper place for us both) with a party of the holy ones, went at three to Mr. Weſley's theatre; then from that to White-

field's

field's till eight, and then ſhut up, to commune with the family compact, page 29. I having had ſo much practice (while a zealot) I really obtained and exhibited a much ſtronger likeneſs of Whitefield than Mr. Foote did. The week before my Covent-Garden exhibition, I met Shuter at the Tabernacle; a great coolneſs had continued for ſome time, as we had not ſpoke, or even looked at each other ſince the breach between us in 1758, but as we were met together in a place of charity and forgiveneſs to all who ſubſcribed to the preacher, we became very ſociable, and before Whitefield's lecture was done we were perfectly reconciled: *we adjourned to the Roſe, and by three the next morning we were ſworn friends,* and continued ſo until his death. Ned Shuter was a lively, ſpirited, ſhrewd companion; a ſuperior in natural whim and humour ſurely never inhabited a human breaſt, for what he ſaid and did was all his own, as it was with difficulty he could read the parts he had to play, and could not write at all; he had attained to ſign an order, but

no

no more. Nature could not here beſtow her gifts to greater advantage, than on poor Ned, as what ſhe gave he made ſhine, not only conſpicuouſly but brilliantly, and to the delight of all who knew him on or off the ſtage; he might truly be dubbed the child of nature. He was no man's enemy but his own, peace, reſt, and happineſs, I hope he now poſſeſſes; for, the poor, the friendleſs and the ſtranger he often comforted, and when ſometimes reduced by his follies, he never could ſee a real object in miſery and reſiſt giving at leaſt half he was worth to his diſtreſſed fellow creature." Page 5, vol. iii. "But, O ye ſaints of your own creating! I will preach to you: Mark! *judge not of plays and players, leſt you be judged*; thoſe who are the moſt cenſorious on the infirmities of others, are uſually moſt notoriouſly guilty of far greater failings themſelves, *and ſanctified methodiſtical ſlander* is of all the *moſt ſevere, bitter and cruel.*"

Page 6. "In the comedy of the Hypocrite, the Colonel ſays he ſuppoſes they go to the play

play for the benefit of the brethren. Cantwell answers, "the charity covereth the sin;" which was actually the case, for in 1757, *as Shuter was bountiful to the Tabernacle, Mr. Whitefield not only permitted, but advised his hearers to attend Shuter's benefit*; but for that night only." Alas, poor Shuter!

It is singular enough that about this time, although I could not write, yet I composed several songs, one of which was sold for a guinea; some were given to the Bristol printers, who printed them, and the ballad-singers sung them about the streets; on which occasions I was as proud as though I had composed an opera. My friend Mr. Jones was my secretary, who before I came to live with him had not the least relish for books, and I had only read a few enthusiastic authors, together with Pomfret's poems; this last I could almost repeat by memory; however I made the most of my little stock of literature, and strongly recommended the purchasing of books to Mr. Jones. But so

ignorant

ignorant were we on the ſubject, that neither of us knew what books were fit for our peruſal, nor what to enquire for, as we had ſcarce ever heard or ſeen even any *title pages*, except a few of the religious ſort, which at that time we had no reliſh for. So that we were at a loſs how to increaſe our ſmall ſtock of ſcience. And here I cannot help thinking that had Fortune thrown proper books in our way, we ſhould have imbibed a juſt taſte for literature, and ſoon made ſome tolerable progreſs, but ſuch was our obſcurity, that it was next to impoſſible for us ever to emerge from it.

As we could not tell what to aſk for, we were aſhamed to go into the bookſellers ſhops; and I aſſure you, my friend, that there are thouſands now in England in the very ſame ſituation: many, very many have come to my ſhop, who have diſcovered an enquiring mind, but were totally at a loſs what to aſk for, and who had no friend to direct them.

"———— Reaſon grows apace, and calls
"For the kind hand of an aſſiduous care.
"Delightful taſk! to rear the tender thought,
"To teach the young idea how to ſhoot,
"To pour the freſh inſtruction o'er the mind,
"To breathe th' enlivening ſpirit, and to fix
"The gen'rous purpoſe in the glowing breaſt."

THOMSON.

One day as my friend Jones and I were ſtrolling about the fair that is annually held in and near St. James's church-yard, we ſaw a ſtall of books, and in looking over the title pages, I met with Hobbes's Tranſlation of Homer's Iliad and Odyſſey. I had ſomehow or other heard that Homer was a great poet, but unfortunately I had never heard of Pope's tranſlation of him, ſo we very eagerly purchaſed that by Hobbes. At this ſtall I alſo purchaſed Walker's poetical paraphraſe of Epictetus's morals; and home we went, perfectly well pleaſed with our bargains.

We that evening began with Hobbes's Homer; but found it very difficult for us to read, owing to the obſcurity of the tranſlation, which together with the indifferent language, and want of poetical merit in the translator, somewhat disappointed us: however we had from time to time many a hard puzzling hour with him.

But as to Walker's Epictetus, although that had not much poetical merit, yet it was very easy to be read, and as easily understood. The principles of the *stoics* charmed me so much, that I made the book my companion wherever I went, and read it over and over in raptures, thinking that my mind was secured against all the smiles or frowns of fortune.

I now grew weary of dissipating my time, and began to think of employing my spare hours in something more satisfactory. For want of something else to do, I went one evening to hear Mr. John Wesley preach in Broadmead, and being completely tired of the way of life that I had lived (more or less) ever since I had been out of my apprenticeship, and happening to have no other pursuit or hobby-

hobby-horſe, there was a kind of vacuity in my mind; in this ſtate I was very ſuſceptible of any impreſſions, ſo that when I came to hear Mr. Weſley, my old fanatical notions returned full upon me, and I was once more carried away by the tide of enthuſiaſm.

My friend Mr. Jones ſoon ſaw with grief and indignation the wonderful alteration in me; who, from a gay, volatile, diſſipated young fellow, was at once metamorphoſed into a dull, moping, praying, pſalm-ſinging fanatic, continually reprehending all about me for their harmleſs mirth and gaiety.

"For Saints themſelves will often be,
"Of gifts that coſt them nothing, free."

HUDIBRAS.

Nothing is more common than to ſee mankind run from one extreme to another: which was my caſe once more.

About this time we left our habitation in Queen-ſtreet and took lodgings of Mr. Jones's mother, on St. Philip's Plain, where lived a brother of Mr. Jones, who was about ſeventeen years of age. Soon after we had removed to this place, the brother, whoſe name was Richard Jones, was permitted to work in the ſame room with my friend and me. They had alſo a ſiſter about twenty years of age, who frequently joined our company.

Our room over-looked the Church-yard, which contributed to increaſe my gloomy ideas; and I had ſo much of the ſpiritual quixotiſm in me, that I ſoon began to think that it was not enough for me to ſave my own ſoul, but I ought in conſcience to attempt the converſion of my companions, who (I really believed) were in the high road to hell, and every moment liable to eternal damnation. Of this charitable diſpoſition are almoſt all the methodiſts; who, as Hudibras ſays,

"Compound for ſins they are inclin'd to,
"By damning thoſe they have no mind to."

The frequency of newly-opened graves, which we ſaw from our windows, furniſhed me with opportunities for deſcanting on the uncertainty

uncertainty of life and all ſublunary enjoyments; I aſſured them that nothing deſerved attention but what related to our everlaſting ſtate, and that they might, on their repentance, receive in one moment the pardon of all their ſins, have a foretaſte of the joys of heaven, and know that their names were enrolled in the book of life. I farther proteſted that they had no time to loſe; that they all ſtood on the very verge of hell, and the breaking-brink of eternal torments; with a great deal more of ſuch edifying ſtuff.

The youngeſt brother ſoon became a convert; and Miſs Betſy was *born again* ſoon after. But I had a tight job to convert my friend John; he held out, and often curſed me heartily, and ſung profane ſongs all day long.

But about four or five weeks after my reconverſion, John was alſo converted, and became a favourite of heaven, ſo that we conſidered ourſelves as a holy community.

"Who knew the ſeat of Paradiſe,
"Could tell in what degree it lies;
"Could deepeſt myſteries unriddle,
"As eaſily as thread a needle."

HUDIBRAS.

A laughable affair happened during my reſidence here. A captain of a ſhip one day brought a parrot as a preſent to a family, the miſtreſs of which being a methodiſt, happened to have one of the preachers call in juſt as the dinner was putting on the table, ſo that the captain and the preacher were both aſked to ſtay. As ſoon as the table was covered, the preacher began a long grace, in the midſt of which *Poll*, who had been put in a corner of the room, cried out, "*D——n your eyes, tip us none of your jaw.*" This, with the immoderate laughter of the captain, entirely diſconcerted the pious chaplain; at laſt he began his grace again, but he had not got to the end before Poll again interrupted him with "*You d——n canting ſon of a b——h.*" By the above it appeared that the

the captain had tutored Poll on purpose to have some fun in this canting family; however, the good lady of the house made it a point of conscience to have Polly converted, but found it utterly impossible to effect that great change in the methodistical way, that is, *instantaneously*, as after she had scolded her six months for speaking bad words, and had actually taught her a part of the Lord's prayer, yet Poll would not entirely leave off her sea language, so that it often happened while the good lady was teaching her to pray, Poll would out with, "*D——n your eyes, tumble up, you lubbers*;" and even after she had preached to her several years, she would not venture to say that Poll was in a state of grace; but be that as it will, Poll obtained the name of Methodist, being called by the neighbours, The Methodist Parrot.

I must inform you also that the poor preacher abovementioned was but just come out of Wales, and understood English but very imperfectly, and in the course of his sermon one day he had forgot the English for the word lamb, and after hammering a good while about it, he out with "Goddymighty's little Mutton, that took away the ſins of the world," which cauſed a good deal of diverſion among the ungodly.

I am,

Dear Friend,

Yours, &c.

LETTER

LETTER XIV.

"——— He was a ſhrewd philoſopher,
"And had read every text and gloſs-over;
"Whate'er the crabbed'ſt author hath,
"He underſtood b'implicit faith;
"Whatever Sceptic could enquire for,
"For every why he had a wherefore;
"Knew more than forty of them do,
"As far as words and terms could go,
"All which he underſtood by rote,
"And as occaſion ſerv'd would quote;
"No matter whether right or wrong,
"They might be either ſaid or ſung."

HUDIBRAS.

DEAR FRIEND,

MR. John Jones and myſelf were now greater friends than ever, ſo that one would on no account ſtir out of the houſe without the other.

Mr. Jones had the advantage of me in temporals, he could get more money than I could; but as to grace, and ſpiritual gifts, I had much the advantage of all our community;

nity; ſo that I was their ſpiritual director, and if they thought that any of their acquaintance held any opinions that were not quite ſound and orthodox, ſuch were introduced to me, in order that I might convince them of their errors. In fact, I was looked upon as an apoſtle, ſo that whatever I aſſerted was received as pure goſpel; nor was any thing undertaken without my advice.

We all worked very hard, particularly Mr. John Jones and me, in order to get money to purchaſe books; and for ſome months every ſhilling we could ſpare was laid out at old book-ſhops, ſtalls, &c. inſomuch that in a ſhort time we had what *we* called a very good library. This choice collection conſiſted of Polhil on precious Faith; Polhil on the Decrees; Shepherd's ſound Believer; Bunyan's Pilgrim's Progreſs; Bunyan's Good News for the vileſt of Sinners; his Heavenly Footman; his Grace abounding to the chief of Sinners; his Life and Death of Mr. Badman; his Holy War in the town of *Manſoul*; Hervey's Meditations; Hervey's Dialogues;

Rogers's

Rogers's Seven Helps to Heaven ; Hall's Jacob's Ladder ; Divine Breathings of a devout Soul ; Adams on the ſecond epiſtle of Peter ; Adams's Sermons on the *black* Devil, the *white* Devil, &c. &c. Collings's Divine Cordial for the Soul ; Pearſe's Soul's Eſpouſal to Chriſt ; Erſkine's Goſpel Sonnets ; the Death of Abel ; The Faith of God's Elect ; Manton on the epiſtle of St. James ; Pamble's Works ; Baxter's Shove for a *heavy-arſed* Chriſtian ; his Call to the Unconverted ; Mary Magdalen's Funeral Tears ; Mrs. Moore's Evidences for Heaven ; Mead's Almoſt a Chriſtian ; The Sure Guide to Heaven ; Brooks on Aſſurance ; God's Revenge againſt Murder ; Brooks's Heaven upon Earth ; The Pathway to Heaven ; Wilcox's Guide to eternal Glory ; Derham's Unſearchable Riches of Chriſt ; his Expoſition of Revelations ; Alleine's Sure Guide to Heaven ; The Sincere Convert ; Watſon's Heaven taken by Storm ; Heaven's Vengeance ; Wall's None but Chriſt ; Ariſtotle's Maſterpiece ; Coles on God's Sovereignty ; Charnock on Providence ; Young's

Short

Short and ſure Guide to Salvation; Weſley's Sermons, Journals, Tracts, &c. and others of the ſame deſcription.

We had indeed a few of a better ſort, as Gay's Fables; Pomfret's Poems; Milton's Paradiſe Loſt; beſides Hobbes's Homer, and Walker's Epictetus, mentioned in my laſt letter.

But what we wanted in judgment in chooſing our library, we made up in application; ſo anxious were we to read a great deal, that we allowed ourſelves but about three hours ſleep in twenty-four, and for ſome months together we never were all in bed at the ſame time; (Sunday nights excepted.) But leſt we ſhould overſleep the time allowed, one of us ſat up to work until the time appointed for the others to riſe, and when all were up, my friend John and your humble ſervant, took it by turns to read aloud to the reſt, while they were at their work.

But this mad ſcheme of ours had nearly been attended with very ſerious conſe-

quences.

quences. One night it being my turn to watch, I removed to the fire-ſide, to read ſome particular paſſage, and the candleſtick which we worked by not being convenient to move about, and there being no other at that time in the room, I ſet up the candle againſt the handle of a pewter pot, and was ſo extremely heavy (owing to much watchfulneſs) that I fell faſt aſleep and had like never to have awaked again; for the candle burned down to the handle of the pot, melted it off, and then fell on the chair on which it ſtood; ſo that Mr. Jones found me in the morning, faſt aſleep, and part of the chair conſumed; which alarmed us all very much, and made us more cautious.

But ſtill we continued our plan of living, ſo that we made a rapid progreſs in what we called ſpiritual and divine knowledge; and were ſoon maſters of the various arguments made uſe of by moſt polemical divines, &c.

And the better to guard my pupils from what I called *falſe doctrines*, I uſed often to engage

engage them in various controverſies, in which I ſometimes took one ſide of the queſtion, ſometimes the other, in order to make them well verſed in controverſy, and acquainted with the ſtrength of their adverſaries. So that I was, by turns, a Calviniſt, an Arminian, an Arian, a Socinian, a Deiſt, and even an Atheiſt. And after they had ſaid all they could to confute me, I would point out where they had failed, and added ſuch arguments as I was maſter of, and in general we were all ſatisfied. But when we happened to have any doubts, we had recourſe to the Bible and commentators of our own ſide of the queſtion, and I aſſure you, my dear friend, this was a very fine hobby-horſe; which, like Aaron's ſerpent, ſwallowed up all the other hobby-horſes.

"Light minds are pleaſed with trifles."

OVID.

I am, dear Friend,

Your, &c.

LETTER

LETTER XV.

"Laugh where you muſt; be candid where you can."

POPE.

"Know then, that always when you come,
"You'll find me ſitting on my bum;
"Or lying on a couch, ſurrounded
"With tables, pens, and books, confounded;
"Wrapt up in lofty ſpeculation,
"As if on the ſafety of the nation."

HUME.

DEAR FRIEND,

IN the courſe of my reading, I learnt that there had been various ſects of philoſophers amongſt the Greeks, Romans, &c. and I well remembered the names of the moſt eminent of them. At an old book-ſhop I purchaſed Plato on the Immortality of the Soul, Plutarch's Morals, Seneca's Morals, Epicurus's Morals, the Morals of Confucius the Chineſe Philoſopher, and a few others. I now can ſcarce help thinking that I received more real benefit from reading and ſtudying them

them and Epictetus, than from all other books that I had read before, or have ever read since that time.

I was but about twenty-two years of age, when I first began to read those fine moral productions; and I assure you, my friend, that they made a very deep and lasting impression on my mind. By reading them, I was taught to bear the unavoidable evils attending humanity, and to supply all my wants by contracting or restraining my desires.

It is now twenty-three years since I first perused them; during which time I do not recollect that I have ever felt one *anxious* painful wish to get money, estates, or any way to better my condition:

"Indeed, my friend, were I to find
"That wealth could e'er my real wishes gain;
"Had e'er disturb'd my thoughtful mind,
"Or cost one serious moment's pain;
"I should have said, that all the rules,
"I learn'd of moralists and schools,
"Were very useless, very vain.

And

And yet I have never ſince that time let ſlip any fair opportunity of doing it. So that all I mean is, that I have not been over *ſolicitous* to obtain any thing that I did not poſſeſs; but could at all times ſay, with St. Paul, that I have learned to be contented in all ſituations, although at times they have been very gloomy indeed. Dryden ſays,

" We to ourſelves may all our wiſhes grant,
" For, nothing coveting, we nothing want."

DRYDEN's Indian Emperor.

And in another place he ſays,

" They cannot want who wiſh not to have more:
" Who ever ſaid an anchoret was poor?"

DRYDEN's Secret Love.

The pleaſures of eating and drinking I entirely deſpiſed, and for ſome time carried this diſpoſition to an extreme. The account of Epicurus living in his garden, at the expence of about a halfpenny per day, and that when he added a little cheeſe to his bread on particular occaſions, he conſidered it as a luxury, filled me with raptures. From that moment

 I began

I began to live on bread and tea, and for a confiderable time did not partake of any other viands, but in thofe I indulged myfelf three or four times a day. My reafons for living in this abftemious manner were in order to fave money to purchafe books, to wean myfelf from the grofs pleafures of eating, drinking, &c. and to purge my mind, and make it more fufceptible of intellectual pleafures. And here I cannot help remarking, that the term *Epicure* when applied to one who makes the pleafures of the table his chief good, cafts an unjuft reflection on *Epicurus*, and conveys a wrong idea of that contemplative and very abftemious philofopher: for although he afferted that pleafure was the chief or fupreme good, yet he alfo as ftrongly afferted, that it was the tranquillity of the mind, and intellectual pleafure, that he fo extolled and recommended.

" Some place the blifs in action, fome in eafe;
" Thofe call it pleafure, and contentment thefe:
" Some, funk to beafts, find pleafure end in pain;
" Some, fwell'd to gods, confefs e'en virtue vain."

POPE.

I con-

I continued the above ſelf-denying life until I left Briſtol, which was on Whitſunday in 1769. I had for ſome time before been pointing out to my friend John Jones ſome of the pleaſures and advantages of travelling, ſo that I eaſily prevailed on him to accompany me towards the Weſt of England; and in the evening we arrived at Bridgewater, where Mr. Jones got work. He was employed by Mr. Caſh, with whom he continued near twelve months, and in the end married Mr. Caſh's daughter, a very pretty and very amiable little woman, with ſome fortune. When my friend was offered work by Mr. Caſh, I prevailed on him to accept of it, aſſuring him that I had no doubt of my being able to get work at Taunton: but in that I was diſappointed, nor could I get a conſtant ſeat of work until I came to Exeter, and of that place I was ſoon tired; but being informed that a Mr. John Taylor of Kingſbridge (forty miles below Exeter) wanted ſuch a hand, I went down, and was gladly received by Mr. Taylor, whoſe name inſpires me with gratitude, as he

 never

never treated me as a journeyman, but made me his companion: Nor was any part of my time ever ſpent in a more agreeable pleaſing manner than that which I paſſed in this retired place, or I believe more profitable to a maſter. I was the firſt man he ever had that was able to make ſtuff and ſilk ſhoes, and it being alſo known that I came from Briſtol, this had great weight with the country ladies, and procured my maſter cuſtomers, who generally ſent for me to take meaſure of their feet, and I was looked upon by all to be the beſt workman in the town, altho' I had not been brought up to ſtuff-work, nor had ever entirely made one ſtuff or ſilk ſhoe before. Nor ſhould I have preſumed to proclaim myſelf a ſtuff-man, had there been any ſuch workmen in the place; but as there were none, I boldly ventured, and ſucceeded very well; nor did any one in the town ever know that it was my firſt attempt in that branch.

During the time that I lived here, I as uſual was obliged to employ one or another of my acquaintance to write my letters for me;

me; this procured me much praiſe among the young men as a good inditer of letters; (I need not inform you that they were not good judges.) My maſter ſaid to me one day, he was ſurprized that I did not learn to write my own letters; and added, that he was ſure that I could learn to do it in a very ſhort time. The thought pleaſed me much, and without any delay I ſet about it, by taking up any pieces of paper that had writing on them, and imitating the letters as well as I could. I employed my leiſure hours in this way for near two months, after which time I wrote my own letters, in a bad hand, you may be ſure; but it was plain and eaſy to read, which was all I cared for: nor to the preſent moment can I write much better, as I never would have any perſon to teach me, nor was I ever poſſeſſed of patience enough to employ time ſufficient to learn to write well; and yet as ſoon as I was able to ſcribble, I wrote verſes on ſome trifle or other every day for years together.

Out of ſome thouſands I at preſent recollect the following, which I placed by the ſide of the figure of a clergyman in his robes, with his hands and eyes lifted up; this image ſtood over the fire-place in my room.

Here's a ſhoemaker's chaplain has negative merit,
As his vice he ne'er flatters or ruffles his ſpirit;
No wages receiving, his conſcience is clear;
Not prone to deceiving, he's nothing to fear.
'Tis true he is ſilent—but that's nothing new;
And if you'd repent, his attitude view;
With uplifted hands all vice to reprove,
How ſolemn he ſtands, his eyes fix'd above!

As a kind of contraſt I will inſert an epigram that I wrote but a few days ſince on an ignorant methodiſt preacher.

A ſtupid fellow told me t'other day,
That by the ſpirit he could preach and pray;
Let none then ſay that miracles have ceas'd,
As God ſtill opes the mouth of beaſt;
And aſſes now can ſpeak as plain
As e'r they could in Balaam's reign.

But I always wrote as faſt as I could, without endeavouring to write well, and that this

this is my present practice I need not inform you.

I came to this place in but a weak state of body, however the healthy situation of the town, together with bathing in the salt water, soon restored me to perfect health. I passed thirteen months here in a very happy manner; but the wages for work being very low, and as I had spent much time in writing hymns to every song-tune that I knew, besides a number of love-verses, letters, &c. I was very poor; and to complete all, I began to keep a deal of company, in which I gave a loose to my natural gaiety of disposition, much more than was consistent with the grave, sedate ideas which I had formed of a religious character; all which made me resolve to leave Kingsbridge, which I did in 1770.

I travelled as far as Exeter the first day; where I worked about a fortnight, and saved sufficient to carry me to Bridgewater, where I worked two or three weeks more. Before

 I ar-

I arrived there Mr. John Jones had gone back to reside at Bristol, but as soon as he heard of my being in Bridgewater, he and his brother Richard sent me an invitation to come to Bristol again and live with them. Finding that I did not immediately comply, they both came to Bridgewater, and declared their intentions of not returning to Bristol without me; so that after a day or two I yielded to their solicitations, and again lived very comfortably with them, their mother and sister.

I think it was about this period, that I went several times to the Tabernacle, and heard Mr. George Whitefield; and of all the preachers that ever I attended, never did I meet with one that had such a perfect command over the passions of his audience. In every sermon that I heard him preach, he would sometimes make them ready to burst with laughter, and the next moment drown them in tears; indeed it was scarce possible for the most guarded to escape the effect.

"He

"He had ſomething t'was thought ſtill more horrid to ſay,
"When his tongue loſt its powers and he fainted away;
"Some ſay 'twas his conſcience that gave him a ſtroke,
"But thoſe who beſt knew him treat that as a joke;
"'Tis a trick which ſtage orators uſe in their need,
"The paſſions to raiſe and the judgment miſlead."

SIMKIN.

In one of my excurſions I paſſed many agreeable hours with the late Mr. La Bute, at Cambridge, who was well known, he having taught French in that univerſity upwards of forty years. He informed me that near forty years ſince, Mr. Whitefield having advertiſed himſelf to preach at Gog-Magog hill, many thouſand people collected together from many miles round. While he was preaching he was elevated on the higheſt ground, and his audience ſtood all round on the declivity; during his ſermon, a young countrywoman, who had come ſome miles to hear him, and waited ſeveral hours, being very faint, owing to the violent heat of the ſun, the breaths of the multitude, as well as the want of refreſhment; and it is very likely much agitated in her mind by the extraordinary

extraordinary doctrines of the preacher, ſhe fell backwards, juſt under the orator, and there lay kicking up her heels. On ſeeing the poor girl lie in a kind of convulſion, ſome of the company moved to aſſiſt her, and the women began to draw down her apron and petticoats over her feet; but Mr. Whitefield cried out, "*Let her alone! let her alone! A glorious ſight! a glorious ſight!*" No doubt the holy man meant that it was a glorious ſight to ſee a ſinner fall before the power of the word; but the young college bucks and wits conſtrued his meaning differently, and put the audience into ſuch immoderate fits of laughing, that even Mr. Whitefield's utmoſt efforts were not able to reſtore their gravity, but he was obliged to diſmiſs his congregation abruptly.

For a long time after this happened, the Cantabs as they reeled homewards in the night-time, diſturbed the ſober inhabitants, by loudly exclaiming, "A glorious ſight! A glorious ſight! as Doctor Squintum ſays."

I am, dear Friend, yours.

LETTER XVI.

"Love, the moſt generous paſſion of the mind,
"The ſofteſt refuge innocence can find;
"The ſafe director of unguided youth,
"Fraught with kind wiſhes, and ſecur'd by truth;
"The cordial drop heav'n in our cup has thrown,
"To make the nauſeous draught of life go down;
"On which one only bleſſing God might raiſe,
"In lands of atheiſts ſubſidies of praiſe;
"For none did e'er ſo dull and ſtupid prove,
"But felt a God, and bleſs'd his pow'r, in love."

Nonpareil.

DEAR FRIEND,

I Muſt now requeſt you to go back with me a few years, as I have not yet made you acquainted with my principal amours. I was about ſeventeen years of age when an adventure diſcovered, that although I was ſo very ſpiritual, as I before informed you, I was notwithſtanding ſuſceptible of another kind of impreſſion.

"Oh, let me ſtill enjoy the cheerful day,
"Till many years unheeded o'er me roll.
"Pleas'd in my age I trifle life away,
"And tell how much I lov'd ere I grew old."

HAMMOND's Love Elegies.

Being at farmer Gamlin's, at Charlton, four miles from Taunton, to hear a methodiſt ſermon, I fell deſperately in love with the farmer's handſome dairy-maid.

"Her home-ſpun dreſs in ſimple neatneſs lies,
"And for no glaring equipage ſhe ſighs.
"She gratefully receives what heav'n has ſent,
"And, rich in poverty, enjoys content.
"Her reputation which is all her boaſt,
"In a malicious viſit ne'er was loſt.
"No midnight maſquerade her beauty wears,
"And health, not paint, the fading bloom repairs.
"If Love's ſoft paſſions in her boſom reign,
"An equal paſſion warms her happy ſwain."

GAY.

At that time I abounded in *ſpiritual gifts*, which induced this honeſt ruſtic maid to be very kind to me, and to walk ſeveral fields with me in my road back to Taunton, talking all the way of her ſpiritual diſtreſs and godly concerns; while I poured heavenly comfort

comfort into her ſoul, and talked ſo long of *divine* Love, until I found that my affection for her was not altogether of that *ſpiritual* nature. And yet,

"We lov'd without tranſgreſſing Virtue's bounds:
"We fix'd the limits of our tendereſt thoughts,
"Came to the verge of honour, and there ſtopp'd;
"We warm'd us by the fire, but were not ſcorch'd.
"If this be ſin, Angels might live with more;
"And mingle rays of minds leſs pure than ours."

DRYDEN's Love Triumphant.

After this you may be ſure that I did not let ſlip any opportunity of hearing ſermons at farmer Gamlin's; and I generally prevailed with Nancy Smith, my charming ſpiritual dairy-maid, to accompany me part of the way home, and at every gate I accompanied my ſpiritual advice with a kiſs.

——" Oh then the longeſt ſummer's day
"Seem'd too too much in haſte; ſtill the full heart
"Had not imparted half: 'twas happineſs
"Too exquiſite to laſt. Of joys departed
"Never to return, how painful the remembrance!

BLAIR's Grave.

But

But alas! theſe comfortable Sunday walks were ſoon at an end; as my charming Nancy Smith, for ſome reaſon or other (I have forgot what) left her place, and went to live as dairy-maid with a farmer in the marſh country, between Bridgewater and Briſtol, ſeventeen miles from Taunton; ſo that I did not ſee her for near two years afterwards; during which time I gave ſpiritual advice to another holy ſiſter, whoſe name was Hannah Allen.

I prevailed on this lovely maid to attend the methodiſt preaching at five o'clock on Monday mornings, and we often met at three or four; ſo that we had an hour or two to ſpend in walking and converſation on ſpiritual affairs. Had you ſeen and heard us on the cold froſty mornings, it would have put you in mind of Milton's *Devils*, whom he repreſents as at times ſtarving with cold:

"Others apart, ſat on a hill, retir'd,
"In thoughts more elevate, and reaſon'd high
"Of Provicence, foreknowledge, will, and fate;

"Fix'd

"Fix'd fate, free-will, foreknowledge abſolute;
"And found no end, in wandering mazes loſt."
Paradiſe Loſt.

But I aſſure you, my friend, that we were ſometimes like the Galatians of old; we began in the *ſpirit*, and ended in the *fleſh*.

With this dear girl I ſpent all my leiſure time, for two or three years; ſo that we enjoyed together hundreds of happy, and I can truly add, *innocent* hours.

"O days of bliſs!
"To equal this
"Olympus ſtrives in vain;
"O happy pair,
"O happy fair!
"O happy, happy ſwain!"
JOANNES SECUNDUS.

But ſtill I never could entirely forget my charming innocent *Dairy-maid.* In fact I had love enough for both, to have taken either for better for worſe; but my being an apprentice, prevented me from marrying at that time.

It

It is true I had the greateſt love for Nancy Smith; but Hannah Allen had the advantage of Nancy, as I could ſee Hannah almoſt every day, and Nancy only once or twice in about three years. However I at laſt fell out with Hannah (on what occaſion I cannot recollect) and I ſent Nancy a letter, which made up matters with her; for, like Sterne, I was "always in love with one goddeſs or other;" and ſoon after that, ſhe came to live for a little time at her father's houſe at Petherton near Bridgewater, ſeven miles from Taunton. This happened during the election at Taunton, when I was changed from a ſtrict methodiſt to a rake; and although the wedding ring was purchaſed, and we were to have been married in a few days, yet the marriage was put off on account of my diſſipated character, ſo that I ſoon after ſet off for Briſtol, as I before informed you: nor did I ſee her after that, until my return from Kingſbridge, when I ſaw her ſeveral times prior to my ſetting off for Briſtol with my friend John Jones, and his brother Richard.

I am, dear Friend, yours, &c.

LETTER XVII.

"The man who by his labour gets
"His bread in independent ſtate,
"Who never begs, and ſeldom eats,
"Himſelf can fix, or change his fate."

PRIOR.

"If you will uſe the little that you have,
"More has not heav'n to give, or you to crave:
"Ceaſe to complain. He never can be poor
"Who has ſufficient, and who wants no more.
"If but from cold, and pining hunger free,
"The richeſt monarch can but equal thee.

HORACE Imitated.

DEAR FRIEND,

I Had not long reſided a ſecond time with my good Briſtol friends, before I renewed my correſpondence with my old ſweetheart Nancy Smith. I informed her that my attachment to Books, together with travelling from place to place, and alſo my total diſregard for money, had prevented me from ſaving any; and that while I remained in a ſingle unſettled ſtate, I was never likely to accumulate it. I alſo preſſed her very much to come to Briſtol to be married, which ſhe ſoon complied with: and married we were, at St. Peter's Church, towards the end of the year 1770; near ſeven years after my firſt making love to her.

"When join'd in hand and heart, to church we went,
"Mutual in vows, and pris'ners by conſent.
"My Nancy's heart beat high, with mix'd alarms,
"But trembling beauty glow'd with double charms.
"In her ſoft breaſt a modeſt ſtruggle roſe,
"How ſhe ſhould ſeem to like the lot ſhe choſe:
"A ſmile, ſhe thought would dreſs her looks too gay:
"A frown might ſeem too ſad, and blaſt the day.
"But while nor this, nor that, her will could bow,
"She walk'd, and look'd, and charm'd, and knew not how.
"Our hands at length th' unchanging Fiat bound,
"And our glad Souls ſprung out to meet the ſound.
"Joys meeting Joys unite, and ſtronger ſhine:
"For paſſion purified is half divine:
"Now NANCY thou art mine, I cry'd—and ſhe
"Sigh'd ſoft—now JEMMY thou art LORD of me!"

A. HILL.

We kept our wedding at the houſe of my friends the Meſſrs. Jones's, and at bed-time retired to ready-furniſhed lodgings, which we had before provided, at half-a-crown per week

week. Our finances were but juſt ſufficient to pay the expences of the day, for the next morning in ſearching our pockets (which we did not do in a careleſs manner) we diſcovered that we had but one halfpenny to begin the world with. It is true we had laid in eatables ſufficient for a day or two, in which time we knew we could by our work procure more, which we very cheerfully ſet about, ſinging together the following ſtrains of Dr. Cotton:

"Our portion is not large indeed,
"But then how little do we need?
"For Nature's calls are few;
"In this the art of living lies,
"To want no more than may ſuffice,
"And make that little do."

The above, and the following ode by Mr. Fitzgerald, did we ſcores of times repeat, even with raptures!

"No glory I covet, no riches I want,
"Ambition is nothing to me:
"The one thing I beg of kind heaven to grant
"Is, a mind independent and free.

"By paſſion unruffled, untainted by pride,
"By Reaſon my life let me ſquare;
"The wants of my nature are cheaply ſupplied,
"And the reſt are but folly and care.

"Thoſe bleſſings which providence kindly has lent,
"I'll juſtly and gratefully prize;
"While ſweet meditation and cheerful content,
"Shall make me both healthy and wiſe.

"In the pleaſures the great man's poſſeſſions diſplay,
"Unenvy'd I'll challenge my part;
"For every fair object my eyes can ſurvey,
"Contributes to gladden my heart.

"How vainly through infinite trouble and ſtrife,
"The many their labours employ;
"When all that is truly delightful in life,
"Is what all, if they will, may enjoy."

After having worked on ſtuff-work in the country, I could not bear the idea of returning to the leather branch; ſo that I attempted and obtained a ſeat of Stuff in Briſtol. But better work being required there than in Kingſbridge, &c. I was obliged to take ſo much care to pleaſe my maſter, that at firſt I could not get more than nine ſhillings a week, and my wife could get but very little, as ſhe was learning to bind ſtuff-ſhoes, and had never been much uſed to her needle; ſo that what with the expence of ready-furniſhed lodging, fire, candles, &c. we had but little left for purchaſing proviſions.

To increaſe our ſtraits, my old friend being ſomewhat diſpleaſed at our leaving him and his relations, took an early opportunity to tell me that I was indebted to him near forty ſhillings, of two years ſtanding. I was not convinced of the juſtice of the claim, but to avoid diſpute, I paid him in about two months, during nearly the whole of which time it was extremely ſevere weather, and yet we made four ſhillings and ſixpence per week pay for the whole of what we con-ſumed in eating and drinking. Strong beer we had none, nor any other liquor (the pure element excepted) and inſtead of tea, or ra-ther coffee, we toaſted a piece of bread; at other times we fried ſome wheat, which when boiled in water made a tolerable ſub-ſtitute for coffee; and as to animal food, we made uſe of but little, and that little we boiled and made broth of.

During the whole of this time we never once wiſhed for any thing that we had not got, but were quite contented, and with a good grace, in reality made a virtue of neceſſity. We

"Trembled not with vain deſires,
"Few the things which life requires."

FRANCIS's Horace.

And the ſubject of our prayer was

"This day be bread and peace our lot,
"All elſe beneath the ſun,
"Thou know'ſt if beſt beſtow'd or not,
"And let thy will be done.

I am, dear Friend,

Your, &c.

LETTER

LETTER XVIII.

" This ſame Monſieur Poverty is a bitter enemy."

JOHN DORY.

" In adverſe hours an equal mind maintain."

FRANCIS's Horace.

DEAR FRIEND,

IN a few days after we had paid the laſt five ſhillings of the debt claimed by my friend Mr. Jones, we were both together taken ſo ill as to be confined to our bed, but the good woman of the houſe, our landlady, came to our room and did a few trifles for us. She ſeemed very much alarmed at our ſituation, or rather for her own, I ſuppoſe, as thinking we might in ſome meaſure become burthenſome to her. We had in caſh two ſhillings and nine-pence, halt crown of which we had carefully locked uı in a box, to be ſaved for a reſource on any extraordinary emergence. This money ſupported

ported us two or three days, in which time I recovered without the help of medicine; but my wife continued ill near ſix months, and was confined to her bed the greateſt part of the time; which illneſs may very eaſily be accounted for.

Before ſhe came to Briſtol, ſhe had ever been uſed to a very active life, and had always lived in the country, ſo that in coming to dwell in a populous city, ſhe had exchanged much exerciſe and good air for a ſedentary life and very bad air; and this I preſume was the cauſe of all her illneſs from time to time, which at length, as unfortunately as effectually, undermined her conſtitution. During her firſt ſix months illneſs, I lived many days ſolely on water-gruel; for as I could not afford to pay a nurſe, much of my time was taken up in attendance on her, and moſt of my money expended in procuring medicines, together with ſuch trifles as ſhe could eat and drink. But what added extremely to my calamity was the being

being within the hearing of her groans, which were caused by the excruciating pains in her head, which for months together defied the power of medicine.

It is impossible for words to describe the keenness of my sensations during this long term; yet as to *myself*, my poverty and being obliged to live upon water-gruel gave me not the least uneasiness.

> " In ruffling seasons I was calm,
> " And smil'd when fortune frown'd."
>
> YOUNG.

But the necessity of being continually in the sight and hearing of a beloved object, a young, charming, handsome, innocent wife,

> " Who sick in bed lay gasping for her breath;
> " Her eyes, like dying lamps sunk in their sockets,
> " Now glar'd, and now drew back their feeble light:
> " Faintly her speech fell from her fault'ring tongue
> " In interrupted accents, as she strove
> " With strong agonies that shook her limbs
> " And writh'd her tortur'd features into forms
> " Hideous to sight."
>
> BELLER's Injur'd Innocence.

How

How I ſupported this long dreary ſcene, I know not; the bare recollection of which is exceedingly painful, even at this diſtance of time. At laſt, when every thing that ſeemed to promiſe relief had been tried in vain, ſome old woman recommended *Cephalic* ſnuff. I own I had not much faith in it; however I procured it, and in a ſhort time after ſhe was much relieved from the intolerable pain in her head, but yet continued in a very bad ſtate of health; her conſtitution having ſuffered ſuch a dreadful ſhock, I thought that no means could be uſed ſo likely to reſtore it, as a removal to her native air. Accordingly I left my ſeat of work at Briſtol, and returned with her to Taunton, which is about ſeven miles from Petherton, her native place. But in Taunton I could not procure ſo much work as I could do; ſo that as ſoon as I thought ſhe could bear the air of Briſtol, we returned thither, where ſhe ſoon relapſed, and we again went back to Taunton. This removing to Taunton was repeated about five times in little more than two years and a half.

But

But at laſt, finding that ſhe had long fits of illneſs at Taunton alſo, as well as at Briſtol, with a view of having a better price for my work I reſolved to viſit London; and as I had not money ſufficient to bear the expences of both to town, I left her all the money I could ſpare, and took a place on the outſide of the ſtage coach, and the ſecond day arrived in the metropolis, in Auguſt 1773, with two ſhillings and ſixpence in my pocket; and recollecting the addreſs of an old townſman, who was alſo a ſpiritual brother.

"Whoſe hair in greaſy locks hung down,
"As ſtrait as candles from his crown,
"To ſhade the borders of his face,
"Whoſe outward ſigns of inward grace
"Were only viſible in ſpiteful
"Grimaces, very ſtern and frightful."

BUTLER's Poſth. Works.

This holy brother was alſo a journeyman ſhoe-maker, who had arrived at the ſummit of his expectations, being able to keep a houſe over his head (as he choſe to expreſs himſelf) that is by letting nearly the whole of of it out in lodgings, he was enabled to pay the rent. This houſe was in White-croſs-ſtreet; which I found out the morning after my arrival, where I procured a lodging, and Mr. Heath, in Fore-ſtreet, ſupplied me with plenty of work.

I laugh'd then and whiſtl'd, and ſung too moſt ſweet,
Saying, juſt to a hair I've made both ends to meet.
Derry-down.

I am,

Dear Friend,

Yours, &c.

LETTER

LETTER XIX.

"I'll travel no more—I'll try a London audience—
"Who knows but I may get an engagement."

Wild Oats.

"When ſuperſtition (bane of manly virtues!)
"Strikes root within the ſoul; it over-runs
"And kills the power of Reaſon."

PHILIPS of Glouceſter.

DEAR FRIEND,

AT this time I was as viſionary and ſuperſtitious as ever I had been at any preceding period, for although I had read ſome ſenſible books, and had thereby acquired a few rational ideas, yet having had a methodiſtical wife for near three years, and my keeping methodiſtical company, together with the gloomy notions which in ſpite of reaſon and philoſophy I had imbibed during the frequent, long, and indeed almoſt conſtant illneſs of my wife, the conſequence was, that thoſe few rational or liberal ideas which

which I had before treaſured up, were at my coming to London in a dormant ſtate, or borne down by the torrent of enthuſiaſtic whims, and fanatical chimeras.

"——— Oh! what a reaſonleſs machine
"Can ſuperſtition make the reas'ner man!"

MILLER's Mahomet.

So that as ſoon as I procured a lodging and work, my next enquiry was for Mr. Weſley's *Goſpel-ſhops*: and on producing my *claſs* and *band* tickets from Taunton, I was put into a claſs, and a week or two after admitted into a band.

But it was ſeveral weeks before I could firmly reſolve to continue in London; as I really was ſtruck with horror for the fate of it; more particularly on Sundays, as I found ſo few went to church, and ſo many were walking and riding about for pleaſure, and the lower claſs getting drunk, quarrelling, fighting, working, buying, ſelling, &c. I had ſeen ſo much of the ſame kind in Briſtol, that I often wondered how God permitted it

to

to ſtand; but London I found infinitely worſe, and ſeriouſly trembled for fear the meaſure of iniquity was quite full, and that every hour would be its laſt. However I at length concluded, that if London was a ſecond *Sodom*, I was a ſecond *Lot*; and theſe comfortable ideas reconciled me to the thought of living in it. Beſides, ſome of Mr. Weſley's people gave me great comfort by aſſuring me, that "the Lord had much people in this city:" which I ſoon diſcovered to be true, as I got acquainted with many of thoſe righteous choſen ſaints, who modeſtly arrogate to themſelves that they are the peculiar favourites of heaven, and conſequently that any place they reſide in muſt be ſafe.

In a month I ſaved money ſufficient to bring up my wife, and ſhe had a pretty tolerable ſtate of health; of my maſter I obtained ſome ſtuff-ſhoes for her to bind, and nearly as much as ſhe could do. Having now plenty of work and higher wages, we were tolerably eaſy in our circumſtances, more ſo

than

than we ever had been, ſo that we ſoon procured a few cloaths. My wife had all her life before done very well with a ſuperfine broad cloth cloak, but now I prevailed on her to have one of ſilk.

Until this winter I had never found out that I wanted a *great coat*, but now I made that important diſcovery; and my landlord ſhewed me one made of a coarſe kind of Bath-coating, which he purchaſed new at a ſhop in Roſemary-lane, for ten ſhillings and ſixpence; ſo that the next half guinea I had to ſpare, away I went to Roſemary-lane (and to my great ſurpriſe) was hauled into a ſhop by a fellow who was walking up and down before the door of a ſlopſeller, where I was ſoon fitted with a great coat of the ſame ſort as that of my landlord. I aſked the price; but how great was my aſtoniſhment, when the honeſt ſlopman told me, that he was ſo taken with my clean, honeſt, induſtrious looks, that he would let *me* have it cheaper than he would his own brother, ſo in one word he would

would oblige *me* with it for five and twenty shillings, which was the very money that it coſt him. On hearing this, I croſſed the ſhop in a trice, in order to ſet off home again, but the door had a faſtening to it beyond my comprehenſion, nor would the good man let me out before I had made him an offer. I told him, I had ſo little money about me that I could not offer any thing, and again deſired that he would let me out. But he perſiſted, and at laſt I told him that my landlord had informed me that he had purchaſed ſuch another coat for ten ſhillings and ſixpence; on which he began to give himſelf airs, and aſſured me that however ſome people came by their goods, that for his part, he always paid for *his*. I heartily wiſhed myſelf out of the ſhop, but in vain; as he ſeemed determined not to part with me until I had made ſome offer. I then told him that I had but ten ſhillings and ſixpence, and of courſe could not offer him any more than I had got. I now expected more abuſe from him, but inſtead of that the patient good man told me, that as he perhaps might get ſomething by me another time, I ſhould have the coat for my half guinea, although it was worth more than double the money.

About the end of November I received an account of the death of my grandfather; and was alſo informed that he had left a will in favour of my grandmother-in-law's relations, who became poſſeſſed of all his effects, except a ſmall freehold eſtate, which he left to my youngeſt brother, becauſe he happened to be called George (which was the name of my grandfather) and ten pounds a piece to each of his other grand-children.

So totally unacquainted was I with the modes of tranſacting buſineſs, that I could not point out any method of having my ten pounds ſent up to London, at leaſt no mode that the executor of the will would approve of; it being ſuch a *prodigious* ſum, that the greateſt caution was uſed on both ſides, ſo that it coſt me about half the money in going down for it, and in returning to town again.

This

This was in extremely hard frofty weather (I think fome time in December) and being on the outfide of a ftage-coach, I was fo very cold, that when I came to the inn where the paffengers dined, I went directly to the fire, which ftruck the cold inward, fo that I had but a very narrow efcape from death. This happened in going down. In returning back to town, I had other misfortunes to encounter. The cold weather ftill continuing, I thought the bafket warmer than the roof, and about fix miles from Salifbury, I went back into the bafket. But on getting out of it, in the inn yard at Salifbury, I heard fome money jingle, and on fearching my pockets, I difcovered that I had loft about fixteen fhillings, two or three of which I found in the bafket, the reft had fallen through on the road; and no doubt the whole of what I had left of my ten pounds would have gone the fame way, had I not (for fear of highwaymen) fewed it up in my cloaths. The lofs of my filver I bore with the temper of a ftoic, and like Epictetus reafoned, that I could not have loſt it, if I had not firſt had it; and that as I had loſt it, why it was all the ſame as though it had never been in my poſſeſſion.

But a more dreadful misfortune befel me the next morning; the extreme ſevere weather ſtill continuing, in order to keep me from dying with cold, I drank ſome purl and gin, which (not being uſed to drink any thing ſtrong) made me ſo drunk, that the coachman put me inſide the carriage for fear I ſhould fall off the roof. I there met with ſome of the jovial ſort, who had alſo drank to keep out the cold, ſo that I found them in high glee; being aſked to ſing them a ſong, I immediately complied, and forgetting that I was one of the holy brethren, I ſung ſong for ſong with the merrieſt of them; only ſeveral times between the acts, I turned up the whites of my eyes, and uttered a few ejaculations, as "Lord forgive me!" "O Chriſt! What am I doing?" and a few more of the ſame pious ſort. However after eating a good dinner, and refraining from liquor, I became nearly

nearly ſober, and by the time I arrived in town quite ſo; though in a terrible agitation of mind, by reflecting on what I had don and was ſo aſhamed of the affair, that I concealed it from my wife, that I might not grieve her righteous ſoul with the knowledge of ſo dreadful a fall: ſo that ſhe with great pleaſure ripped open the places in my clothes, which contained my treaſure, and with an heart full of gratitude, piouſly thanked providence for affording us ſuch a ſupply, and hoped that the Lord would enable us to make a good uſe of it.

I am,

Dear Friend,

Yours, &c.

LETTER XX.

" Now ſince thro' all the race of man we find,
" Each to ſome darling paſſion is inclin'd,
" Let Books be ſtill the bias of my mind."

Anonym.

" Fixt in an elbow chair at eaſe,
" I chooſe companions as I pleaſe."

Swift.

DEAR FRIEND,

WITH the remainder of the money we purchaſed houſhold goods, but as we then had not ſufficient to furniſh a room, we worked hard, and lived ſtill harder, ſo that in a ſhort time we had a room furniſhed with our own goods; and I believe that it is not poſſible for you to imagine with what pleaſure and ſatisfaction we looked round the room and ſurveyed our property: I believe that Alexander the Great never reflected on his immenſe acquiſitions with half the heart-felt enjoyment which we experienced on this capital attainment.

After

After our room was furniſhed, as we ſtill enjoyed a better ſtate of health than we did at Briſtol and Taunton, and had alſo more work and higher wages, we often added ſomething or other to our ſtock of wearing apparel. Nor did I forget the old-book ſhops: but frequently added an old book to my ſmall collection, and I really have often purchaſed books with the money that ſhould have been expended in purchaſing ſomething to eat; a ſtriking inſtance of which follows:

At the time we were purchaſing houſhold goods, we kept ourſelves very ſhort of money, and on Chriſtmas-eve we had but half-a-crown left to buy a Chriſtmas dinner. My wife deſired that I would go to market, and purchaſe this feſtival dinner, and off I ſet for that purpoſe; but in the way I ſaw an old-book ſhop, and I could not reſiſt the temptation of going in; intending only to expend ſixpence or ninepence out of my half-crown. But I ſtumbled upon Young's Night Thoughts—down went my half-crown—and

I haſtened home, vaſtly delighted with the acquiſition. When my wife aſked me where was our Chriſtmas dinner ? I told her it was in my pocket.—" In your pocket (ſaid ſhe) that is a ſtrange place. How could you think of ſtuffing a joint of meat into your pocket ?" I aſſured her that it would take no harm. But as I was in no haſte to take it out, ſhe began to be more particular, and enquired what I had got, &c. On which I began to harangue on the ſuperiority of intellectual pleaſures over ſenſual gratifications, and obſerved that the brute creation enjoyed the latter in a much higher degree than man. And that a man, that was not poſſeſſed of intellectual enjoyments, was but a two-legged brute.

I was proceeding in this ſtrain: " And ſo, (ſaid ſhe) inſtead of buying a dinner, I ſuppoſe you have, as you have done before, been buying *books* with the money ?" I then confeſſed I had bought Young's Night Thoughts: " And I think (ſaid I) that I have acted

wiſely ;

wiſely; for had I bought *a dinner*, we ſhould have eaten it to-morrow, and the pleaſure would have been ſoon over, but ſhould we live fifty years longer, we ſhall have the *Night Thoughts* to feaſt upon." This was too powerful an argument to admit of any farther debate; in ſhort, my wife was convinced. Down I ſat, and began to read with as much enthuſiaſm as the good doctor poſſeſſed when he wrote it; and ſo much did it excite my attention as well as approbation, that I retained the greateſt part of it in my memory. A couplet of Perſius, as Engliſhed, might have been applied to me:

" ——— For this you gain thoſe meager looks,
" And ſacrifice your dinner to your books."

Sometime in June 1774, as we ſat at work in our room, Mr. Boyd, one of Mr. Weſley's people, called and informed me that a little ſhop and parlour were to be let in Featherſtone-ſtreet; adding, that if I was to take it, I might there get ſome work as a maſter. I without heſitation told him that

that I liked the idea, and hinted that I would ſell books alſo. Mr. Boyd then aſked me how I came to think of ſelling books? I informed him that until that moment it had never once entered into my thoughts; but that when he propoſed my taking the ſhop, it inſtantaneouſly occurred to my mind, that for ſeveral months paſt I had obſerved a great increaſe in a certain old-book ſhop; and that I was perſuaded I knew as much of old books as the perſon who kept it. I farther obſerved, that I loved books, and that if I could but be a bookſeller, I ſhould then have plenty of books to read, which was the greateſt motive I could conceive to induce me to make the attempt. My friend on this aſſured me, that he would get the ſhop for me, and with a laugh added, "when *you* are Lord Mayor, you ſhall uſe all your intereſt to get *me* made an Alderman." Which I engaged not to forget to perform.

My *private library* at this time conſiſted of Fletcher's Checks to Antinomianiſm, &c.

5 volumes;

5 volumes; Watts's Improvement of the Mind; Young's Night Thoughts; Wake's Tranſlation of the Apoſtolical Epiſtles; Fleetwood's Life of Chriſt; the firſt twenty numbers of Hinton's Dictionary of the Arts and Sciences; ſome of Weſley's Journals, and ſome of the pious lives publiſhed by him; and about a dozen other volumes of the latter ſort, beſides odd magazines, &c. And to ſet me up in ſtile, Mr. Boyd recommended me to the friends of an holy brother lately gone to heaven, and of them I purchaſed a bagful of old books, chiefly divinity, for a guinea.

With this ſtock, and ſome odd ſcraps of leather, which together with all my books were worth about five pounds, I opened ſhop on Midſummer-day, 1774, in Feathe-ſtone-ſtreet, in the pariſh of St. Luke; and I was as well pleaſed in ſurveying my little ſhop with my name over it, as was Nebuchadnezzar, when he ſaid "Is not this great Babylon that I have built?" and my good wife

wife often perceiving the pleaſure that I took in my ſhop, piouſly cautioned me againſt ſetting my mind on the riches of this world, and aſſured me that it was all but vanity. "You are very right, my dear (I ſometimes replied) and to keep our minds as ſpiritual as we can, we will always attend our claſs and band meetings, hear as many ſermons, &c. at the Foundery on week days as poſſible, and on ſabbath days we will mind nothing but the good of our ſouls: our ſmall beer ſhall be fetched in on Saturday nights, nor will we dreſs even a potatoe on the ſabbath. We will ſtill attend the preaching at five o'clock in the morning; at eight go to the prayer meeting; at ten to the public worſhip at the Foundery; hear Mr. Perry at Cripplegate, at two; be at the preaching at the Foundery at five; meet with the general ſociety at ſix; meet in the united bands at ſeven, and again be at the prayer meeting at eight; and then come home and read and pray by ourſelves."

I am, dear Friend, yours, &c.

LETTER XXI.

" ——— Strange viciſſitudes of human fate!
" Still alt'ring, never in a ſteady ſtate;
" Good after ill, and after pain delight;
" Alternate, like the ſcenes of day and night.
" Since every one who lives, is born to die,
" And none can boaſt intire felicity:
" With equal mind what happens let us bear,
" Nor joy, nor grieve too much for things beyond our care.
" Like pilgrims, to the appointed place we tend:
" The world's an Inn, and death's the journey's end.

DRYDEN's Palemon and Arcite.

DEAR FRIEND,

NOtwithſtanding the obſcurity of the ſtreet, and the mean appearance of my ſhop, yet I ſoon found cuſtomers for what few books I had, and I as ſoon laid out the money in other old traſh which was daily brought for ſale.

At that time Mr. Weſley's people had a ſum of money which was kept on purpoſe to lend out, for three months, without intereſt

to

to ſuch of their ſociety whoſe characters were good, and who wanted a temporary relief. To increaſe my little ſtock, I borrowed five pounds out of this fund, which was of great ſervice to me.

In our new ſituation we lived in a very frugal manner, often dining on potatoes, and quenching our thirſt with water, being abſolutely determined if poſſible to make ſome proviſion for ſuch diſmal times as ſickneſs, ſhortneſs of work, &c. which we had been ſo frequently involved in before, and could ſcarce help expecting to be our fate again. My wife foreboded it much more than I did, being of a more melancholy turn of mind.

"A ſad prophetic Spirit dwells with woe."

I lived in this ſtreet ſix months, and in that time increaſed my ſtock from five pounds, to twenty-five pounds.

"London—

"London——the public there are candid and generous, and before my merit can have time to create me enemies, I'll save money, and a fig for the Sultan and Sophy."

ROVER.

This immense stock I deemed too valuable to be buried in Featherstone-Street; and a shop and parlour being to let in Chiswell-Street, No. 46, I took them. This was at that time, and for fourteen years afterwards a very dull and obscure situation: as few ever passed through it, besides Spitalfield weavers on *hanging days*, and methodists *on preaching nights*; but still it was much better adapted for business than Featherstone-Street.

A few weeks after I came into Chiswell-Street, I bade a final adieu to the *gentle craft*, and converted my little stock of leather, &c. into old books; and a great sale I had, considering my stock; which was not only extremely small, but contained very little variety, as it principally consisted of divinity; for as I had not much knowledge, so I seldom ventured out of my depth. Indeed, there

there was one claſs of books, which for the firſt year or two that I called myſelf a bookſeller, I would not ſell, for ſuch was my ignorance, bigotry, ſuperſtition (or what you pleaſe) that I conſcientiouſly deſtroyed ſuch books as fell into my hands which were written by freethinkers; for really ſuppoſing them to be dictated by the devil, I would neither read them myſelf, nor ſell them to others.

You will perhaps be ſurpriſed when I inform you, that there are in London (and I ſuppoſe in other populous places) perſons who purchaſe every article which they have occaſion for (and alſo many articles which they have no occaſion for) at ſtalls, beggarly ſhops, pawnbrokers, &c. under the idea of purchaſing *cheaper* than they could at reſpectable ſhops, and of men of property. A conſiderable number of theſe kind of cuſtomers I had in the beginning, who forſook my ſhop as ſoon as I began to appear more reſpectable, by introducing better order, poſſeſſing more valuable books, and having acquired

acquired a better judgment, &c. Notwithstanding which, I declare to you, upon my honour, that these very bargain-hunters have given me double the price that I now charge for thousands and tens of thousands of volumes. For as a tradesman increases in respectability and opulence, his opportunities of purchasing increase proportionably, and the more he buys and sells, the more he becomes a judge of the real value of his goods. It was for want of this experience and judgment, stock, &c. that for several years I was in the habit of charging more than double the price I now do for many thousand articles. But professed bargain-hunters often purchase old *locks* at the stalls in Moorfields, when half the wards are rusted off or taken out, and give more for them than they would have paid for new locks to any reputable ironmonger. And what numerous instances of this infatuation do we meet with daily at sales by auction, not of books only, but of many other articles! Of which I could here adduce a variety of glaring instances: but (not to tire you) a few of recent date ſhall ſuffice.—At the ſale of Mr. Rigby's books at Mr. Chriſtie's, Martyn's Dictionary of Natural Hiſtory ſold for *fifteen guineas*, which then ſtood in my catalogue at *four pounds fifteen ſhillings*; Pilkington's Dictionary of Painters, at *ſeven guineas*, uſually ſold at three; Francis's Horace, *two pounds eleven ſhillings*, and many others in the ſame manner. At Sir George Colebrook's ſale, the octavo edition of the Tatler ſold for *two guineas and a half.* At a ſale a few weeks ſince, Rapin's Hiſtory, in folio, the two firſt volumes only (inſtead of five) ſold for upwards of *five pounds!* I charge for the ſame from *ten ſhillings and ſixpence* to *one pound ten ſhillings*; and I ſell great numbers of books to pawnbrokers, who ſell them out of their windows at much higher prices, the purchaſers believing that they are buying bargains, and that ſuch articles have been pawned; and it is not only books which pawnbrokers purchaſe, but various other matters, and they always purchaſe the worſt kind of very article. I will even add that many ſhops which

are

are *called* pawnbrokers, never take in any pawns, yet can live by ſelling things which are ſuppoſed to be kept over time.

I went on proſperouſly until ſome time in September, 1775, when I was ſuddenly taken ill of a dreadful fever; and eight or ten days after, my wife was ſeized with the ſame diſorder.

At that time I only kept a boy to help in my ſhop, ſo that I fear, while I lay ill, my wife had too much care and anxiety on her mind. I have been told that before ſhe was confined to her bed ſhe walked about in a delirious ſtate; in which ſhe did not long continue, but contrary to all expectation died, in enthuſiaſtic rant, on the ninth of November, ſurrounded with ſeveral methodiſtical preachers.

> "Invidious death! how doſt thou rend in ſunder
> "Whom love has knit and ſympathy made one?
> "A tie ſo ſtubborn."——
>
> BLAIR's Grave.

She was in reality one of the beſt of women; and although for about four years ſhe was ill the greateſt part of the time, which involved me in the very depth of poverty and diſtreſs, yet I never once repented having married her.

> " ——— ſtill buſy meddling memory,
> " In barbarous ſucceſſion, muſters up
> " The paſt endearments of our ſofter hours,
> " Tenacious of his theme."
>
> BLAIR's Grave,

'T is true ſhe was enthuſiaſtical to an extreme, and of courſe very ſuperſtitious and viſionary, but as I was very far gone myſelf, I did not think that a fault in her.

Indeed ſhe much exceeded me, and moſt others that ever fell under my obſervation, as ſhe in reality *totally* neglected and diſregarded every kind of pleaſure *whatever*, but thoſe of a ſpiritual (or viſionary) nature. Methinks I here ſee you ſmile: but I aſſure you ſhe made *no* exception; but was a complete devotee, and what is more remarkable, without pride or ill-nature.

> " Intentions ſo pure, and ſuch meekneſs of ſpirit,
> " Muſt of courſe, and of right, Heaven's kingdom inherit."
>
> SIMKIN.

I am, dear Friend, yours.

LETTER XXII.

"I've ſtrange news to give you! but when you receive it,
"'Tis impoſſible, Sir, that you ſhould believe it;
"But as I've been told this agreeable ſtory,
"I'll digreſs for a moment to lay it before ye."

DEAR SIR,

A Friend of mine, of whoſe veracity I entertain the higheſt opinion, has favored me with an account of a lady, who has to the full as much, indeed more of the ſpirit, but without the good-nature of Nancy Lackington. The fact is as follows:

"'Tis true 'tis pity: and pity 'tis it's true."

Mr. R—t, a genteel tradeſman with whom I am acquainted, having loſt his ſecond wife early in 1790, courted and married one of the holy ſiſters a few months afterwards. They had lived together about ſix months, when Mr. R—t, one Sunday, being a ſober religious man, took down Doddridge's Lectures, and began to read them to his wife and family.

But this holy ſiſter found fault with her huſband for reading ſuch learned rational diſcourſes, which ſavoured too much of human reaſon and vain philoſophy, and wiſhed he would read ſomething more ſpiritual and edifying. He attempted to convince her that Dr. Doddridge was not only a good rational divine, but to the full as ſpiritual as any divine ought to be; and that to be more ſpiritual he muſt be leſs rational, and of courſe become fanatical and viſionary. But theſe obſervations of the huſband ſo diſpleaſed his ſpiritual wife, that ſhe retired to bed, and left her huſband to read Doddridge's Lectures as long as he choſe to his children by a former wife.

The next morning while Mr. R—t was out on buſineſs, this holy ſiſter, without ſaying one ſyllable to any perſon, packed up all her clothes, crammed them into a hackney coach, and away ſhe went. Mr. R—t, poor ſoul! on coming home diſcovered his immenſe loſs, and in an almoſt frantic ſtate, ſpent the firſt fortnight in fruitleſs attempts to diſcover her retreat.

" Three weeks after her elopement, I was " (ſays Mr. R—t) going down Cheap- " ſide one day, and ſaw a lady ſomething " like my wife, but as ſhe was ſomewhat " diſguiſed, and I could not ſee her face, I " was not ſure. At laſt I ventured to look " under her bonnet, and found, that, ſure " enough, it was ſhe. I then walked three " times backwards and forwards in Cheap- " ſide, endeavouring to perſuade her to re- " turn with me, or to diſcover where ſhe " lived: but ſhe obſtinately refuſed to re- " turn, or to let me ſee her retreat; and " here (ſays Mr. R—t) I begged that ſhe " would grant me a kiſs; but ſhe would not " willingly. However after ſome buſtle in " the ſtreet, I took a farewel kiſs. Poor " dear ſoul! (ſigh'd he) ſhe is rather *too* " *ſpiritual!* for notwithſtanding I laid by " her ſide near ſix months, ſhe never would " be prevailed upon to do any thing carnal; " and although I did all in my power to get

" the better of her ſpiritual ſcruples, yet ſhe
" was always ſo in love with Chriſt her hea-
" venly ſpouſe, that when ſhe eloped from
" me, ſhe was, I aſſure you, as good a vir-
" gin as when I married her."

I muſt give you one more ſtory of the ſame nature with the preceding.

A gentleman of London happening to be on a viſit at Briſtol about three years ſince, fell in love with a handſome young lady who was one of the holy ſiſterhood; after a few weeks acquaintance he made her an offer of his perſon and fortune, and the young lady after proper inquiry had been made into the gentleman's family, fortune, &c. conſented to make our lover happy. They were ſoon after married, and the ſame day ſet off in a poſt-chaiſe towards London, in order to ſleep the firſt night at an inn, and ſo ſave the lady the bluſhes occaſioned by the jokes common on ſuch occaſions; this happy couple had been in bed about an hour when the cry of murder alarmed the houſe, this alarm pro-

ceeding

ceeding from the room that was occupied by the bride and bridegroom, drew the company that way; the inn-keeper knocked at the door and demanded admittance, our Benedict appeared at the door, and informed the host that his lady had been taken suddenly ill in a kind of fit he believed, but that she was better; and after the innkeeper's wife had been sent into the room to see the young lady, and had found her well, all retired to bed.

They had, however, not lain more than two hours, when the cry of murder, fire, &c. again alarmed the house, and drew many out of their beds once more.

Our young gentleman then dressed himself, and opening the door, informed the company that he had that morning been married to the young lady in bed, and that being married, he had insisted on being admitted to the privilege of an husband, but that the young lady had talked much about the good of her poor soul, her spiritual husband, &c. and that instead of granting what he conceived to be the right of every huſband, ſhe had thought proper to diſturb all in the houſe. He added, that having been thus made very ridiculous, he would take effectual care to prevent a repetition of the ſame abſurd conduct.

He then ordered a poſt-chaiſe and ſet off for London, leaving our young ſaint in bed to enjoy her ſpiritual contemplations in their full extent, nor has he ever ſince paid her any attention.

Some time ſince being in a large town in the Weſt, ſhe was pointed out to me by a friend, as ſhe was walking in the ſtreet.

The above puts me in mind of what Ovid ſays was practiſed by young maids on the feſtival of the celebrated nymph *Anna Perenna*, thus tranſlated by I know not who:

" With promiſes the amorous god ſhe led,
" And with fond hopes his eager paſſion fed,
" At length 'tis done, the goddeſs yields, ſhe cry'd;
" My pray'rs have gain'd the victory o'er pride.

" With

"With joy the god prepares the golden bed;
"Thither, her face conceal'd, is Anna led,
"Just on the brink of bliss, she stands confess'd;
"The disappointed lover is her jest,
"While rage and shame alternate swell his breast.

I am informed from good authority that there are now in Mr. Wesley's society, in London, some women who ever since they were converted, have refused to sleep with their husbands, and that some of those will not pay the least attention to any temporal concern whatever, being as they term it, wholly wrapped up in divine contemplation, having their souls absorbed in divine love, so as not to be interrupted by the trifling concerns of a husband, family, &c.

I am,

Dear Friend,

Yours,

LETTER

LETTER XXIII.

"Women that leave no ſtone unturn'd,
"In which the cauſe might be concern'd."

HUDIBRAS.

"The *man without ſin*, the *methodiſt* Rabbi,
"Has perfectly cur'd the chloroſis of Tabby:
"And if right I can judge from her ſhape and face,
"She ſoon may produce an infant of grace.
"Now they ſay that all people in her ſituation
"Are very fine ſubjects for regeneration."

New Bath Guide.

DEAR FRIEND,

BECAUSE ſome of the holy ſiſters are in their amours altogether ſpiritual, you are by no means to underſtand that they are all totally diveſted of the carnal propenſity.

Some of theſe good creatures are ſo far from thinking that their huſbands are too carnal in their affections, that they really think that they are not enough ſo; and inſtances are not wanting, in which, owing to their

their having hufbands too fpiritual, they have been willing to receive affiftance from the hufbands of other women.

It is but about a year fince a certain celebrated preacher ufed to adminifter carnal confolation to the wife of his clerk. This holy communication was repeated fo often, and fo open, that at laft it came to the clerk's ears, who watching an opportunity, one day furprized the pious pair at their *devotion*, and fo *belaboured* the preacher with his walking-ftaff, that the public were for near a month deprived of the benefits refulting from his remarkable gift of eloquence.

As I am got into the ftory-telling way, I cannot refift the temptation of telling another.

A certain holy fifter who lately kept a houfe in a country village, within ten miles of London; and *took in* (as they called it) Mr. Wefley's preachers, by taking *in* is only meant, that when they came in their turn to preach

preach in the village ſhe uſed to ſupply each with victuals and a bed; (*no doubt* but they ſlept *alone.*) This lady was ſo very remarkable for her *ſpiritual experience* and divine gifts, that ſhe attracted many to her houſe, beſides ſuch as came in the regular courſe of their duty, and among the former a preacher from London, from whom I learnt the affair. This preacher happening to want a wife, and being very ſpiritually-minded, actually married her in December 1790, merely for her great gifts and grace, as her fortune was not above the fiftieth part as much as his own; and as to perſon, ſhe is ſcarce one degree above uglineſs itſelf; although her huſband is well-proportioned, and upon the whole a handſome man. They had not been married a week, when this ſimple preacher diſcovered that his gifted gracious ſaint was an incarnate devil, who had married him only to rob, plunder, and ——— him, and in a few months between her and her gallants, they bullied him out of a ſettlement to the amount of four times the

ſum

ſum ſhe brought him, and the poor pious preacher thinks that he has cheaply got rid of her.

> " Ah, fooliſh woman! may ſhe one day ſee
> " How deep ſhe 's plung'd herſelf in infamy,
> " And with true penitence waſh out the ſtain;—
> " But—miſchief on't—why ſhould I pray in vain;
> " For ſhe's but harden'd at the name of grace,
> " No bluſh was ever ſeen t' adorn her face."
>
> GOULD.

The reaſon why I intereſt myſelf in his behalf is, becauſe I am confident that he really is an honeſt well-meaning man at the bottom; but withal one that does not poſſeſs the greateſt ſhare of underſtanding, and who being formerly but a mean mechanic, never had any education; but although he is a great enthuſiaſt, yet he is one of the good-natured inoffenſive ſort, who will do no harm to any perſon, but on the contrary all the good in his power. I am only ſorry, as he lately was an honeſt uſeful tradeſman, that he ſhould have ſo much ſpiritual quixotiſm in him, as at thirty years of age to ſhut up his ſhop and turn preacher, without being able

able to read his primer; which I can aſſure you is the caſe. But here, my friend, you ſee I forgot that theſe heavenly teachers only ſpeak as the Spirit giveth utterance, and that of courſe all human learning is entirely ſuperfluous.

" —— " As he does not chuſe to cull,
" His faith by any ſcripture rule;
" But by the vapours that torment
" His brains, from hypocondria ſent,
" Which into dreams and viſions turn,
" And make his zeal ſo fiercely burn,
" That reaſon loſes the aſcendant,
" And all within grows independant,
" He proves all ſuch as do accord
" With him the choſen of the Lord;
" But that all others are accurſt,
" 'Tis plain in Canticles the firſt."

BUTLER's Poſth. Works.

A few years ſince the methodiſt-preachers got footing in Wellington (the famous birth-place of your humble ſervant) and eſtabliſhed a ſociety there, ſoon after which one of their preachers (at Collompton, a neighbouring town) happened to like a young ſervant girl, who was one of the holy ſiſters, ſhe having gone

gone through the new birth, better than his wife, becauſe ſhe was an unenlightened, unconverted woman. But this ſervant girl happening to be with child, the news ſoon reached Wellington; and a very wealthy gentleman who entertained the preachers there followed the preacher of Collompton's example, and got his own pious maid with child.

"Bleſſed ſhe tho' once rejected,
"Like a little wandering ſheep;
"Poor maid, one morning was elected
"By a viſion in her ſleep."

After this ſome of the ſociety in Wellington began to have all things in common, and ſeveral more of the holy ſiſters proved prolific; which ſo alarmed the pariſh, that ſome of the heads of it inſiſted that the preachers ſhould not be permitted to preach there any longer. "For, if (ſaid they) the methodiſt-ſociety continues, we ſhall have the pariſh full of baſtards."

A ſimilar affair happened at a country town, ten or twelve miles from Oxford, about two years ſince, where a very handſome powerful preacher made converts of a great number of women, both married and ſingle, who were wonderfully affected, and great numbers flocked to his ſtandard; but he had not laboured there more than a year, before the churchwardens were made acquainted with his powerful operations on fine young female ſaints, who all ſwore baſtards to this holy, ſpiritual labourer in the vineyard; upon which the gentlemen of the town exerted themſelves, and prevented the farther propagation of methodiſm; as

"The ladies by ſympathy ſeem'd to diſcover
"The advantage of having a ſpiritual lover.
"They were ſadly afraid that wives, widows, and miſſes
"Would confine to the —— all their favors and kiſſes."

The author of a letter to Dr. Coke and Mr. More, publiſhed ſince the firſt edition of my Memoirs, informs us, that a gentleman of Cheſham had a daughter about ſeventeen years of age, which he put into the hands

hands of a methodist parson, to have her converted, and was exceedingly kind and liberal to him; and we are informed that this rascal converted her first, and debauched her afterwards.

So you see, my dear friend, by the above examples (were it necessary, I could give you many more) that not all the converted and sanctified females are thereby become so absorbed in the spiritual delights of the mystical union, as to have lost all relish for carnal connections; as we find that many among them are blessed with a mind so capacious, as to be able to participate in the pleasures of both worlds.

I am,

Dear Friend,

Yours.

LETTER XXIV.

"It was not good for man to be alone:
"An equal, yet the subject, is design'd
"For thy soft hours, and to unbend the mind."

DRYDEN.

"Woman, man's chiefest good, by heaven design'd
"To glad the heart, and humanize the mind;
"To sooth each angry care, abate each strife,
"And lull the passions as we walk through life."

Art of Living in London.

DEAR FRIEND,

AFTER a long digression, I must now return to my own affairs.

I continued in the above-mentioned dreadful fever many weeks, and my life was despaired of by all that came near me. During which time, my wife, whom I affectionately loved, died and was buried, without my once having a sight of her. What added much to my misfortunes, several nurses that were hired to take care of me and my wife, proved

proved ſo abandoned and depraved as to have loſt all ſenſe of moral obligation, and every tender feeling for one who to all appearance was juſt on the point of death: ſeveral of theſe monſters in female ſhape robbed my drawers of linen, &c. and kept themſelves drunk with gin, while I lay unable to move in my bed, and was ready to periſh, partly owing to want of cleanlineſs and proper care. Thus ſituated, I muſt inevitably have fallen a victim, had it not been for my ſiſter Dorothy, wife of Mr. Northam of Lambeth, and my ſiſter Elizabeth, wife of Mr. Bell in Soho. Theſe kind ſiſters, as ſoon as they were informed of the deplorable ſtate in which I lay, notwithſtanding ſome miſunderſtanding which ſubſiſted between us, and prevented me from ſending for them, haſtened to me, and each ſat up with me alternately, ſo that I had one or the other with me every night; and, contrary to all expectation, I recovered. But this recovery was in a very ſlow manner.

As ſoon as I was able to enquire into the ſtate of my affairs, I found that Mr. Wheeler, ſack and rope-maker in Old-ſtreet, and Meſſrs. Bottomley and Shaw, carpenters and ſaſh-makers in Bunhill-row, had ſaved me from ruin, by locking up my ſhop, which contained my little *all*. Had not this been done, the nurſes would no doubt have contrived means to have emptied my ſhop, as effectually as they had done my drawers.

The above gentlemen not only took care of my ſhop, but alſo advanced money to pay ſuch expences as occurred; and as my wife was dead, they aſſiſted in making my will in favour of my mother.

Theſe worthy gentlemen belong to Mr. Weſley's ſociety (and notwithſtanding they have imbibed many enthuſiaſtic whims) yet would they be an honour to any ſociety, and are a credit to human nature. I hope that I never ſhall recollect their kindneſs without being filled with the warmeſt ſentiments of gratitude towards them.

"He

"He that hath Nature in him muſt be grateful:
"'Tis the Creator's primary great Law,
"That links the chain of being to each other,
"Joining the greater to the leſſer nature,
"Tying the weak and ſtrong, the poor and powerful,
"Subduing men to brutes, and even brutes to men."

On my recovery I alſo learnt that Miſs Dorcas Turton (the young woman that kept the houſe, and of whom I then rented the ſhop, parlour, kitchen and garret) having out of kindneſs to my wife, occaſionally aſſiſted her during her illneſs, had caught the ſame dreadful diſorder, ſhe was then very dangerouſly ill, and people ſhunned the houſe as much as if the plague had been in it. So that when I opened my ſhop again, I was ſtared at as though I had actually returned from the other world; and it was a conſiderable time before many of my former cuſtomers could credit that I really was in exiſtence, it having been repeatedly reported that I was dead.

Miſs Dorcas Turton, was a charming young woman, and you muſt now be made farther acquainted with her. She is the daughter of Mr. Samuel Turton of Staffordſhire; her mother by marriage, ſtill retained her maiden name, which was Miſs Jemima Turton, of Oxfordſhire. Mr. Samuel Turton had a large fortune of his own, and about twenty thouſand pounds with his wife Miſs Jemima, but by an unhappy turn for gaming he diſſipated nearly the whole of it, and was obliged to have recourſe to trade to help ſupport his family.

"'Tis loſt at dice, what ancient honour won,
"Hard, when the father plays away the ſon!

He opened a ſhop as a ſaddler's ironmonger, but as he was but little acquainted with trade, and as his old propenſity to gaming never quitted him, it is no wonder that he did not ſucceed in his buſineſs; and to crown all his other follies, he was bound for a falſe friend in a large ſum; this completed his ruin.

His wife died in Jan. 1773, and his final ruin enſued a few months after; ſo that from that

that time to his death he was partly ſupported by his daughter Miſs Dorcas Turton, who cheerfully ſubmitted to keep a ſchool, and worked very hard at plain work, by which means ſhe kept her father from want. The old gentleman died a few months after I came into the ſhop. Being partly acquainted with this young lady's goodneſs to her father, I concluded that ſo amiable a daughter was very likely to make a good wife; I alſo knew that ſhe was immoderately fond of books, and would frequently read until morning; this turn of mind in her was the greateſt of all recommendations to me, who having acquired a few ideas, was at that time reſtleſs to increaſe them: ſo that I was in raptures with the bare thoughts of having a woman to read with, and alſo to read to me.

"Of all the pleaſures, noble and refin'd,
"Which form the taſte and cultivate the mind,
"In every realm where ſcience darts its beams,
"From Thale's ice to Afric's golden ſtreams,
"From climes where Phœbus pours his orient ray,
"To the fair regions of declining day,

"The

"The "Feast of Reason" which from READING springs
"To reas'ning man the highest solace brings.
"'Tis BOOKS a lasting pleasure can supply,
"Charm while we live, and teach us how to die."

LACKINGTON'S Shop Bill.

I embraced the first opportunity after her recovery to make her acquainted with my mind, and as we were no strangers to each others characters and circumstances, there was no need of a long formal courtship; so I prevailed on her not to defer our union longer than the 30th of January, 1776, when for the second time I entered into the holy state of matrimony.

——"Wedded Love is founded on esteem,
"Which the fair merits of the mind engage:
"For those are charms that never can decay,
"But Time, which gives new whiteness to the swan,
"Improves their lustre."

FENTON.

I am,

Dear Friend,

Yours.

LETTER

LETTER XXV.

"Reaſon re-baptiz'd me when adult:
"Weigh'd true from falſe, in her impartial ſcale.
"Truth, radiant goddeſs! ſallies on my ſoul!
"And puts deluſion's duſky train to flight."

YOUNG.

"All the myſtic lights were quench'd."

LEE.

DEAR FRIEND,

I Am now in February 1776, arrived at an important period of my life. Being lately recovered from a very painful, dangerous, and hopeleſs illneſs, I found myſelf once more in a confirmed ſtate of health, ſurrounded by my little ſtock in trade, which was but juſt ſaved from thieves, and which to me was an immenſe treaſure. Add to the above, my having won a ſecond time in a game where the odds were ſo much againſt me; or to uſe another ſimile, my having drawn another prize in the lottery of wedlock, and thus like John Buncle repaired the

loſs

loſs of one very valuable woman by the acquiſition of another ſtill more valuable.

"O woman! let the libertine decry,
"Rail at the virtuous love he never felt,
"Nor wiſh'd to feel.—Among the ſex there are
"Numbers as greatly good as they are fair;
"Where rival virtues ſtrive which brightens moſt,
"Beauty the ſmalleſt excellence they boaſt;
"Where all unite ſubſtantial bliſs to prove,
"And give mankind in them a taſte of joys above."

HAWKWARD.

Reflecting on the above united circumſtances, I found in my heart an unuſual ſenſation, ſuch as until then I had been a ſtranger to: my mind began to expand, intellectual light and pleaſure broke in and diſpelled the gloom of fanatical melancholy; the ſourneſs of my natural temper which had been much increaſed by ſuperſtition, (called by Swift, "the ſpleen of the ſoul,") in part gave way, and was ſucceeded by cheerfulneſs, and ſome degree of good-nature.

It was in one of theſe cheerful moods that I one day took up the Life of John Buncle; and it is impoſſible for my friend to imagine with

with what eagerneſs and pleaſure I read through the whole four volumes of this whimſical, ſenſible, pleaſing work; it was written by Thomas Amory, Eſq. (who was living in the year 1788, at the great age of 97) and I know not of any work more proper to be put into the hands of a poor ignorant bigotted ſuperſtitious methodiſt; but the misfortune is, that ſcarce one of them will read any thing but what ſuits with their own narrow notions, ſo that they ſhut themſelves up in darkneſs, and exclude every ray of intellectual light; which puts me in mind of the enthuſiaſts on the banks of the Ganges, who will not look at any thing beyond the tip of their noſes. By the time I had gone through the laſt volume,

> "My ſoul had took its freedom up."
>
> GREEN.

I alſo received great benefit from reading Coventry's Philemon to Hydaſpes; it conſiſts of dialogues on falſe religion, extravagant devotion, &c. in which are many very curious remarks on viſionaries of various ages and

and ſects. The works is complete in five parts octavo. There has alſo been a decent Scotch edition, publiſhed in twelves, both editions are now rather ſcarce.

I now began to enjoy many innocent pleaſures and recreations in life, without the fear of being eternally damn'd for a laugh, a joke, or for ſpending a ſociable evening with a few friends, going to the play-houſe, &c. &c.

In ſhort I ſaw that true religion was no way incompatible with, or an enemy to rational pleaſures of any kind. As life (ſays one) is the gift of heaven, it is religion to enjoy it.

> " Fools by exceſs make varied pleaſure pall,
> " The wiſe man's moderate, and enjoys them all."
>
> VOLTAIRE by Franklin.

I now alſo began to read with great pleaſure the rational and moderate divines of all denominations: and a year or two after I began with metaphyſics, in the intricate though pleaſing labyrinths of which I have occaſionally

ally ſince wandered, nor am I ever likely to find my way out.

"Like a guide in a miſt have I rambled about,
"And now come at laſt where at firſt I ſet out;
"And unleſs for new lights we have reaſon to hope,
"In darkneſs it muſt be my fortune to grope."

I am not in the leaſt uneaſy on that head, as I have no doubt of being in my laſt moments able to adopt the language of one of the greateſt men that ever exiſted:

"Great God, whoſe being by thy works is known,
"Hear my laſt words from thy eternal throne:
"If I miſtook, 'twas while thy law I ſought,
"I may have err'd, but thou wert in each thought,
"Fearleſs I look beyond the opening grave,
"And cannot think the God who being gave,
"The God whoſe favours made my bliſs o'erflow,
"Has doom'd me, after death, to endleſs woe."

In the mean time I can ſincerely adopt the following lines of Mr. Pope.

"If I am right, thy grace impart,
"Still in the right to ſtay;
"If I am wrong! O teach my heart,
"To find the better way."

Having

Having begun to think rationally, and reaſon freely on religious matters, you may be ſure I did not long remain in Mr. Weſley's ſociety. What is remarkable, I well remember that ſome years before, Mr. Weſley told his ſociety in Broadmead, Briſtol, in my hearing, that he could never keep a bookſeller ſix months in his flock, (all fanatics are enemies to reaſon.) He was then pointing out the danger that attended cloſe reaſoning in matters of religion and ſpiritual concerns, in reading controverſies, &c. at that time I had not the leaſt idea of my ever becoming a bookſeller: but I no ſooner began to give ſcope to my reaſoning faculties than the above remarkable aſſertion occurred to my mind.

But that which rather haſtened my departure from methodiſm was this. The methodiſt preachers were continually reprobating the practice of maſters and miſtreſſes keeping ſervants at home on Sundays, to dreſs dinners, which prevented them from hearing the word of God (by the word of God

God they mean their own jargon of nonsense); assuring them if the souls of such servants were damned, they might in a great measure lay their damnation at the doors of such masters and mistresses, who rather than eat a cold dinner, would be guilty of breaking the sabbath, and risking the souls of their servants. But how great was my surprize on discovering that these very men who were continually preaching up fasting, abstinence, &c. to their congregations, and who wanted others to dine off cold dinners, or eat bread and cheese, &c. would themselves not even *sup*, without roasted fowls, &c.

This I found to be fact, as I several times had occasion after attending the preaching to go into the kitchen behind the *old Foundery*, (which at that time was Mr. Wesley's preaching house;) there I saw women who had been kept from hearing the sermon, &c. they being employed in roasting fowls, and otherwise providing good suppers for the preachers.

"So," said I, "you lay burthens on other men's shoulders, but will not so much as touch them yourselves with one of your fingers."

A ridiculous instance of the same nature happened also some years since at Taunton. One of Mr. Wesley's preachers, whose name was Cotterrell, assured his congregation from time to time, that every baker that baked meat on Sundays would be damned, and every person that partook of such meat would also be damned; on which a poor baker shut up his oven on Sundays; the consequence was, that he lost his customers, as such bakers as baked their victuals on Sunday, had their custom on other days, so that the poor baker's family was nearly reduced to the workhouse; when one Sunday passing before the door where he knew the preacher was to dine, he was very much surprised to see a baked leg of pork carried into the house, and after a few minutes reflections he rushed in and found the pious preacher eating part of the baked leg of pork, on which

which he bid farewel to the methodiſts, and again took care for his family.

It perhaps is worth remarking, that many poor hair-dreſſers in Mr. Weſley's ſociety are reduced to extreme poverty, they cannot get employment, as they will not dreſs hair on Sundays; and I find that a poor milk woman, who until the beginning of this year 1792, maintained her family in a decent manner, was lately frightened out of her underſtanding by a methodiſt preacher; her crime was, the ſelling milk on Sundays. The poor wretch is now confined in Bedlam, and her five children are in a workhouſe.

I at this time know a bookſeller, who being a methodiſt, is ſo conſcientious as to have his hair dreſſed on the evening of every Saturday, and to prevent its being diſcompoſed in the night, he on thoſe nights always ſleeps in his elbow chair. Indeed ſome tell the ſtory different, and ſay, that his hair is dreſſed on Saturday morning, and by ſleeping in his chair he ſaves the expence of dreſſing on Sundays; others ſay, that the firſt is the fact, and that he hinted at it in his ſhop-bills, in order that the public may know where to find a tradeſman that had a very tender conſcience.

I was one day called aſide and a hand-bill was given me; and thinking it to be a quack doctor's bill for a certain diſeaſe, I expreſſed my ſurpriſe at its being given to me in ſuch a particular manner; but on reading it I found it contained a particular account of the wonderful converſion of a John Biggs, when he was twenty-one years of age. Mr. Biggs ſays, that ever ſince that time he has had *communion with God his Father every hour*. He publiſhes this bill (he ſays) for the glory of God; but that the public might have an opportunity of dealing with this wonderful ſaint and perfectly holy man, he put his addreſs in capitals, John Biggs, No. 98, Strand. I keep this bill as a curioſity.

I am, dear Friend, yours.

LETTER

LETTER XXVI.

" Good morrow to thee: How doſt do?
" I only juſt call'd in, to ſhew
" My love, upon this bleſſed day,
" As I by chance came by this way.

BUTLER's Poſth. Works.

" Let not your weak unknowing hand
" Preſume God's bolts to throw,
" And deal damnation round the land,
" On each you judge his foe."

DEAR FRIEND,

I Had no ſooner left Mr. Weſley's ſociety, and begun to talk a little more like a rational being, but I found that I had incurred the hatred of ſome, the pity of others, the envy of many, and the diſpleaſure of *all* Mr. Weſley's—*old women!* So that for a long time I was conſtantly teaſed with their impertinent nonſenſe. I believe that never was a poor devil ſo plagued.

" Superſtition is dreadful in her wrath,
" Her dire Anathema's againſt you dart."

HENRIADE.

Some as they paſſed by my door in their way to the Foundery would only make a ſtop and lift up their hands, turn up the whites of their eyes, ſhake their heads, groan, and paſs on. Many would call in and take me aſide, and after making rueful faces, addreſs me with, "Oh, Brother Lackington! I am very ſorry to find that you who began in the Spirit are now like to end in the fleſh. Pray brother, do remember Lot's wife." Another would interrupt me in my buſineſs, to tell me, that "he that putteth his hand to the plough, and looketh back, is unfit for the kingdom." Another had juſt called as he was paſſing by, to caution me againſt the bewitching ſnares of proſperity. Others again called to know if I was as happy then as I was when I conſtantly ſought the Lord with my brethren, in prayer meeting, in claſs, in band, &c. When I aſſured them that I was more happy, they in a very ſolemn manner aſſured me, that I was under a very great deluſion of the devil; and when I by chance happened to laugh

laugh at their enthusiastic rant, some have run out of my shop, declaring that they were afraid to stay under the same roof with me, lest the house should fall on their heads. Sometimes I have been accosted in such an alarming manner as though the house was on fire, with "Oh! brother! brother! you are fast asleep! and the flames of hell are taking hold of you!"

A certain preacher assured me, in the presence of several gentlemen, that the devil would soon toss me about in the flames of hell with a pitchfork. This same eloquent mild preacher used occasionally to strip to his shirt to *dodge* the devil.

Mr. E. a gentleman of my acquaintance, going through some alley, one Sunday, hearing a very uncommon noise, was led by curiosity to the house from whence it proceeded, and there he saw elevated above an assembly of old women, &c. this taylor, stript in his shirt, with his wig off, and the collar of his shirt unbuttoned, sweating, foaming at the mouth, and bellowing like a baited bull. In the above manner it ſeems he would often amuſe himſelf and his congregation for near two hours,

> "Curſing from his ſweating tub,
> "The cavaliers of Belzebub."
>
> BUTLER's Poſth. Works.

Some of the *Tabernacle* ſaints aſſured me, that I never had one grain of ſaving grace, and that when I thought myſelf a child of God, I was only deluded by the devil, who being now quite ſure of me, did not think it worth his while to deceive me any longer. Others adviſed me to take care of ſinning againſt light and knowledge, and piouſly hoped that it was not quite *too late*; that I had not (they hoped) committed the *unpardonable* ſin againſt the Holy Ghoſt. Others again, who happened to be in a better humour, often told me that they ſhould ſee me brought back to the true ſheepfold, as they really hoped I had once been in a ſtate of grace, and if ſo, that I always was in grace,

in

in ſpite of all I could do: the Lord would never quit his hold of me; that I might fall *foully*, but that it was impoſſible for me to fall *finally*, as in the end I ſhould be brought back on the ſhoulders of the everlaſting goſpel, for when God came to number his jewels, not one would be miſſing.

One of theſe righteous men, after paſſing ſome encomiums on me for my moral character, aſſured me that I had by no means fallen ſo low as many of God's dear children had fallen, but fall as low as they poſſibly can, ſaid he, they are ſtill God's children, for altho' they may "be black with ſin they are fair within." He then read to me the following paſſage out of a pamphlet written againſt Mr. Fletcher by Mr. R. Hill. "David "ſtood as completely juſtified in the everlaſting "righteouſneſs of Chriſt, at the time when "he cauſed Uriah to be murdered, and was "committing adultery with his wife, as he "was in any part of his life. For all the ſins "of the elect, be they more or be they leſs,

"be

"be they paſt, preſent, or to come, were "for ever done away. So that every one "of thoſe *elect* ſtand ſpotleſs in the ſight of "God." Is not this a very comfortable kind of doctrine? The pernicious conſequences of ſuch tenets impreſſed on the minds of the ignorant followers of theſe quacks in religion, muſt be obvious to every perſon capable of reflection, They have nothing to do but to enliſt themſelves in the band of the elect, and no matter then how criminal their life!

Thus, my dear friend, I was for a long time coaxed by ſome, threatened with all the tortures of the damned by others, and conſtantly teaſed ſome how or other by all the methodiſts who came near me.

"Surrounded by foes, as I ſat in my chair,
"Who attacked like dogs that are baiting a bear."

I at laſt determined to laugh at all their ridiculous perverſions of the ſcripture, and their ſpiritual cant. The conſequence (as might

might be expected) was, they piously and charitably consigned me over to be tormented by the devil, and every where declared that I was turned a downright atheist. But the aspersions of such fanatics gave me no concern, for

"——— If there's a power above us,
"(And that there is, all nature cries aloud
"Through all her works) he must delight in Virtue;
"And that which he delights in must be happy."

ADDISON's Cato.

And no matter "when or where." After relating such ridiculous stuff as the above, I think that I cannot conclude this better than with Swift's humorous and satirical account of the day of judgment; so humorous that I would not have quoted it had it not been written by a divine of the Church of England.

" With a whirl of thought oppress'd,
" I sunk from reverie to rest,
" An horrid vision seiz'd my head,
" I saw the graves give up their dead:

" Jove

"Jove arm'd with terrors bursts the skies,
"And thunder roars, and light'ning flies!
"Amaz'd, confus'd, its fate unknown,
"The world stands trembling at his throne!
"While each pale sinner hung his head,
"Jove nodding, shook the heavens and said,
"Offending race of human kind,
"By nature, reason, learning blind;
"You who thro' frailty stept aside,
"And you who never fell thro' pride,
"You who in different sects were sham'd,
"And come to see each other damn'd!
"(So some folks told you, but they knew,
"No more of Jove's designs than you)
"The world's mad business now is o'er,
"And I resent those pranks no more,
"—I to such blockheads set my wit!
"I damn such fools! go, go, you're bit."

I am,

Dear Friend,

Yours.

LETTER

LETTER XXVII.

" In London ſtreets is often ſeen
" A hum-drum ſaint with holy mein,
" His looks moſt primitively wear
" An antient Abrahamick air,
" And like bad copies of a face,
" The good original diſgrace."

BUTLER's Poſth. Works.

DEAR FRIEND,

IT being generally known that I had for many years been a ſtrict methodiſt, ſince I have freed myſelf from their ſhackles, I have been often aſked if I did not believe or rather know, that the methodiſts were a vile ſect of hypocrites altogether? My reply has been uniformly in the negative. I am certain that they are not in general ſo. The major part of them indeed are very ignorant (as is the caſe with enthuſiaſts of every religion); but I believe that a great number of the methodiſts are ſincere, honeſt, friendly people; in juſtice to thoſe of that

that deſcription it may not be amiſs to obſerve, that many artful, ſly, deſigning perſons, having noticed their character, connections, &c. and knowing that a religious perſon is in general ſuppoſed to be honeſt and conſcientious, have been induced to join their ſocieties, and by aſſuming an appearance of extraordinary ſanctity, have the better been enabled to cheat and defraud ſuch as were not guarded againſt their hypocritical wiles.

> "Making religion a diſguiſe,
> "Or cloak to all their villanies."
>
> BUTLER's Poſth. Works.

I have alſo reaſon to believe that there are not a few, who think that they can as it were afford to cheat and defraud, on the ſcore of having right notions of religion in their heads, hearing what they deem orthodox teachers, going to prayer-meetings, &c.

There are again others who think, that grace is ſo free and ſo eaſy to be had, or in other words, that as they can have pardon

for

for all kinds of ſins, and that at any time whenever they pleaſe, they under this idea make very little conſcience of running up large ſcores, to which practice I fear ſuch doctrines as I noticed in my laſt, from the pen of Mr. Hill, have not a little contributed.

I have often thought that great hurt has been done to ſociety by the methodiſt preachers, both in town and country, attending condemned malefactors, as by their fanatical converſation, viſionary hymns, bold and impious applications of the ſcriptures, &c. many dreadful offenders againſt law and juſtice, have had their paſſions and imaginations ſo worked upon, that they have been ſent to the other world in ſuch raptures, as would better become martyrs innocently ſuffering in a glorious cauſe, than criminals of the firſt magnitude.

A great number of narratives of theſe ſudden converſions and triumphant exits have been compiled, many of them publiſhed, and circulated

circulated with the greatest avidity, to the private emolument of the editors, and doubtless to the great edification of all sinners, long habituated to a course of villainous depredations on the lives and properties of the honest part of the community; and many such accounts as have not appeared in print, have been assiduously proclaimed in all the methodist chapels and barns, throughout the three kingdoms; by which the good and pious of every denomination have been scandalized, and notorious offenders encouraged to persevere, trusting sooner or later, to be honoured with a similar degree of notice, and thus by a kind of hocus pocus, be suddenly transformed into saints.

The following remarks made by the compilers of the Monthly Review for 1788, page 286, are so applicable to the present subject, that I hope my introducing the passage will not be deemed improper. After mentioning a couplet in one of the methodistical hymns, where it is said

"*Believe* and all your ſin's forgiven."
"Only *believe* and yours is heaven."

they proceed thus:

"Such doctrine no doubt muſt be comfortable to poor wretches ſo circumſtanced as thoſe were to whom this pious preacher had the goodneſs to addreſs his diſcourſe; but ſome (and thoſe not men of ſhallow reflection) have queſtioned whether it is altogether right, thus to free the moſt flagitious outcaſts of ſociety from the terrors of an *after-reckoning*; ſince it is too well known, that moſt of them make little account of their puniſhment in *this* world. Inſtead of the "fearfull *looking for of* (future) *judgment*;" they are enraptured with the proſpect of a joyful flight "to the expanded arms of a loving Saviour—longing to embrace his long loſt children." Surely this is not the way (humanly ſpeaking) to check the alarming progreſs of moral depravity; to which, one would think *no* kind of *encouragement* ought to be given."

I muſt obſerve farther, that the unguarded manner in which the methodiſt preachers make tenders of pardon and ſalvation, has induced many to join their fraternity, whoſe conſciences wanted very large plaiſters indeed! many of thoſe had need to be put under a courſe of mortification and penance, but they generally adopt another method; a few quack noſtrums, which they call faith and aſſurance, drys up the wound, and they then make themſelves as hateful by affecting to have ſqueamiſh conſciences, as they really have been obnoxious, for having conſciences of very wide latitude indeed. And notwithſtanding the affected change, they often are as bad, or worſe than ever. As a friend, permit me to adviſe you never to purchaſe any thing at a ſhop where the maſter of it crams any of his pious nonſenſe into his ſhop-bill, &c. as you may be aſſured you will nine times out of ten find them, in the end, arrant hypocrites, and as ſuch, make no ſcruple of cheating in the way of trade, if poſſible.

This

This puts me in mind of one of theſe pious brethren in Petticoat-lane who wrote in his ſhop-window, " Rumps and Burs ſold here, and Baked Sheep's heads will be continued every night, *if the Lord permit.*" The Lord had no objection: ſo Rumps, Burs, and Baked *Sheep's heads* were ſold there a long time. And I remember to have ſeen on a board, near Bedminſter-down, " Tripe and cow-heels ſold here as uſual, except on the Lord's-day, which *the Lord help me to keep.*" And on my enquiring about the perſon who exhibited this remarkable ſhew-board, at the inn juſt by, I was informed that the pious Tripe-ſeller generally got drunk on Sundays, after he returned from the barn-preaching; which accounts for his not ſelling tripe on that day, having full employment (though poſſibly not ſo inoffenſive) elſewhere.

I alſo ſaw in a village near Plymouth in Devonſhire, " Roger Tuttel, *by God's grace and mercy*, kills rats, moles, and all ſorts of vermin and venomous creatures." But I need not have gone so far, as, no doubt you must remember that a few years since, a certain pious common-council man of the metropolis, advertised in the public papers for a porter that could carry *three hundred* weight and *serve the Lord*. Of the same worthy personage I have heard it asserted, that so very conscientious is he, that he once staved a barrel of beer in his cellar, because he detected it *working* on the sabbath-day, which brought to my recollection four lines in drunken Barnaby's Journey:

" To Banbury came I; O prophane one!
" Where I saw a puritane one,
" Hanging of his cat on Monday,
" For killing of a mouse on Sunday.

Mr. L——e, a gentleman of my acquaintance informs me, that a methodist neighbour of his, in St. Martin's-lane, who keeps a parcel of fowls, every Saturday night, makes a point of conscience of tying together the legs of every cock he has, in order to prevent

prevent them from breaking the ſabbath, by treading the hens on Sundays.

I have a few more obſervations to make on this remarkable ſect, but fearing I have already tired you, ſhall reſerve them for my next.

> " Seeming devotion doth but gild the knave,
> " T[illegible]s neither faithful, honeſt, juſt, or brave,
> " But where religion does with virtue join,
> " It makes a hero like an angel ſhine."
>
> WALLER.

I am,

Dear Friend,

Yours.

LETTER XXVIII.

"Under this ſtone reſts Hudibras,
"A Knight as errant as e'er was:
"The controverſy only lies,
"Whether he was more fool than wiſe;
"Full oft he ſuffer'd bangs and drubs,
"And full as oft took pains in tubs:
"And for the good old Cauſe ſtood buff,
"'Gainſt many a bitter kick and cuff,
"Of which the moſt that can be ſaid,
"He pray'd and preach'd, and preach'd and pray'd."

BUTLER's Poſth. Works.

DEAR FRIEND,

IT is very remarkable that while I was writing the laſt five lines of my former letter to you, on Wedneſday the 2d of March 1791, I received the news of the death of Mr. John Weſley, who I am informed, died that morning at his own houſe, in the City-road, Moorfields, in the Eighty-eighth year of his age. He had no illneſs, but the wheels of the machine being worn out, it ſtopt of courſe. As I am on the ſub-ject

ject of methodism, I hope you will not deem it impertinent, if I devote a few lines to this great parent of a numerous sect, whom I well knew, and feel a pleasure in speaking of with some respect.

Several days preceding his interment, being laid in his coffin, in his gown and band, he was exposed to the view of all who came and the public; and I suppose that forty or fifty thousand persons had a sight of him. But the concourse of people was so great, that many were glad to get out of the crowd without seeing him at all; and although a number of constables were present, yet the pick-pockets contrived to ease many of their purses, watches, &c.

To prevent as much as possible the dreadful effects of a mob, he was interred on Wednesday March the 9th, between five and six o'clock in the morning, in the burial ground behind his own chapel in the City-road. After which Dr. Whitehead (the physician) preached his funeral sermon; but notwithſtanding the early hour, many thouſands attended more than the chapel would hold, although it is very large.

As ſoon as it was known that Mr. Weſley was deceaſed, a number of needy brethren deemed it a fair opportunity of profiting by it, and each immediately ſet his ingenuity to work to compoſe what he choſe to call a *life* of him; and for ſome weeks ſince the funeral the chapel-yard and its vicinity has exhibited a truly ludicrous ſcene, on every night of preaching, owing to the different writers and venders of theſe haſty performances exerting themſelves to ſecure a good ſale; one bawling out, that *his* is the *right* life, a ſecond with a pious ſhake of the head, declares *his* the real life, a third proteſts *he* has got the *only genuine* account; and a fourth calls them all vile cheats and impoſtors, &c. ſo that between all theſe competitors, the ſaints are ſo divided and perplexed in their opinions, that ſome decline purchaſing either; others willing " to try all, and keep that which is good,

good," buy of each of theſe reſpectable venders of the life and laſt account of that celebrated character; while the unintereſted paſſenger is apt to form a concluſion that the houſe of prayer is again become a den of thieves. Thus we ſee thoſe holy candidates for heaven are ſo influenced by ſelf-intereſt that it

"Turns meek and ſecret ſneaking ones
"To Raw-heads fierce and bloody bones."

HUDIBRAS.

I cannot help thinking that Mr. John Weſley, the father of the methodiſts, was one of the moſt reſpectable enthuſiaſts that ever lived; as it is generally thought that he believed all that he taught others, and lived the ſame pious exemplary life, that he would have his followers practiſe. The ſale of his numerous writings produced nett profits to the amount of near TWO THOUSAND POUNDS per annum; and the weekly collection of the claſſes in London and Weſtminſter amounted to a very large ſum; beſides this, great ſums were collected, at the ſacraments

ments and love-feafts, for quarterly tickets, private and public fubfcriptions, &c. &c. In a pamphlet which was publifhed in the beginning of this year 1792, by an old member of their fociety, it is afferted that for the laft ten years, the fums collected in Great Britain and Ireland, have amounted to no lefs than FOUR HUNDRED THOUSAND POUNDS per annum. Befides the above, many private collections are made in all his focieties throughout the three kingdoms, fo that Mr. Wefley might have amaffed an immenfe fortune, had riches been his object. But inftead of accumulating wealth, he expended all his own private property; and I have been often informed, from good authority, that he never denied relief to a poor perfon that afked him. To needy tradefmen I have known him to give ten or twenty pounds at once. In going a few yards from his ftudy to the pulpit, he generally gave away an handful of half-crowns to poor old people of his fociety. He was indeed charitable to an extreme, as he often gave to unworthy

objects,

objects, nor would he keep money ſufficient to hold out on his journies. One of his friends informs me that he left but £4. 10s. behind him: and I have heard him declare that he would not die worth twenty pounds, except his books for ſale, which he has left to the "general methodiſt fund, for carrying on the work of God, by itinerant preachers," charged only with a rent of eighty-five pounds a year, which he has left to the wife and children of his brother Charles.

His learning and great abilities are well known. But I cannot help noticing that in one of his publications (ſtepping out of his line) he betray'd extreme weakneſs and credulity, though no doubt his intentions were good. What I allude to is his "*Primitive Phyſic*, a work certainly of a dangerous tendency, as the majority of remedies therein preſcribed are moſt aſſuredly inefficacious, and many of them very dangerous, if adminiſtred. The conſequence of the firſt is,

that

that while poor ignorant people are trying theſe remedies, (beſides the very great probability of their miſtaking the caſe) the diſeaſes perhaps become ſo inveterate as to reſiſt the power of more efficacious remedies properly applied, and with regard to thoſe of a highly dangerous nature, how raſh to truſt them in the hands of ſuch uninformed people as this book was almoſt ſolely intended for, eſpecially when ſanctioned by the name of an author whoſe influence impreſſed the minds of the unfortunate patients with the moſt powerful conviction. Many fatal effects, I fear, have been produced by a blind adherence to this compilation; which carries with it more the appearance of being the production of an ignorant opinionated old woman, than of the man of ſcience and education. One melancholy inſtance is freſh in my memory; a much eſteemed friend having fallen an immediate ſacrifice to an imprudent application of one of theſe remedies.

A very worthy phyſician to whom the community is highly indebted for his indefatigable and ſucceſsful exertions in the cauſe of humanity, publiſhed ſome very judicious "Remarks on the Primitive Phyſic," which however, for obvious reaſons, were not ſo generally noticed as the ſubject deſerved; as almoſt all the admirers of Mr. Weſley's work conſiſted of his followers, (ſufficiently numerous indeed to enſure a very extenſive ſale) theſe were too bigoted to condeſcend to peruſe any production tending to enlighten their underſtandings; and the public at large, not having paid much attention to it, did not conceive themſelves ſo materially intereſted in the "Remarks," though I am firmly of opinion, if they are peruſed with that candour with which they appear to be written, they will have a very beneficial tendency in guarding the public againſt the miſchief too frequently ariſing from the "Primitive Phyſic," and other quack publications, as abſurd as they are injurious.

Permit

Permit me juſt to give you one ſpecimen of the author's wonderful abilities, by quoting a receipt, which if not an *infallible remedy*, muſt at leaſt be acknowledged to be a ſingular one.

"To cure a windy Cholic."

"Suck a healthy woman daily; this (ſays Mr. Weſley) was tried by my father."

Should you, my dear friend, be deſirous of peruſing a variety of remedies, not equally *judicious* as well as *efficacious* with thoſe of Mr. Weſley, you will meet with ample ſatisfaction by turning to "*Dom Pernety's Voyage to the Falkland Iſlands*," page 153 to 162. quarto edition.

Some of the receipts there inſerted are ſo truly *curious*, I can ſcarce refrain from treating you with a ſpecimen or two, but being at the ſame time not *very* delicate, I muſt decline inſerting them, for like Simpkin,

"I pity the ladies ſo modeſt and nice."

Should

Should you, however, deem it worth the trouble of turning to the volume, I am confident the ſubject muſt excite a ſmile at the amazing credulity of the writer, as well as his folly in expoſing ſuch wretched traſh to the public eye, indeed I can hardly perſuade myſelf he could be ſerious when he wrote them.

The two following receipts I muſt give you, one being no doubt an effectual remedy for a grievous complaint of that uſeful quadruped the horſe, the other at leaſt equally certain for the cure of one of the moſt dangerous diſorders human nature is ſubject to.

"To Cure a Foundered Horſe."

"Let him take one or two ſpoonfuls of *common ſalt* in half a pint of water!"

"For a malignant Fever."

"A live tench applied to the feet for *twelve hours*, then buried *quietly*, or thrown down *the houſe of office*, and the patient will ſoon recover."

But

But as I well know you do not possess the faith either of a methodist or a papist, to put implicit trust in whatever the teachers of either choose to write or say, I fear lest I have bestowed on you labour in vain, I therefore decline quoting any more of those extraordinary remedies.

It was a circumstance peculiarly happy for the practitioners of physic, though no doubt a terrible misfortune to the public, that the difference in religious principles of these two reverend gentlemen proved an effectual bar to the union of their medical abilities, which appear so exactly correspondent; had such an event taken place, that horrid monster *disease* might by this time have been banished from the earth, and the sons of Æsculapius would be doomed to feed on their own compositions or starve! The Rev. Dr. Fordyce, in a late publication, has also given the world a remedy for the cramp, as *delicate* as efficacious.

But here, I think I see you smile at my censuring Mr. Wesley for *stepping out of his line*,

line, when at the very moment I am committing the ſame error by obtruding my judgment upon the ſcience of phyſic.—I ſhall only reply, Many thought I did the ſame when I commenced bookſeller; and a friend once taught me the adage, (be not offended, 'tis the only ſcrap of Latin I ſhall give you) "*Ne Sutor ultra crepidam.*" But the event has proved it otherwiſe, and I flatter myſelf every candid and judicious perſon capable of judging will think with me on the above ſubject.——But to reſume my narrative.

What a pity that ſuch a character as Mr. Weſley ſhould have been a dupe and a rank enthuſiaſt! A believer in dreams, viſions, immediate revelations, miraculous cures, witchcraft, and many other ridiculous abſurdities, as appears from many paſſages of his Journals, to the great diſgrace of his abilities and learning; which puts me in mind of Sir Iſaac Newton's Expoſition of the Revelations, Milton's Paradiſe Regained, Dr. Johnſon's unmanly Devotions, &c. &c.

and (to compare ſmall things with greater) J. L.'s turning author. However, we may ſafely affirm that Mr. Weſley was a good ſincere and honeſt one, who denied himſelf many things; and really thought that he diſregarded the praiſe and blame of the world, when he was more courted, reſpected, and followed than any man living, and he ruled over a hundred and twenty thouſand people with an abſolute ſway, and the love of power ſeems to have been the main ſpring of all his actions. I am inclined to believe that his death will be attended with conſequences ſomewhat ſimilar to thoſe which followed the death of Alexander the Great. His ſpiritual generals will be putting in their pretenſions, and ſoon divide their maſter's conqueſts. His death happened at a time rather critical to the methodiſts, as the *Swedenborgians*, or *New Jeruſalemiſts*, are gaining ground very faſt: Many of the methodiſts, both preachers and hearers, are already gone over to their party, many more will now, undoubtedly, follow; and the death of that great female champion

of

of methodiſm, the Counteſs of Huntingdon, which has ſince happened, will in all probability occaſion another conſiderable defection from *that* branch of methodiſts, and an additional reinforcement to the Swedenborgians; a proof of the fondneſs of mankind for novelty, and the marvellous, even in religious matters.

I ſhall conclude my remarks on the methodiſts in my next.

I am,

Dear Friend,

Yours.

LETTER XXIX.

"More haughty than the reſt, the — race,
"Appear with belly gaunt, and famiſh'd face:
"Never was ſo deform'd a babe of grace."

DRYDEN.

Their ſermons

"Are olios made of conflagration,
"Of gulphs, of brimſtone, and damnation,
"Eternal torments, furnace, worm,
"Hell-fire, a whirlwind, and a ſtorm;
"With Mammon, Satan, and perdition,
"And *Belzebub* to help the diſh on;
"*Belial*, and *Lucifer*, and all
"The nicknames which *Old Nick* we call.

DEAR FRIEND,

ALTHOUGH Mr. Weſley was poſſeſſed of a very great ſhare both of natural and acquired abilities, yet I ſuppoſe it ſcarcely neceſſary to inform you, that this is by no means the caſe with his preachers in general; for although there are amongſt them ſome truly ſenſible, intelligent men, yet the major part are very ignorant and extremely illiterate: many of theſe excellent ſpiritual

ſpiritual guides cannot even read a chapter in the bible, though containing the deep myſteries which they have the raſhneſs and preſumption to pretend to explain. Many others cannot write their own names.. But ſo great is the ignorance of Mr. Weſley's people in general, that they often neglect the more rational and ſenſible of their preachers, and are better pleaſed with ſuch as are even deſtitute of common ſenſe; really believing that the incoherent nonſenſe which they from time to time pour forth, is dictated by the Holy Spirit; for which ſeveral reaſons may be aſſigned.

It is always obſervable, that the more ignorant people are, the more confidence they poſſeſs. This confidence, or *impudence*, paſſes with the vulgar, as a mark of their being in the right; and the more the ignorance of the preachers is diſcovered, the more are they brought down to their own ſtandard. Again, the more ignorant preachers having very contracted ideas of real religion and manly virtue, of courſe ſupply the want of it with a ridiculous fuſs about trifles, which paſſes with the ignorant for a more ſanctified deportment, and hence ariſes much of the miſchief which has been ſo juſtly charged on the methodiſts. For by making the path to heaven ſo very narrow, and beſet with ten thouſand bugbears, many deſpairing to be ever able to walk in it, have thrown off all religion and morality, and ſunk into the abyſs of vice and wickedneſs. Others have their tempers ſo ſoured as to become loſt to all the tender connexions of huſband, wife, father, child, &c. really believing that they are *literally* to *hate* father, mother, &c. for Chriſt's ſake. Many have in a fit of deſpondency put a period to their exiſtence, it having become a burthen too intolerable to be borne. Some have been ſo infatuated with the idea of faſting to mortify the fleſh, that their ſtrict perſeverence in it has been productive of the moſt ſerious conſequences: Two inſtances of which lately occurred in one family, in the City Road—The miſtreſs was deprived of her ſenſes, and the maid *literally* fasted herself to death; and Bedlam and private mad-houses now contain many, very many melancholy instances of the dreadful effects of religious despondency; not to mention the hundreds that have died from time to time in such places, and the numerous suicides which have been traced to the same source.

Mr. Bentley says, in his letter to the members of the house of commons, dated May 12th, 1791, that although he had a fortune of one thousand pounds, and naturally liked good living, yet that he lived on horse and ass flesh, barley bread, stinking butter, &c. and when he found that his eating such things gave offence to his neighbours, he left off eating ass flesh, and only lived on vegetables, as the common sort of food by their dearness hurt his conscience.

A few years since I saw in a field not seven miles from China-hall, a man tossing up his bible in the air. This he often repeated, and raved at a strange rate. Amongst other things, (pointing to a building at ſome diſtance) "*That* (ſaid he) is the *devil's* houſe, and it ſhall not ſtand three days longer!" On the third day after this I ſaw with ſurprize an account in one of the public papers of that very building having been ſet on fire, and burnt to the ground, and thus the poor itinerant diſciples of Theſpis loſt the whole of their wardrobe and ſcenery.

This religious maniac ſoon after preached very often in Smithfield and Moorfields; but he did not wholly depend on the operations of the Holy Spirit, as at laſt he ſeldom began to preach until he was nearly drunk, or filled with another kind of ſpirit, and then he was "a very powerful preacher indeed." But the good man happening ſeveral times to exert himſelf rather too much, had nearly tumbled headlong out of his portable pulpit; theſe accidents the mob *uncharitably* aſcribed to the liquor that he had drank, and with mud, ſtones, dead cats, &c. drove him off every time he came, until at laſt our preacher took his leave of them with ſaying "that

he

he perceived it was in vain to attempt their converſion, as he ſaw that God had given them over to the hardneſs of their hearts."

But although this holy man deſerted them, yet other ſpiritual knights-errant were not wanting, ſo that a little time before the heaps of ſtones which lay for years in Moorfields were removed for the purpoſe of building on the ſpot, I have ſeen five or ſix in a day preaching their initiation ſermons from thoſe elevated ſituations, until they could collect a ſufficient ſum of money to purchaſe pulpits. Some of theſe excellent preachers received the whole of their divine education and took up their degrees in Moorfields, and in due time, after having given ample and ſatisfactory proofs of being properly qualified, have been admitted to profeſſorſhips in the noble College ſituated on the ſouth ſide of thoſe fields, generally known by the name of *Bedlem*. You muſt know, Sir, that many of the lazy part of the community ſet up ſtalls in Moorfields to buy and ſell apples, old iron, &c. ſeveral of theſe having heard ſuch edifying diſcourſes frequently repeated as they ſat at their ſtalls, and obſerving the ſucceſs which thoſe kind of preachers met with, boldly reſolved to make trial of *their* ſpiritual gifts on the heaps of ſtones, and have now totally abandoned their ſtalls, and are gone forth as embaſſadors of heaven, though without being furniſhed with any diplomas as ſuch. One of theſe who cannot read, lately informed me that he had quitted all temporal concerns for the good of poor ignorant ſinners. However after all, "there is (poſſibly) a pleaſure in being mad, which none but madmen know." The ſubject of methodiſm is ſo fertile a one, that were I diſpoſed to enlarge thereon, my correſpondence would be extended to a very conſiderable length; but inſtead of purſuing it, I think it better to apologize for having ſo long digreſſed from the main ſubject of my narrative.

But before I take my leave of the ſubject, I will in few words inform you how the preachers were governed and ſupported. Mr.

Mr. Weſley every year ordered the major part of his travelling preachers in great Britain and Ireland, which were upwards of two hundred in number, to meet together, one year at London, the next at Briſtol, and the following at Mancheſter; this meeting he called a conference. At thoſe conferences, the buſineſs of the whole ſociety was tranſacted, new preachers admitted, and ſome turned off, or ſilenced; complaints heard, differences adjuſted, &c. Mr. Weſley having divided Great Britain into circuits, at thoſe conferences, he appointed the preachers to every circuit for the following year, and as he well knew the general want of abilities among his preachers, he limited their time of preaching in one circuit to a year, and ſo in ſome meaſure, made up the want of abilities by variety, moſt of thoſe circuits had three or four preachers every year, and in many country places, they had but one ſermon a week from the travelling preachers, ſo that each preacher preached about twelve ſermons in the year, (ſometimes it may be

twenty)

twenty) at each place. In every circuit one of the preachers was called the aſſiſtant; to him the various contributions were paid, and of him might be had any of Mr. Weſley's publications. He alſo admitted new members, or turned out any who were judged unworthy of bearing the high appellation of a methodiſt.

Each itinerant preacher had a horſe found him, which, with himſelf, is maintained by ſome brother or ſiſter wherever they go, as the preachers do not put up at any inn, and yet they have as regular ſtages to call at as the coaches have, they having made converts at convenient diſtances in moſt parts of Great Britain and Ireland.

Each travelling preacher was then allowed twelve pounds a year, to find himſelf cloaths, pay turnpikes, &c. beſides what they could get privately out of the old women's pockets. But beſides thoſe circuit-preachers, there "are in the year 1790, in Europe and America, thirteen or fourteen hundred," of local

holders-

holdersforth, who do not preach out of their own neighbourhood, and those in general are the most ignorant of all.

Many of the circuit-preachers only travel until they can marry a rich widow, or some ignorant young convert with money, which has often been the cause of great unhappiness, in many respectable families. The following poetical description of the methodist preachers, is so much to my purpose, that I must insert it:

" Every *mechanic* will commence
" *Orator*, without *mood* or *tense*;
" *Pudding* is *pudding* still they know,
" Whether it has a plum or no:
" So, tho' the preacher have no skill,
" A *sermon* is a *sermon* still.

" The Bricklay'r throws his trowel by,
" And now *builds mansions in the sky*;
" The *Cobler*, touch'd with *holy pride*,
" Flings his *old shoes* and *last* aside,
" And now devoutly sets about
" Cobbling of *souls*, that *ne'er wear out*;
" The *Baker* now *a preacher* grown,
" Finds *man lives not by bread alone*,
" And now his customers he feeds
" With *pray'rs*, with *sermons*, *groans*, and *creeds*;

" The

" The *Tinman*, mov'd by warmth within,
" *Hammers* the *gospel* just like *tin*;
" *Weavers inspir'd*, their *shuttles* leave,
" *Sermons* and *flimsy hymns* to weave;
" *Barbers* unreap'd will leave the chin,
" To trim, and shave the *man within*;
" The *Waterman* forgets *his wherry*,
" And opens a *celestial ferry*;
" The *Brewer*, bit by frenzy's grub,
" The *mashing* for the *preaching* tub
" Resigns, *those waters* to explore,
" Which if you drink, you thirst no more;
" The *Gard'ner*, weary of his trade,
" Tir'd of the mattock and the spade,
" Chang'd to *Apollos* in a trice,
" *Waters the plants* of *paradise*;
" The *Fishermen* no longer set
" For *fish* the meshes of their net,
" But catch, like *Peter*, *men of sin*,
" For *catching* is to *take them in*."

I now take a final leave of methodism, with assuring you, that in giving a general idea of the tenets and practices of a numerous sect who have excited much public attention, I have invariably had in view to " speak of them as they are, nothing to extenuate, nor set down aught in malice." Should you wish to see the errors of the methodists particularly

ticularly exposed, you may read Bishop Lavington's "Enthusiasm of the methodists and baptists compared." It is esteemed a very good work, it will amuse as well as instruct you. In my next, I intended to have resumed the account of my own affairs; but an extraordinary publication, will tempt me to add, one letter more on the methodists.

I am,

Dear Friend,

Yours.

LETTER XXX.

"Religion, faireſt maid on earth,
"As meek as good, who drew her breath
"From the bleſt union when in heaven;
"Pleaſure was bride to virtue given;
"Religion ever pleas'd to pray,
"Poſſeſs'd the precious gift one day;
"Hypocriſy of cunning born,
"Crept in and ſtole it ere the morn."

CHURCHILL.

DEAR FRIEND,

ALTHOUGH I was many years in connexion with Mr. Weſley's people, it ſeems, according to a pamphlet publiſhed a few months after the firſt edition of my Memoirs, that I was but ſuperficially acquainted with Mr. Weſley and his preachers. The pamphlet is entitled, "A Letter to the Rev. T. Coke, L.L.D. and Mr. H. Moore." To which is added, "An Appeal and Remonſtrance to the People called Methodiſts, by an old Member of the Society." This old member informs us, that he has been acquainted

quainted with the methodiſts twenty-eight years, and if their preachers are but half as bad as he has drawn them, they are a deteſtable ſet of ſly deceiving villains. The letter was occaſioned by Dr. Coke and Mr. Moore's propoſals for publiſhing Mr. Weſley's Life, in oppoſition to that advertiſed (under the ſanction of the executors) to be written by Dr. Whitehead.

And we are informed that after Mr. Weſley's manuſcripts and private papers had been given up to Dr. Whitehead, and the Doctor appointed to write his Life, and this Life announced to the public by the executors as the only authentic work, on a miſunderſtanding taking place between Dr. Whitehead and the preachers, becauſe the Doctor would not ſubmit his work to be inſpected, altered, &c. and alſo becauſe the Doctor would not conſent to give to the preachers at the conference, nearly the whole of the profits derived from his labours, they then ſent a circular letter ſigned by nine of their head preachers, to all their ſocieties, and adviſe them *to return the ſubſcriptions that they had taken for Doctor Whitehead's Life of Mr. Weſley, and to procure all the ſubſcriptions in their power for another Life of Mr. Weſley,* to be written by Dr. Coke and Mr. Moore.

The following quotations I think will pleaſe you, page 8, &c. "That Mr. Weſley was a great man is an undeniable truth; *that* is comparitively:—Great amongſt little people."

"Nothing can exhibit his character as an ambitious man, more than the following anecdote, which I can give from the moſt authentic authority. When a boy he was in the Charter-Houſe ſchool; the Rev. A. *Tooke,* the author of the *Pantheon,* was then maſter, and obſerving that his pupil, who was remarkably forward in his ſtudies, yet he conſtantly aſſociated with the inferior claſſes; and it was his cuſtom to be ſurrounded by a number of the little boys, haranguing them. Mr. Tooke, once accidentally broke in upon him when in the middle of an oration, and interrupted him, by deſiring him to follow him to the parlour. Mr. Weſley, offended by being thus abruptly de-

prived

prived of an opportunity of diſplaying his ſuperior abilities, obeyed his maſter very reluctantly. When they had got into the parlour Mr. Tooke ſaid to him : " John, I wonder that you who are ſo much above the lower forms ſhould conſtantly aſſociate with them, for you ſhould now conſider yourſelf as a man, and affect the company of the bigger boys, who are your equals." Our hero, who could hardly ſtifle his reſentment whilſt his maſter ſpoke, boldly replied :—" *Better to rule in hell, than ſerve in heaven.*"

" Mr. Tooke diſmiſſed his pupil with this remarkable obſervation to an aſſiſtant maſter.— That boy though deſigned for the church will never get a living in it: for his ambitious ſoul will never acknowledge a ſuperior, or be confined to a pariſh.

" That he was ſuperior to the prejudices he inculcated to his followers, and with what contempt he ſometimes treated the lay-preachers, the following will ſhew.—Being at ſupper one Sunday night, (a ſhort time before his death) with ſeveral of the preachers, one of them obſerved that whenever Mr. Weſley travelled, he was always invited to the houſes of the neighbouring nobility and gentry; but when the preachers travelled, no notice was taken of them, which he could not account for. Mr. Weſley replied, " It was the way of the world to court the great, but I ſay, love me love my dog!" enjoying his triumph with a hearty laugh at their expence."

After this old member's letter comes his Appeal and Remonſtrance to the Methodiſts, which, as coming from an old methodiſt, contains ſome very extraordinary aſſertions and facts, and letters more extraordinary. I ſhall give you ſome extracts from it in page 28. "Faith is the ground-work of (methodiſt) evidence—it precludes the neceſſity of every virtue—it is to be feared it has ſent more of its votaries to Bedlam than to heaven—is to wiſe men a ſtumbling block, an unintelligible jargon of myſtical nonſenſe, which common ſenſe and common honeſty reject."

Page 30, &c. "It has been computed thatthe contributions raiſed among the members of the different ſocieties in Great-Britain and Ireland for theſe laſt ten years, has amounted to no leſs than FOUR HUNDRED THOUSAND POUNDS per annum. It has been further proved that about one eighth part of this ſum is appropriated to the purpoſes

poſes for which it was raiſed, and the remainder is diſpoſed of at the diſcretion of the conference, the preachers, and the ſtewards. This calculation does not include the enormous ſums known to be raiſed privately by the influence of the preachers in their reſpective circuits, under the various pretenſions of diſtreſs, &c.

" However, I do not pretend to vouch for the accuracy of this calculation, yet I think it by no means exaggerated. What has come within my own knowledge I can aſſert with confidence, and I challenge any one to refute it.

" Of *Kingſwood School*, I can ſpeak with certainty: for this foundation, many thouſands have been raiſed which never were, and I believe never were intended to be applied to that charity. During eight years that I was at Kingſwood, it not only ſupported itſelf, but produced a conſiderable annual ſurplus.

" One of the maſters of King's School, being deficient in his accounts, he was judged an improper perſon to enjoy any place of truſt, and was accordingly diſmiſſed, and appointed to a circuit as a *travelling preacher*—but any will do for that, who has but *impudence* and *hypocriſy*—no matter whether he poſſeſſes a grain of *honeſty*. Now if this was the caſe with reſpect to Kingſwood, may we not conclude that the ſame iniquitous principle pervaded the adminiſtration of the finances in all the different departments?

Page 33, &c. " O how long, ye *ſheep*, will ye be the prey of *wolves* who fleece and devour you at pleaſure! and, ye *fools*, be the dupes of *knavery* and *hypocriſy*?

" Open your eyes, and behold the *villain* and *hypocrite* unmaſked, in inſtances of the moſt flagitious crimes, and deeds of the blackeſt dye! perpetrated by wretches, whom you tamely ſuffer to devour your ſubſtance, and whom you cheerfully contribute to ſupport in idleneſs and luxury, which brings into contempt the goſpel, and whoſe example has done more harm to religion, than that of the moſt abandoned and profligate open ſinner: admitting at the ſame time that there may be, and I hope there are, ſome honeſt and ſincere men amongſt them.

" To begin then with the late Rev. J. Weſley. As the founder and head, he muſt be conſidered as the *primum mobile*, or firſt mover of this mighty machine of *hypocriſy*, *fraud*, and *villainy*! Yet were his motives originally laudable in their intention, virtuous in their object, but unhappy in their conſequences. This I will endeavour to make appear, by an impartial review of his life, character, and conduct. I flatter myſelf that I am in ſome meaſure qualified, being totally di-

veſted

vested of prejudice, and having no interest either in representing him as a *saint* or a *devil.*

" From what I have observed during near twenty-eight years that I have known him, I have uniformly found him ambitious, imperious, and positive even to obstinacy. His learning and knowledge various and general, but superficial; his judgment too hasty and decisive to be always just—his penetration acute; yet was he constantly the dupe to his credulity and his unaccountable and universal good opinion of mankind. Humane, generous, and just. In his private opinions liberal to a degree inconsistent with strict Christianity; in his public declarations rigid almost to intolerance. From this observation of the inconsistency of his private opinions and public declarations, I have often been inclined to doubt his sincerity, even in the profession of the Christian faith. In his temper impetuous, and impatient of contradiction; but in his heart, a stranger to malice or resentment; incapable of particular attachment to any individual; he knew no ties of blood or claims of kindred; never violently or durably affected by grief, sorrow or any of the passions to which humanity is subject; susceptible of the grossest flattery, and the most fulsome panegyric was constantly accepted and rewarded. In his views and expectations, sanguine and unbounded, but though often disappointed, never dejected; of his benevolence and charity much has been said; but it is to be observed, benevolence is but a passive virtue, and his charity was no more than bribery; he knew no other use of money but to give it away, and he found out that an hundred pounds would go farther in half crowns than in pounds; so that his charity was little more than parade, as he hardly ever essentially relieved an object of distress: in fact his charity was no more than putting his money to interest, as the example excited his followers to the practice of the same virtue, and doubled their subscriptions and contributions. In his constitution warm, and consequently amorous; in his manner of living luxurious and strictly epicurean and fond of dishes highly relished, and fond of drinking the richest wines, in which he indulged often, but never to excess. He was indebted more to his commanding, positive, and authoritative manner, than to any intrinsically superior abilities.

"Having thus given the outlines of his character, I shall only observe, that he appears to have been more a philosopher than a christian: and shall then proceed to some anecdotes and circumstances which will corroborate my assertions, and justify my conclusion.

As the *work of God*, as it is called, was the sphere of action in which he was more particularly and

and conſpicuouſly engaged, and as I have ventured to queſtion the ſincerity of his profeſſions, it is proper that I ſhould ſtate my reaſons for ſo doing. Firſt then of converſion: in the *methodiſtical* ſenſe of the word, for in the true ſenſe, I apprehend to be neither more or leſs, than forſaking vice and practiſing virtue; but however, the methodiſtical ſenſe imports quite a different thing, and it is in that ſenſe we ſhall view it. I have made it an invariable obſervation, that Mr. Weſley, although he was often in the company of ſenſible men, who were capable of forming an opinion, and preſumed to judge for themſelves by the light of nature, the evidence of the ſenſes, and the aid of reaſon and philoſophy; but of ſuch, he never attempted the converſion. In his own family and amongſt his relations, he never attempted, or if he did attempt, he never ſucceeded: except now and then with a female, in whom he found a heart ſuſceptible of any impreſſion he pleaſed to give. It is remarkable, that even the children of Mr. C. W. were never converted—becauſe they, and moſt of his relations, poſſeſſed ſenſe enough to diſcover hypocriſy, and honeſty enough to reject the advantage they might have derived from aſſuming it. But what is ſtill more extraordinary, is, that out of ſo many hundred, who have been educated at *Kingſwood*, in the moſt rigid diſcipline of methodiſm, hardly any have embraced their tenets, or become

members

members of the ſociety. The reaſon is pretty obvious, they were taught too much to imbibe the ridiculous prejudices the founder wiſhed to be inſtilled into their minds: philoſophy and methodiſm, are utterly incompatible. When the human mind is informed by the ſtudy of philoſophy, it expands itſelf to the contemplation of things.

"It is true indeed, the *work* was ſometimes attended with power among the children at *Kingſwood*. *Converſions* were frequent; but never durable. I myſelf was converted ſome ten or a dozen times; but unluckily, my *claſs leader* was detected in having ſtolen a pair of ſilver buckles. This was a dreadful ſtroke to the *work*, and a glorious triumph to the *wicked one*. The whole fabric of *faith*, *grace*, and all its concomitant vices, as *hypocriſy*, &c. &c. experienced a total overthrow! The ſerious boys, as they were called by way of eminence, fell into the utmoſt contempt, and ever after, the *leader* of a *claſs* was ſtiled *Captain* of the *Gang*: a *convert* and a *thief*, were ſynonimous terms.

"A general converſion among the boys, was once effected, by the late excellent Mr. *Fletcher*: one poor boy only excepted, who unfortunately reſiſted the influence of the Holy Spirit; for which he was ſeverely flogged, which did not fail of the deſired effect, and impreſſed proper notions

of

of religion on his mind. Unhappily these operations of the Spirit, though violent, were but of short duration.

"As the conversion of men and women, is a more serious concern than that of children, I will describe one, to which I was an eye witness among the poor Colliers at *Kingswood*. One of those presumptuous and impious fanatical wretches, who assume the character of ministers of God, and take upon them in his most holy name, to denounce his curses and vengeance against those who are far less guilty than themselves: a fellow of this description, of the name of *Sanderson*, preaching to a congregation of ignorant, but harmless people; this fellow, took upon himself in the name of God, to condemn them all to eternal damnation, painting their deplorable state in the most dreadful colours: some of his hearers were soon evidently affected by this discourse, which he took care to improve, and taking the advantage of the kindling spark, addressed himself more particularly to them, whom he soon "made roar for the disquietude of their souls." The whole congregation were quickly affected in the like manner, one and all exclaimed "What shall I do to be saved? Oh! I'm damned! I'm damned! I'm damned to all eternity! What shall I do? Oh! Oh! Oh! Our performer observing to what a state he he had reduced his audience, redoubled his threats of divine wrath and vengeance, and with a voice terrible as thunder, demanded, "; Is there any backſliders in the preſence of God?" A dead and ſolemn pauſe enſued—till he exclaimed "Here is an old grey-headed ſinner:" at the ſame time ſtriking with his hand violently on the bald pate of an honeſt old man who ſat under the deſk; the poor man gave a deep groan; whether from conviction, or from the pain of the blow, I know not, for it was far from being gentle. The farce was not yet concluded: when they were ſtrongly *convulſed* with theſe *convictions*, he fell down upon his knees, and with the greateſt fervency, accompanied with abundance of tears, he intreated the Lord in mighty prayer, to have compaſſion on the poor deſponding ſinners whom he had brought to a proper ſenſe of their danger: the prayer continued about ten minutes, accompanied by the ſighs and groans of the converted and alarmed ſinners, in concert making a moſt divine harmony: when ſuddenly ſtarting up, he pretended to have received a gracious anſwer to his prayer, and with a joyful and ſmiling countenance, pointing towards the window, exclaimed: —Behold the Lamb! Where! Where! Where! was the cry of every contrite and returning ſinner, (and they were all of that deſcription) There! (continued the preacher, extending his arms towards the window where he pretended firſt to

have

have eſpied the Lamb.) In Heaven! In *Cœlo*! making interceſſion for your ſins! And I have his authority to proclaim unto you—" your ſins are forgiven—depart in peace."—O, my deareſt brethren, how ſweet is the ſound of thoſe extatic words. " Behold the lamb of God, who taketh away the ſins of the world!" But could you but feel the peculiar energy, the divine force, the rapturous and cheering import of the *original*, your mouths would be filled with praiſe, and your hearts with divine joy, holy exultation, and unſpeakable gratitude.—Only mark the ſound of the words, even that will convey an inexpreſſible pleaſure to your ſouls, " *Hecca Hangus Dei! Ki dollit pekkaltus Monday!*" The ſchool-boys (who were ſeated in a pew detached from the congregation on account of their prophane and contemptuous behaviour during ſervice) immediately burſt into a loud laugh, on one of the congregation ſaying, " O the bleſſed man! We ſhall ſee him again on MONDAY."

In ſome pages following we have an account of the methodiſt preacher's firſt converting his benefactor's daughter, and then debauching her; alſo of a preacher at Beverly, in Yorkſhire, that collected fifteen pounds for a poor man in great diſtreſs, and

gave

gave him only fifteen ſhillings, reſerving to himſelf fourteen pounds five ſhillings for the trouble of collecting it, with which, and twenty pounds more he was entruſted with, he decamped the next day, to the aſtoniſhment of the ſimple on whom he had impoſed.

I wiſh the author as he propoſes may ſoon give us a more particular account of the methodiſts, preachers, and people, and alſo of ſome of Mr. Weſley's private opinions, &c.

This pamphlet concludes with very curious letters written by Mr. J. Weſley, and he informs us in a note that the publiſher has his addreſs in order to direct any perſon to the author where they may ſee the original letters. I here give you the whole of theſe extraordinary letters.

Page 50, &c.

" DEAR SIR,

FOR your obliging letter which I received this morning, I return you thanks.

" Our opinions for the moſt part perfectly coincide reſpecting the ſtability of the connexion,

after

after my head is laid in the duſt. This, however, is a ſubject, about which I am not ſo anxious as you ſeem to imagine; on the contrary, it is a matter of the utmoſt indifference to me; as I have long foreſeen that a diviſion muſt neceſſarily enſue, from cauſes ſo various, unavoidable and certain, that I have long ſince given over all thoughts and hopes of ſettling it on a permanent foundation. You do not ſeem to be aware of the moſt effective cauſe that will bring about a diviſion. You apprehend the moſt ſerious conſequences from a ſtruggle between the preachers for power and pre-eminence, and there being none among them of ſufficient authority or abilities to ſupport the dignity, or command the reſpect and exact the implicit obedience which is ſo neceſſary to uphold our conſtitution on its preſent principles. This is one thing that will operate very powerfully againſt unity in the connexion, and is, perhaps, what I might poſſibly have prevented, had not a ſtill greater difficulty ariſen in my mind: I have often wiſhed for ſome perſon of abilities to ſucceed me as the head of the church I have with ſuch indefatigable pains, and aſtoniſhing ſucceſs eſtabliſhed; but convinced that none but very ſuperior abilities would be equal to the undertaking, was I to adopt a ſucceſſor of this deſcription, I fear he might gain ſo much influence among the people, as to uſurp a ſhare, if not the whole of that abſolute and uncontrolable

power

power, which I have hitherto, and am determined I will maintain ſo long as I live: never will I bear a rival near my throne.—You no doubt, ſee the policy of continually changing the preachers from one circuit to another at ſhort periods: for ſhould any of them become popular with their different congregations, and inſinuate themſelves into the favour of their hearers, they might poſſibly obtain ſuch influence, as to eſtabliſh themſelves independently of me, and the general connexion. Beſides the novelty of the continual change, excites curioſity, and is the more neceſſary, as few of our preachers have abilities to render themſelves in any degree tolerable, any longer than they are new.

The principal cauſe which will inevitably effect a diminution and diviſion in the connexion after my death, will be the failure of ſubſcriptions and contributions towards the ſupport of the cauſe, for money is as much the ſinews of religious, as of military power. If it is with the greateſt difficulty that even I can keep them together, for want of this very neceſſary article, I think no one elſe can. Another cauſe, which with others will effect the diviſion, is the diſputes and contentions that will ariſe between the preachers and the parties that will eſpouſe their ſeveral cauſes, by which means much truth will be brought to light, which will reflect ſo much to their diſadvantage, that the

eyes

eyes of the people will be opened to ſee their motives and principles, nor will they any longer contribute to their ſupport, when they find all their pretenſions to ſanctity and love are founded on motives of intereſt and ambition. The conſequence of which will be, a few of the moſt popular will eſtabliſh themſelves in the reſpective places where they have gained ſufficient influence over the minds of the people; the reſt muſt revert to their original humble callings. But this no way concerns me: I have attained the object of my views, by eſtabliſhing a name that will not ſoon periſh from the face of the earth; I have founded a ſect which will boaſt my name, long after my diſcipline and doctrines are forgotten.

"My character and reputation for ſanctity is now beyond the reach of calumny; nor will any thing that may hereafter come to light, or be ſaid concerning me, to my prejudice, however true, gain credit.

"My unſoil'd name, th' auſtereneſs of my life,
Will vouch againſt it,
And ſo the accuſation overweigh,
That it will ſtifle in its own report,
And ſmell of calumny."

Another cauſe that will operate more powerfully and effectually than any of the preceding, is the rays of philoſophy which begins now to pervade all ranks, rapidly diſpelling the miſts of

 ignorance,

ignorance, which has been long in a great degree the mother of devotion, of ſlaviſh prejudice, and the enthuſiaſtic bigotry of religious opinions: the decline of the papal power is owing to the ſame irreſiſtible cauſe, nor can it be ſuppoſed that methodiſm can ſtand its ground, when brought to the teſt of truth, reaſon, and philoſophy.

I am, &c.

I. W."

City Road, Thurſday Morn.

Our Author informs us that the following was written to a very amiable and accompliſhed lady, ſome years ago. The lady was about three and twenty years of age.

" MADAM,

" IT is with the utmoſt diffidence I preſume to addreſs ſuperior excellence: emboldened by a violent, yet virtuous paſſion, kindled by the irreſiſtible rays, and encouraged by the ſweetly attractive force, of tranſcendent beauty, the elegant ſimplicity of your manners, the faſcinating melody of your voice, and above all, the inexpreſſible fire of an eye, that the extravagance of the Muſes has given to the goddeſs of love: but which Nature has beſtowed on you alone.

" They ſparkle with the right *Promethean* fire!"

" Believe

" Believe me, my dear Madam, this is not the language of romance; but the genuine exuberant effusions of an enraptured soul. The impression of your charms was no less instantaneous than irresistible: when first I saw you, so forcibly was I struck with admiration and love of your divine perfections, that my soul was filled with sensations so wild and extravagant, yet delightful and pure! —But I will not indulge in declaring what are my real sentiments, lest I should incur a suspicion of flattery. Your mind, superior to fulsome panegyric, unsusceptible of the incense of affected adulation, would, with just indignation, spurn at those impertinent compliments, which are commonly offered with a view to impose upon the vanity and credulity of the weaker part of your sex: I will not attempt it; but confine myself to the dictates of sincerity and truth, nor shall a compliment escape my pen, that is not the sentiment of a devoted heart.

" As beauty has no positive criterion, and fancy alone directs the judgment and influences the choice, we find different people see it in various lights, forms, and colours, I may therefore, without a suspicion of flattery declare, that in my eye you are the most agreeable object, and most perfect work of created nature: nor does your mind seem to partake less of the divinity than your person.

"I view thee over with a lover's eye;
No fault haſt thou, or I no fault can ſpy."

"The reaſon I did not before declare myſelf, was the profound and reſpectful diſtance I thought it became me to obſerve, from a conſcious ſenſe of my own comparative unworthineſs to approach, much leſs to hope for favour from, the quintеſſence of all female perfection.—Forgive me, my dear Eliza, and compaſſionate a heart too deeply impreſſed with your divine image, ever to be eraſed by time, nor can any power, but the cold hand of death, ever obliterate from my mind the fond imagination and ſweet remembrance of Eliza's charms! Nor can even death itſelf divide the union that ſubſiſts between kindred ſouls.

"Yeſterday, my dear Eliza, the charms of your converſation detained me too late to meet the *penitents*, as I had promiſed to do; but

"With thee converſing, I forget
All times, all ſeaſons, and their change."

"I hope however, the diſappointment of my company did not deprive them of a bleſſing.

"This being my birth-day, reflexions on the revolution of years and the ſhortneſs of life, naturally intrude on my mind. I am now *eighty-one* years of age, and I thank God I enjoy the ſame vigor of conſtitution I poſſeſſed at *twenty-one!*

None

None of the infirmities that uſually accompany years, either corporal or mental; and I think it not impoſſible that I may fulfil my hundred years, the reſidue of which ſhall be devoted to love and Eliza.

I. W."

I ſent a perſon to the author of the above pamphlet, to deſire him to give me a ſight of the original of the preceding letters; but he returned for anſwer, that he had ſent them back to the perſons to whom they were written.

I am,

Dear Friend,

Yours.

LETTER XXXI.

"Paſſion, 'tis true, may hurry us along;
"Sometimes the juſt may deviate into wrong."

VOLTAIRE by Franklin.

DEAR FRIEND,

MY new wife's attachment to books was a very fortunate circumſtance for us both, not only as it was a perpetual ſource of rational amuſement, but alſo as it tended to promote my trade: her extreme love for books made her delight to be in the ſhop, ſo that ſhe ſoon became perfectly acquainted with every part of it, and (as my ſtock increaſed) with other rooms where I kept books, and could readily get any article that was aſked for. Accordingly, when I was out on buſineſs, my ſhop was well attended. This conſtant attention, and good uſage, procured me many cuſtomers; and I ſoon perceived that I could ſell double and treble the quantity of books if I had a larger ſtock. But how

how to enlarge it, I knew not, except by ſlow degrees, as my profits ſhould enable me; for as I was almoſt a ſtranger in London, I had but few acquaintances, and theſe few were not of the opulent ſort. I alſo ſaw that the town abounded with cheats, ſwindlers, &c. who obtained money and other property, under falſe pretences, of which the credulous were defrauded, which often prevented me from endeavouring to borrow, leſt I ſhould be ſuſpected of having the ſame bad deſigns.

I was ſeveral times ſo hard put to it, for caſh to purchaſe parcels of books which were offered to me, that I more than once pawned my watch, and a ſuit of cloaths, and twice I pawned ſome books for money to purchaſe others; but I ſoon was tired of pawnbrokers, and at that time they were not ſo reſtricted, as now, in reſpect to intereſt, and thinking myſelf impoſed on, by being charged more than was reaſonable, I never redeemed the laſt parcel at all; for, indeed, they were books that I had bought extremely cheap, ſo that I borrowed more money on them than they coſt me, and in ſo doing repaid myſelf what I had been overcharged. "I confeſs we *were* poor; but, while that is the worſt our enemies can ſay of us, we are content."

Soon after I commenced bookſeller, I became acquainted with what Pope calls "the nobleſt work of God," an HONEST man. This was Mr. JOHN DENIS, an oilman in Cannon-ſtreet (father of the preſent Mr. John Denis, bookſeller.) This gentleman had often viſited me during my long illneſs, and having ſeen me tranquil and ſerene when on the very point of death, he formed a favourable concluſion that I too muſt be an honeſt man, as I had ſo quiet a conſcience at ſuch an awful period. Having retained theſe ideas of me after my recovery, and being perfectly well acquainted with my circumſtances, he one day offered to become a partner in my buſineſs, and to advance money in proportion to my ſtock. This confidential

confidential offer I ſoon accepted; early in 1778 he became partner; and we very ſoon laid out his money in ſecond-hand books, which increaſed the ſtock at once to double.

I ſoon after this propoſed printing a ſale catalogue, to which, after making a few objections, Mr. Denis conſented. This catalogue of twelve thouſand volumes (ſuch as they were) was publiſhed in 1779. My partner's name was not in the title-page, the addreſs was only "J. LACKINGTON and Co. No. 46, Chiſwell-ſtreet." This our firſt publication produced very oppoſite effects on thoſe who peruſed it; in ſome it excited much mirth, in others an equal proportion of anger. The major part of it was written by me, but Mr. Denis wrote many pages of it; and as his own private library conſiſted of ſcarce old myſtical and alchymical books, printed above a century ago, many of them were in bad condition; this led him to inſert *neat* in the catalogue to many articles, which

were

were only neat when compared with ſuch as were in very bad condition; ſo that when we produced ſuch books as were called *neat* in our catalogue, we often got ourſelves laughed at, and ſometimes our *neat* articles were heartily *damned*. We had alſo a deal of trouble on another ſcore; Mr. Denis inſerted a number of articles without the authors names, and aſſured me that the books were well known, and to mention the authors was often uſeleſs. The fact was, Mr. Denis knew who wrote thoſe articles; but was ſoon convinced that many others did not, as we were often obliged to produce them merely to let our cuſtomers ſee who were the authors: we however took twenty pounds the firſt week the books were on ſale, which we thought a large ſum. The increaſe of our ſtock augmented our cuſtomers in proportion; ſo that Mr. Denis, finding that his money turned to a better account in bookſelling than in the funds, very ſoon lent the ſtock near two hundred pounds, which I ſtill turned to a good

account.

account. We went on very friendly and prosperously for a little more than two years; when one night Mr. Denis hinted that he thought I was making purchases too fast, on which I grew warm, and reminded him of an article in our partnership agreement by which I was to be sole purchaser, and was at liberty to make what purchases I should judge proper. I also reminded him of the profits which my purchases produced, and he reminded me of his having more money in the trade than I had. We were indeed both very warm; and on my saying, that if he was displeased with any part of my conduct, he was at liberty to quit the partnership, he in great warmth replied that he would. The above passed at Mr. Denis's house in Hoxton-square, I then bade him good night. When Mr. Denis called at the shop the next day, he asked me if I continued in the same mind I was in the preceding night? I assured him that I did. He then demanded of me whether I insisted on his keeping his word to quit the partnership?

I replied,

I replied, I did not *inſiſt* on it, as I had taken him a partner for three years, nearly one third part of which time was unexpired; but, I added, that, as I had always found him ſtrictly a man of his word, I ſuppoſed he would prove himſelf ſo in the preſent inſtance, and not aſſert one thing at night and another in the morning. On which he obſerved, that as he was not provided with a ſhop, he muſt take ſome time to look for one. I told him that he might take as long a time as he thought neceſſary. This was in March 1780. He appointed the twentieth of May, following. On that day we accordingly diſſolved the partnerſhip; and, as he had more money in the trade than myſelf, he took my notes for what I was deficient, We parted in great friendſhip, which continued to the day of his death; he generally called every morning to ſee us, and learn our concerns, and we conſtantly informed him of all that had paſſed the preceding day; as how much caſh we had taken, what were the profits, what purchaſes we had made, what bills

bills we had to pay, &c. and he ſometimes lent me money to help to pay them.

At his death he left behind him in his private library the beſt collection of ſcarce, valuable, myſtical, and alchymical books, that ever was collected by one perſon. In his lifetime he prized theſe kind of books above every thing; in collecting them he never cared what price he paid for them. This led him to think, after he became a bookſeller, that other book-collectors ſhould pay their money as freely as he had done his, which was often a ſubject of debate between him and me, as I was for ſelling every thing cheap, in order to ſecure thoſe cuſtomers already obtained, as well as increaſe their numbers.

Mr. Denis was, at the time of his death, about fifty years of age. He informed me that in his childhood and youth he was weakly to an extreme, ſo that no one who knew him ever thought he could live to be

twenty

twenty years of age; however he enjoyed an uninterrupted ſtate of health for nearly the laſt thirty years of his life; this he aſcribed to his ſtrictly adhering to the rules laid down by *Cornaro* and *Tryon* in their books on Health, Long Life and Happineſs. His unexpected death was in conſequence of a fever caught by ſitting in a cold damp room.

O'er the ſad reliques of a friend ſincere,
The happieſt mortal, ſure, may ſpare a tear.

I am,

Dear Friend,

Yours.

LETTER

LETTER XXXII.

"There is a tide in the affairs of men,
"Which taken at the flood leads on to fortune,
"Omitted, all the voyage of their life
"Is bound in ſhallows and in miſeries;
"On ſuch a foul ſea are we now afloat,
"And we muſt take the current when it ſerves,
"Or loſe our ventures."

SHAKESPEARE's Julius Cæſar.

DEAR FRIEND,

IT was ſome time in the year ſeventeen hundred and eighty, when I reſolved from that period to give no perſon whatever any credit. I was induced to make this reſolution from various motives: I had obſerved, that where credit was given, moſt bills were not paid within ſix months, many not within a twelvemonth, and ſome not within two years. Indeed, many tradeſmen have accounts of ſeven years ſtanding; and ſome bills are never paid. The loſſes ſuſtained by the intereſt of money in long credits, and by thoſe bills that were not paid at

all;

all; the inconveniences attending not having the ready-money to lay out in trade to the beſt advantage, together with the great loſs of time in keeping accounts, and collecting debts, convinced me, that if I could but eſtabliſh a ready-money buſineſs, *without any exceptions*, I ſhould be enabled to ſell every article very cheap. When I communicated my ideas on this ſubject to ſome of my acquaintances, I was much laughed at and ridiculed; and it was thought, that I might as well attempt to rebuild the tower of Babel, as to eſtabliſh a large buſineſs without giving credit. But notwithſtanding this diſcouragement, and even *You*, my dear friend, expreſſing your doubts of the practicability of my ſcheme, I determined to make the experiment; and began by marking in every book the loweſt price that I would take for it; which being much lower than the common market prices, I not only retained my former cuſtomers, but ſoon increaſed their numbers. But, my dear Sir, you can ſcarce imagine what difficulties I encountered for ſeveral

years

years together. I even ſometimes thought of relinquiſhing this my favorite ſcheme altogether, as by it I was obliged to deny credit to my very acquaintance; I was alſo under a neceſſity of refuſing it to the moſt reſpectable characters, as *no exception* was, or now is made, not even in favour of nobility; my porters being ſtrictly enjoined, by one general order, to bring back all books not previouſly paid for, except they receive the amount on delivery. Again, many in the country found it difficult to remit ſmall ſums that are below bankers notes, and others to whom I was a ſtranger, did not like to ſend the money firſt, as not knowing how I ſhould treat them, and ſuſpecting by the price of the articles, there muſt certainly be ſome deception. Many unacquainted with my plan of buſineſs, were much offended, until the advantages accruing to them from it were duly explained, when they very readily acceded to it. As to the anger of ſuch, who though they were acquainted with it, were ſtill determined to deal on credit only, I conſidered that as of little conſequence, from an opinion that ſome of them would have been as much enraged when their bills were ſent in, had credit been given them.

I had alſo difficulties of another nature to encounter; when firſt I began to ſell very cheap, many came to my ſhop prepoſſeſſed againſt my goods, and of courſe often ſaw faults where none exiſted; ſo that the beſt editions were merely from prejudice deemed very bad editions, and the beſt bindings ſaid to be inferior workmanſhip, for no other reaſon, but becauſe I ſold them ſo cheap; and I often received letters from the country, to know if ſuch and ſuch articles were REALLY as I ſtated them in my catalogues, and *if they* REALLY *were the beſt editions, if* REALLY *in calf; and* REALLY *elegantly bound*; with many other *reallys.* Oh my friend! I *really* was afraid for ſome years that I ſhould be *really* mad with vexation. But theſe letters of *reallys* have for years happily ceaſed, and the public are now *really*

and

and thoroughly convinced that I will not aſſert in my catalogues what is not *really* true. But imagine, if you can, what I muſt have felt, on hearing the very beſt of goods depreciated, on no other account whatever, but becauſe they were not charged at a higher price.

It is alſo worth obſerving, that there were not wanting among the bookſellers, ſome who were mean enough to aſſert that all my books were bound in ſheep; and many other unmanly artifices were practiſed, all of which ſo far from injuring me, as baſely intended, turned to my account; for when gentlemen were brought to my ſhop by their friends, to purchaſe ſome trifling article, or were led into it by curioſity, they were often very much ſurpriſed to ſee many thouſands of volumes in elegant and ſuperb bindings. The natural concluſion was, that if I had not held forth to the public better terms than others, I ſhould not have been ſo much envied and miſrepreſented. So that whether I am righteous or not, all theſe afflictions have worked together for my good. But I aſſure you, that my temporal ſalvation was not effected without "*conditions.*" As every envious tranſaction was to me an additional ſpur to exertion, I am therefore not a little indebted to Meſſrs. ENVY, DETRACTION, and Co. for my preſent proſperity; though I aſſure you, this is the only debt I am determined not to pay. Green ſays,

" Happy the man who innocent,
" Grieves not at ills he can't prevent:
" And when he can't prevent foul play,
" Enjoys the follies of the fray."

SPLEEN.

I am,

Dear Friend,

Yours.

LETTER

LETTER XXXIII.

"Conſtant at ſhop and Change, his gains were ſure:
"His givings rare; ſave half-pence to the poor."

DEAR FRIEND,

IN the firſt three years after I refuſed to give credit to any perſon, my buſineſs increaſed much, and as the whole of my profit (after paying all expences) was laid out in books, my ſtock was continually enlarged, ſo that my Catalogues in the year ſeventeen hundred and eighty-four, were very much augmented in ſize. The firſt contained Twelve thouſand, and the ſecond Thirty thouſand volumes: this increaſe was not merely in numbers, but alſo in value, as a very great part of theſe volumes were *better*, that is, books of an higher price. But notwithſtanding the great increaſe of my buſineſs, I ſtill met with many difficulties on account of my ſelling books cheap; one of theſe I confeſs I did not foreſee: as the more convinced the public were of my act-ing ſtrictly conformable to the plan I had adopted, the more this objection gained ground, and even to the preſent day is not *entirely* done away. This difficulty was, in making private purchaſes of libraries and parcels of books, many of my cuſtomers for ſeveral years had no objection to *buying* of me becauſe I ſold cheap, but were not equally inclined to *ſell* me ſuch books as they had no uſe for, or libraries that were left them at the death of relations, &c. They reaſoned (very plauſibly, it muſt be confeſſed) thus: "Lackington ſells very cheap; he therefore will not give much for what is offered him for ſale. I will go to thoſe who ſell very dear; as the more they ſell their books for, the more they can afford to give for them."

This mode of reaſoning, however ſpecious it ſeems at firſt, will on due reflection appear nugatory and erroneous, for the following reaſons:

I believe no one ever knew or heard of a covetous man that would ſell his goods *cheap*: But

But every one has heard of ſuch characters ſelling *very dear*; and when a covetous perſon makes a purchaſe, is it likely that he ſhould offer a generous price? Is he not when buying influenced by the ſame avaritious diſpoſition as when ſelling? And on the other hand, I cannot help thinking (I am aware of the inference) that one who has been conſtantly ſelling cheap for a ſeries of years muſt poſſeſs ſome degree of generoſity; that this diſpoſition has prevailed in me when I have been called to purchaſe, and when libraries or parcels of books have been ſent to me, thouſands in the three kingdoms can witneſs. And however paradoxical it may appear, I will add, that I can afford to give more for books now, than I could if I ſold them much dearer. For, were I to ſell them dear, I ſhould be ten times longer in ſelling them; and the expences for warehouſe-room, inſurance from fire, together with the intereſt of the money lying long in a dead ſtock, would prevent my giving a large price when books were offered for ſale.

But it did not appear in this point of view to the public in the more early ſtages of my buſineſs, until being often ſent for after other bookſellers had made offers for libraries, and finding that I would give more than they had offered, it was communicated from one to another until it became publickly known; and the following method which I adopted ſome years ſince has put the matter beyond the ſhadow of a doubt.

When I am called upon to purchaſe any library or parcel of books, either myſelf or my aſſiſtants carefully examine them, and if deſired to fix a price, I mention at a word the utmoſt that I will give for them, which I always take care ſhall be as much as any bookſeller can afford to give: but if the ſeller entertains any doubts reſpecting the price offered, and chooſes to try other bookſellers, he pays me five per cent. for valuing the books; and as he knows what I have valued them at, he tries among the trade, and when he finds that he cannot get any greater ſum offered, on returning to me, he not

only

only receives the price I at firſt offered, but alſo a return of the five per cent. which was paid me for the valuation.

But to ſuch as fix a price on their own books I make no charge, either taking them at the price at which they are offered to me, or if that appear too much, immediately declining the purchaſe.

This equitable mode I have the pleaſure to find has given the public the utmoſt ſatisfaction.

I am,

Dear Friend,

Yours.

LETTER

LETTER XXXIV.

" Behold, Sir Balaam, now a man of ſpirit,
" Aſcribes his gettings to his parts and merit."

Pope.

" Weak truth cannot your reputation ſave,
" The knaves will all agree to call you knave:
" Wrong'd ſhall he live, inſulted, o'er oppreſt,
" Who dares be leſs a villain than the reſt."

Satyr againſt Man.

DEAR FRIEND,

WHEN I was firſt initiated into the various manoeuvres practiſed by bookſellers, I found it cuſtomary among them, (which practice ſtill continues) that when any books had not gone off ſo rapidly as expected, or ſo faſt as to pay for keeping them in ſtore, they would put what remained of ſuch articles into private ſales, where only bookſellers are admitted, and of them only ſuch as were invited by having a catalogue ſent them. At one of theſe ſales I have frequently ſeen ſeventy or eighty thouſand volumes ſold after dinner, including books

books of every deſcription, good, bad and indifferent; by this means they were diſtributed through the trade.

When firſt invited to theſe trade ſales, I was very much ſurpriſed to learn, that it was common for ſuch as purchaſed remainders, to *deſtroy* one half or three fourths of ſuch books, and to charge the full publication price, or nearly that, for ſuch as they kept on hand; and there was a kind of ſtanding order amongſt the trade, that in caſe any one was known to ſell articles under the publication price, ſuch a perſon was to be excluded from trade ſales; ſo blind were copy-right-holders to their own intereſt.

For a ſhort time I cautiouſly complied with this cuſtom, but I ſoon began to reflect that many of theſe books ſo deſtroyed, poſſeſſed much merit, and only wanted to be better known; and that if others were not worth ſix ſhillings, they were worth three or two, and ſo in proportion for higher or lower priced books.

From

From that time I resolved not to destroy any books that were worth saving, but to sell them off at half, or a quarter of the publication prices. By selling them in this cheap manner, I have disposed of many hundred thousand volumes, many thousands of which have been intrinsically worth their original prices. This part of my conduct, however, though evidently highly beneficial to the community, and even to booksellers, created me many enemies among the trade; some of the meaner part of whom, instead of employing their time and abilities in attending to the increase of their own business, aimed at reducing mine; and by a variety of pitiful insinuations and dark inuendoes, strained every nerve to injure the reputation I had already acquired with the public, determined, (as they *wisely* concluded) thus to effect my ruin; which indeed they daily prognosticated, with a demon-like spirit, must inevitably very speedily follow. This conduct, however, was far from intimidating me, as the effect proved directly opposite to what they wished for and

expected,

expected, and I found the reſpect and confidence of the public continually increaſing, which added very conſiderably to the number of my cuſtomers: It being an unqueſtionable fact, that before I adopted this plan, great numbers of perſons were very deſirous of poſſeſſing ſome particular books, for which however (from various motives) they were not inclined to pay the original price; as ſome availed themſelves of the opportunity of borrowing from a friend, or from a circulating library, or having once read them, though they held the works in eſteem, might deem them too dear to purchaſe; or they might have a copy by them, which from their own and family's frequent uſe (or lending to friends) might not be in ſo good a condition as they could wiſh, though rather than purchaſe them again at the full price, they would keep thoſe they had; or again, they might be deſirous to purchaſe them to make preſents of; or they might have a commiſſion from a correſpondent in the country, or abroad, and wiſh to gain a ſmall

ſmall profit on the articles for their trouble, not to mention the great numbers that would have been given to the poor.

Thouſands of others have been effectually prevented from purchaſing, (though anxious ſo to do) whoſe circumſtances in life would not permit them to pay the full price, and thus were totally excluded from the advantage of improving their underſtandings, and enjoying a rational entertainment. And you may be aſſured, that it affords me the moſt pleaſing ſatisfaction, independent of the emoluments which have accrued to me from this plan, when I reflect what prodigious numbers in inferior or *reduced* ſituations of life, have been eſſentially benefited in conſequence of being thus enabled to indulge their natural propenſity for the acquiſition of knowledge, on eaſy terms: nay, I could almoſt be vain enough to aſſert, that I have thereby been highly inſtrumental in diffuſing that general deſire for READING, now ſo prevalent among the inferior orders of ſociety;

ciety; which moſt certainly, though it may not prove equally inſtructive to all, keeps them from employing their time and money, if not to *bad*, at leaſt to *leſs rational* purpoſes.

How happy ſhould I have deemed myſelf in the earlier ſtage of my life, if I could have met with the opportunity which every one capable of reading may now enjoy, of obtaining books at ſo eaſy a rate: Had that been the caſe, the Catalogue of my *juvenile library*, with which I preſented you in a former letter, would have made a more reſpectable appearance, and I might poſſibly have been enabled when I purchaſed Young's Night Thoughts for a *Chriſtmas dinner*, to have at the ſame time bought a joint of meat, and thus enjoyed both a mental and corporeal feaſt, as well as pleaſed my wife, (which I need not inform you the ladies ſay every good huſband ought to do.) But after all, quere, Whether if I had enjoyed ſuch an advantage, ſhould I ever have thought of commencing bookſeller? If not, ſhould I

have

have been the *great man* I now feel myſelf, and hope *you* acknowledge me to be? In my next I will make a few obſervations on purchaſing manuſcripts, bookſeller's liberality, author's turning publiſhers, &c. in the mean time,

I am,

Dear Friend,

Yours.

LETTER

LETTER XXXV.

"High in the world of letters, and of wit,
"Enthron'd like Jove behold opinion sit!
"As ſymbols of her ſway, on either hand
"Th' unfailing urns of praiſe and cenſure ſtand;
"Their mingled ſtreams her motley ſervants ſhed
"On each bold author's ſelf-devoted head."

HAYLEY.

DEAR FRIEND,

I Promiſed in my laſt to give you a few remarks on purchaſing manuſcripts; and as I ſeldom make ſuch purchaſes, and but rarely publiſh any new books, I think you may fairly credit me for impartiality. Nothing is more common than to hear authors complaining againſt publiſhers, for want of liberality in purchaſing their manuſcripts. But I cannot help thinking that moſt of theſe complaints are groundleſs; and that were all things conſidered, publiſhers (at leaſt many of them) would be allowed to poſſeſs more liberality than any other ſet of tradeſmen, I mean ſo far as relates to the purchaſing manuſcripts and copy-right.

Not to trouble you with a long enumeration of inſtances in confirmation of this aſſertion, I ſhall barely mention the following:

It is owing to the encouragement of bookſellers that the public is poſſeſſed of that valuable work Johnſon's Dictionary; and the ſame liberality to the doctor in reſpect to that publication, his edition of Shakeſpeare, and the Engliſh Poets will always reflect honour on the parties. So ſenſible was the doctor of this, that he aſſerted bookſellers were the beſt Macaenas's.

The late Sir John Hawkins, Dr. Cullen, the preſent Dr. Robertſon, Mr. Gibbon, Dr. Knox, &c. &c. are all ſtriking inſtances of the truth of my obſervation.

As I feel a pleaſure in mentioning acts of liberality wherever they occur, ſuffer me to quote

quote the following paſſage from Sir John Hawkins's Life of Dr. Johnſon.

"The bookſellers with whom Mr. Chambers had contracted for his dictionary, finding that the work ſucceeded beyond their expectations, made him a voluntary preſent of, I think, 500l. Other inſtances of the like generoſity have been known of a profeſſion of men, who, in the debates on the queſtion of literary property, have been deſcribed as ſcandalous monopolizers, fattening at the expence of other men's ingenuity, and growing opulent by oppreſſion."

It is confidently aſſerted, that the late Dr. Hawkeſworth received ſix thouſand pounds for his compilation of Voyages, if ſo (and I have never heard it contradicted) I leave it to any conſiderate perſon to judge, whether in paying ſo enormous a price, the publiſhers did not run a great riſk, when it is conſidered how great the expences of bringing forward ſuch a work, muſt have been. I have alſo been informed that David Mallet, Eſq. was offered two thouſand pounds for Lord Bolingbroke's Philoſophical Works, which he refuſed.

It ought alſo to be conſidered, that frequently the money which is paid for the copy, is but trifling, compared with the expence of printing, paper, advertiſing, &c. and hundreds of inſtances may be adduced of publiſhers having ſuſtained very great loſſes, and many have been made bankrupts, through their liberality in purchaſing manuſcripts and publiſhing them; and on the other hand, it muſt be acknowledged that ſome publiſhers have made great fortunes by their copy rights, but their number is comparatively ſmall.

It ſhould alſo be remarked that authors in general, are apt to form too great expectations from their productions, many inſtances of which I could give you, but I will only produce one.

A gen-

A gentleman a few years ſince ſhewed a manuſcript to a publiſher, which he refuſed to purchaſe, but offered to be the publiſher if the gentleman would print it, &c. at his own expence, which he readily agreed to do, the publiſher then deſired to know how many copies ſhould be printed, on which the gentleman began to compute how many families there were in Great Britain, and aſſured the publiſher that every family would at *leaſt* purchaſe one copy, but the publiſher not being of the ſame opinion, our author then ſaid that he would print ſixty thouſand copies *only*, but added, he was afraid that another edition could not be got ready as ſoon as it would be wanted. However, after a long debate, the publiſher prevailed on him to print only *twelve hundred and fifty*, inſtead of *ſixty thouſand*, but promiſed in caſe another edition ſhould be wanted in haſte, to make the printers work night and day in order not to diſappoint the public. This work was ſoon afterwards publiſhed and advertiſed at a great rate and for a long time, but to the infinite mortification of our author, not one hundred copies were ſold, not even enough indeed to pay for the advertiſements. In the preceding inſtance I am perſuaded the publiſher did his beſt to promote the ſale of the work; but in general where authors keep their own copy-right they do not ſucceed, and many books have been conſigned to oblivion, through the inattention and miſmanagement of publiſhers, as moſt of them are envious of the ſucceſs of ſuch works as do not turn to their own account; very many juſt complaints are made on this head, ſo that I am fully of opinion that for authors to ſucceed well they ſhould ſell their copy-rights, or be previouſly well acquainted with the characters of their publiſhers.

As I have before obſerved, there are ſome authors who become their own publiſhers, but that mode will ſeldom or never anſwer, as fifty to one might be ſold by being exposed to view, and recommended in booksellers shops, where ladies and gentlemen are continually calling to purchase some books, and to turn over others, and often by dipping into publications are led to purchase such as they had no intention to buy. But authors should be reminded that there are many who would not go to private houses to look over books when they are not certain to purchase, and where, if they do purchase, they are to take them home in their pockets, or be at the trouble of sending for them, which is not the case when they purchase at a bookseller's shop. And all authors should be sure to give the full allowance to the trade, or their works can never have a great sale, as no bookseller can reasonably be expected to promote the sale of a work in which he is abridged of his usual profits, and the more liberality authors exercise towards the trade, the greater will be their profits in the end. For it is inconceivable what mischief booksellers *can* and often *will* do to authors, as thouſands of books are yearly written for to London that are never ſent; and in theſe caſes many plauſible reaſons are aſſigned by them for ſuch omiſſions, and in ſuch caſes, what redreſs can an author have for ſo eſſential an injury?

I am,

Dear Friend,

Yours.

LETTER

LETTER XXXVI.

" Thoſe who would learning's glorious kingdom find,
" The dear-bought treaſure of the trading mind,
" From many dangers muſt themſelves acquit,
" And more than Scylla and Charybdis meet.
" Oh! what an ocean muſt be voyaged o'er,
" To gain a proſpect of the ſhining ſtore!
" Reſiſting rocks oppoſe th' enquiring ſoul,
" And adverſe waves retard it as they roll.
" The little knowledge now which man obtains,
" From outward objects and from ſenſe he gains;
" He like a wretched ſlave muſt plod and ſweat,
" By day muſt toil, by night that toil repeat,
" And yet, at laſt, what little fruit he gains,
" A beggar's harveſt glean'd with mighty pains!"

POMFRET.

DEAR FRIEND,

ALTHOUGH the reſult of the plan which I adopted for reducing the price of books, as mentioned in my laſt, was a vaſt increaſe of purchaſers, yet at the ſame time I found a prodigious accumulation of my expences; which will not appear ſtrange, when I inform you that I made pro-

proportionably large purchaſes, ſuch as two hundred copies of one book, three hundred of another, five hundred of a third, a thouſand of a fourth, two thouſand of a fifth, nay, ſometimes I have purchaſed ſix thouſand copies of one book, and at one time I actually had no leſs than TEN THOUSAND COPIES of Watts's Pſalms, and the ſame number of his Hymns in my poſſeſſion. In addition to theſe, I purchaſed very large numbers of many thouſand different articles, at trade ſales of all ſorts, as bankrupt ſales, ſales of ſuch as had retired from buſineſs, others cauſed by the death of bookſellers, ſales to reduce large ſtocks, annual ſales, &c. that you may form ſome idea, I muſt inform you that at one of the above ſales, I have purchaſed books to the amount of five thouſand pounds in one afternoon. Not to mention thoſe purchaſed of authors, and town and country bookſellers, by private contract, &c. to a very conſiderable amount. My expences were alſo exceedingly increaſed by the neceſſity I was under of keeping each article in

a variety

a variety of different kinds of bindings, to ſuit the various taſtes of my cuſtomers: Beſides paying my bills for the above, I was always obliged to find ready money to pay for libraries and parcels of ſecond-hand books, which after a while poured in upon me from town and country. So that I often look back with aſtoniſhment at my courage (or temerity, if you pleaſe) in purchaſing, and my wonderful ſucceſs in taking money ſufficient to pay the extenſive demands that were perpetually made upon me, as there is not another inſtance of ſucceſs ſo rapid and conſtant under ſuch circumſtances. Some indeed there have been, who for two or three years, purchaſed away very faſt, but could not perſevere, as they were unable to ſell with equal rapidity: for no one that has not a quick ſale can poſſibly ſucceed with large numbers. For ſuppoſing that a bookſeller expends a thouſand pounds in the purchaſe of four articles (I have often done that in only one article) and theſe are bought at a quarter the uſual price, the intereſt of the money is fifty pounds a year; beſides which ſome allowance muſt be made for warehouſe-room, inſurance from fire, &c. ſo that granting he might ſell a few of each article every year at four times the price he firſt paid for them, yet if he does not ſell enough to pay the intereſt and other expences of thoſe that remain, he is, after all, on the loſing ſide; which has been the caſe with the major part of ſuch as have purchaſed a large number of one book, and I have known many inſtances of bookſellers purchaſing articles at a quarter the price, and ſelling them at the full price, and yet have not had two per cent. for their money

For ſeveral years together I thought I ſhould be obliged to deſiſt from purchaſing a large number of any one article; for although by not giving any credit I was enabled to ſell very cheap, yet the heavy ſtock of books in ſheets often diſheartened me, ſo that I more than once reſolved to leave off purchaſing all ſuch articles where the number was very large. But, ſomehow or other, a torrent of

buſineſs

buſineſs ſuddenly poured in upon me on all ſides, ſo that I very ſoon forgot my reſolution of not making large purchaſes, and now find my account in firmly adhering to that method; and being univerſally known for making large purchaſes, moſt of the trade in town and country, and alſo authors of every deſcription are continually furniſhing me with opportunities. In this branch of trade it is next to impoſſible for me ever to have any formidable rivals, as it requires an uncommon exertion, as well as very uncommon ſucceſs, and that for many years together, to riſe to any great degree of eminence in that particular line. This ſucceſs muſt be attained too, without the aid of *novelty*, which I found to be of very great ſervice to me: And ſhould any perſon begin on my plan and ſucceed extremely well, he could never ſuperſede me, as I am ſtill enlarging my buſineſs every year, and the more it is extended the cheaper I can afford to ſell; ſo that though I may be purſued, I cannot be overtaken, except I ſhould (as ſome others

have

have done) be ſo infatuated and blinded by proſperity, as to think that the public would continue their favors, even though the plan of buſineſs were reverſed. But as the firſt king of Bohemia kept his country ſhoes by him, to remind him from whence he was taken, I have put a motto on the doors of my carriage, conſtantly to remind me to what I am indebted for my proſperity, viz.

"SMALL PROFITS DO GREAT THINGS."

And I aſſure you, Sir, that reflecting on the means by which I have been enabled to ſupport a carriage, adds not a little to the pleaſure of riding in it. I believe I may, without being deemed cenſorious, aſſert, that there are ſome who ride in their carriages, who cannot reflect on the means by which they were acquired with an equal degree of ſatisfaction to that experienced by,

Dear Friend,

Yours.

LETTER

LETTER XXXVII.

"Books, of all earthly things my chief delight;
"My exercife by day, and dreams by night;
"Difpaffion'd mafters, friends without deceit,
"Who flatter not; companions ever fweet;
"With whom I'm always cheerful, from whom rife,
"Improv'd and better, if not good and wife;
"Grave, faithful counfellors, who all excite,
"Inftruct, and ftrengthen to behave aright;
"Admonifh us, when fortune makes her Court,
"And when fhe's abfent, folace and fupport.
"Happy the man to whom ye are well known.
"'Tis his own fault if ever he's alone."

Anonymous.

DEAR FRIEND,

IT has been afked, times innumerable, how I acquired any tolerable degree of knowledge, fo as to enable me to form any ideas of the merits or demerits of books; or how I became fufficiently acquainted with the prices that books were commonly fold for, fo as to be able to buy and fell; particularly books in the learned and

and foreign languages. Many have thought that from the beginning I always kept ſhopmen to furniſh me with inſtructions neceſſary to carry on my buſineſs; but you and all my old friends and acquaintances well know that not to have been the caſe; as for the firſt thirteen years after I became a bookſeller, I never had one ſhopman who knew any thing of the worth of books, or how to write a ſingle page of a catalogue properly, much leſs to compile the whole. I always wrote them myſelf, ſo long as my health would permit: Indeed I continued the practice for years after my health was much impaired by too conſtant an application to that and reading; and when I was at laſt obliged to give up writing them, I for ſeveral catalogues ſtood by and dictated to others; even to the preſent time I take ſome little part in their compilation; and as I ever did, I ſtill continue to fix the price to every book that is ſold in my ſhop, except ſuch articles as are both bought and ſold again while I am out of town. I have now many aſſiſtants in my

ſhop,

ſhop, who buy, ſell, and in ſhort tranſact the major part of my buſineſs.

As to the little knowledge of literature I poſſeſs, it was acquired by dint of application. In the beginning I attached myſelf very cloſely to the ſtudy of divinity and moral philoſophy, ſo that I became tolerably acquainted with all the points controverted between the divines; after having read the great champions for chriſtianity, I next read the works of Toulmin, Lord Herbert, Tindal, Chubb, Morgan, Collins, Hammond, Woolſton, Annet, Mandeville, Shafteſbury, D'Argens, Bolingbroke, Williams, Helvetius, Voltaire, and many other free-thinkers. I have alſo read moſt of our Engliſh poets, and the beſt tranſlations of the Greek, Latin, Italian and French poets; nor did I omit to read Hiſtory, Voyages, Travels, Natural Hiſtory, Biography, &c. At one time I had a ſtrong inclination to learn French, but as ſoon as I was enabled to make out and abridge title-pages, ſo as to inſert them right in my catalogues, I left off for what appeared to me more pleaſing as well as more neceſſary purſuits; reflecting that as I began ſo late in life, and had probably but a very ſhort period to live, (and I paid ſome regard to what Helvetius has aſſerted, viz. that "No man acquires any new ideas after he is forty-five years of age.") I had no time to beſtow on the attainment of languages. I therefore contented myſelf with reading all the tranſlations of the claſſics, and inſerting the originals in my Catalogues as well as I could; and when ſometimes I happened to put the *Genitive* or *Dative* caſe inſtead of the *Nominative* or *Accuſative*, my cuſtomers kindly conſidered this as a venial fault, which they readily pardoned, and bought the books notwithſtanding.

As I have indefatigably uſed my beſt endeavours to acquire knowledge, I never thought I had the ſmalleſt reaſon to be aſhamed on account of my deficiency, eſpecially as I never made pretenſions to erudition, or affected to poſſeſs what I knew I

was

was deficient in. Dr. Young's couplet, you will therefore think equally applicable to many others as well as myſelf:

"Unlearned men of books aſſume the care,
"As eunuchs are the guardians of the fair."
Love of Fame.

I had like to have forgot to inform you, that I have alſo read moſt of our beſt plays, and am ſo fond of the Theatre, that in the winter ſeaſon I have often been at Drury-Lane or Covent-Garden four or five evenings in a week. Another great ſource of amuſement as well as knowledge, I have met with in reading almoſt all the beſt novels; by the *beſt*, I mean thoſe written by Cervantes, Fielding, Smollet, Richardſon, Miſs Burney, Voltaire, Sterne, Le Sage, Goldſmith, and ſome others. And I have often thought, with Fielding, that ſome of thoſe publications have given us a more genuine hiſtory of Man, in what are called Romances, than is ſometimes to be found under the more reſpectable titles of Hiſtory, Biography, &c.

In order to obtain ſome ideas in Aſtronomy, Geography, Electricity, Pneumatics, &c. I attended a few lectures given by the late eminent Mr. Ferguſon, the preſent very ingenious Mr. Walker, and others; and for ſome time ſeveral gentlemen ſpent two or three evenings in a week at my houſe, for the purpoſe of improvement in ſcience. At theſe meetings we made the beſt uſe of our time with globes, teleſcopes, microſcopes, electrical machines, air pumps, air guns, *a good bottle of wine*, and *other philoſophical* inſtruments—

The mention of which revives in my memory the loſs I ſuſtained by the premature death of a worthy philoſophical friend, whom you have met, when you occaſionally did us the honor of making one of the evening party, and benefiting us by your inſtructions. I could ſay much in his praiſe, but ſhall forbear, as another friend, who was alſo one of this (I may truly ſay) *rational aſſembly* has compoſed what I think a juſt character of him, free from that fulſome

panegyric

panegyric which too often degrades thoſe it is meant to celebrate, and conveys to all who knew the parties, the idea of having been deſigned as a burleſque inſtead of an encomium; however, as you may not have ſeen it (though in print) and it will engroſs but a very little of your time to peruſe, I ſhall here beg leave to inſert it.

" On Sunday, May 24, 1789, died at his " houſe in Worſhip-ſtreet, Moorfields, aged " 50, Mr. Ralph Tinley; one who had not " dignity of birth or elevated rank in life to " boaſt of, but who poſſeſſed what is far ſu- " perior to either, a ſolid underſtanding, " amiable manners, a due ſenſe of religion, " and an induſtrious diſpoſition. Inſtead of " riches, Providence bleſſed him with a good " ſhare of health, and a mind contented with " an humble ſituation. Thoſe hours which " he could ſpare from a proper attention to " the duties of a huſband and a father, and " manual labour as a ſhoemaker, were inceſ- " ſantly employed in the improvement of " his mind in various branches of ſcience;

" in many of which he attained a profici-
" ency, totally divested of that affectation of
" superiority which little minds assume.
" These qualities rendered him respected by
" all who knew him, as an intelligent man,
" and a most agreeable companion. Among
" other acquisitions, ENTOMOLOGY was his
" peculiar delight. Thus far the prospect is
" pleasing. It is a painful task to add, that
" this amiable person fell a victim to an un-
" happy error in taking a medicine. The
" evening previous to his decease he spent in
" a philosophical society, of which he had
" many years been a member, and where
" his attendance had been constant; but
" finding himself indisposed, he in the
" morning early had recourse to a phial of
" antimonial wine, which had long been in
" his possession, and of which only a small
" part remained. This, most unfortunately!
" he swallowed; and it having by long ma-
" ceration, acquired an extraordinary degree
" of strength, and being rendered turbid by
" mixing with the metallic particles, it pro-

" duced

"duced the effect of a violent poison, occa-
"sioning almost instantaneous death. May
"his fate prove a warning to others to be
"careful how they venture to confide in
"their own judgment in so intricate a science
"as medicine!—His valuable cabinet of in-
"sects, both foreign and domestic, supposed
"to be one of the completest (of a private
"collection) in the kingdom, all scientifi-
"cally arranged with peculiar neatness, and
"in the finest preservation, will (if it falls
"into proper hands,) remain a monument of
"his knowledge and application."—But to proceed.

I cannot help regretting the disadvantages I labor under by having been deprived of the benefits of an early education, as it is a loss that can scarcely be repaired, in any situation. How much more difficult then was it for me to attain any degree of proficiency, when involved in the concerns of a large business?

"Without a genius learning soars in vain,
"And without learning, genius sinks again;
"Their force united, crowns the sprightly reign."

ELPHINSTON'S Horace.

 The

The inſtructions that I received from men and books were often like the ſeeds ſown among thorns, the cares of the world choked them. So that although I underſtand a little of many branches of literature, yet my knowledge is, after all, I freely confeſs, but ſuperficial; which indeed I need not have told you. However, ſuperficial as it is, it not only affords me an endleſs ſource of pleaſure, but it has been of very great uſe to me in buſineſs, as it enabled me to put a value on thouſands of articles, before I knew what ſuch books were commonly ſold at: 'tis true I was ſometimes miſtaken, and have ſold a very great number of different articles much lower than I ought, even on my own plan of ſelling very cheap, yet that never gave me the ſmalleſt concern; But if I diſcovered that I had (as ſometimes was the caſe) ſold any articles too dear, it gave me much uneaſineſs; for whether I had any other motives I will leave to ſuch as are acquainted with me to determine, but I reaſoned thus; If I ſell a book too dear, I perhaps loſe that

cuſtomer

cuſtomer and his friends for ever, but if I ſell articles conſiderably under their real value, the purchaſer will come again and recommend my ſhop to his acquaintances, ſo that from the principles of ſelf-intereſt I would ſell cheap; I always was inclined to reaſon in this manner, and nine years ſince a very trifling circumſtance operated much upon my mind and fully convinced me my judgment was right on that head. Mrs. Lackington had bought a piece of linen to make me ſome ſhirts; when the linen-draper's man brought it into my ſhop, three ladies were preſent, and on ſeeing the cloth opened, aſked Mrs. L. what it coſt per yard: on being told the price, they all ſaid it was very cheap, and each lady went and purchaſed the ſame quantity, to make ſhirts for their huſbands, thoſe pieces were again diſplayed to their acquaintances, ſo that the linen-draper got a deal of cuſtom from that very circumſtance; and I reſolved to do likewiſe. However trifling this anecdote may appear, you will pardon me for intro-

ducing

ducing it, when you reflect that it was productive of very beneficial consequences, and that many great effects have arisen from as trivial causes. We are even told that Sir Isaac Newton would probably never have studied the system of gravitation had he not been under an apple tree, when some of the fruit loosened from the branches and fell to the earth, and it was the question of a simple gardener that led Galileo to study and discover the weight of the air.

I am,

Dear Friend,

Yours.

LETTER

LETTER XXXVIII.

" ——Honeſt Engliſhmen, who never were abroad,
" Like England only, and its taſte applaud.
" Strife ſtill ſubſiſts, which yields the better gout;
" Books or the world, the many or the few.
" True taſte to me is by this touchſtone known,
" That's always beſt that's neareſt to my own."

Man of Taſte.

DEAR FRIEND,

IT has been long ſince remarked, that a perſon may be well acquainted with books, or in other words, may be a very learned man, and yet remain almoſt totally ignorant of men and manners, as Mallet remarks of a famous divine:

" While Bentley, long to wrangling ſchools confin'd,
" And but by books acquainted with mankind,
" Dares, in the fulneſs of the pedant's pride,
" ———————Tho' no judge decide."

Verbal Criticiſm.

Hence many fine chimerical ſyſtems of law, government, &c. have been ſpun out of of the prolific brains of the learned, which have only ſerved to amuſe others as learned and as unacquainted with mankind as the authors, and have frequently produced a number of remarks, replies, obſervations, ſevere (not to ſay ſcurrilous) criticiſms, and new ſyſtems and hypotheſes; theſe again gave birth to freſh remarks, rejoinders, &c. *ad*——(*infinitum*, I was going to ſay—but I beg pardon, having promiſed to give you no more Latin.) Theſe learned men, after tiring themſelves and the public, have generally left them juſt as wiſe on the ſubject as when they began, nay often

"From the ſame hand how various is the page?
"What civil war their brother pamphlets rage?
"Tracts battle tracts, ſelf-contradictions glare."

YOUNG.

The reading and ſtudying of Hiſtory, Voyages, Travels, &c. will no doubt contribute much to that kind of knowledge, but will not alone be ſufficient. In order to become a proficient in that uſeful branch of knowledge,

knowledge, "MAN KNOW THYSELF!" was a precept of the antient philoſophers. But I can ſcarce think it poſſible for any man to be well acquainted with himſelf, without his poſſeſſing a tolerable degree of knowledge of the rest of mankind. In the former part of my life I ſaw a deal of what is called *low life*, and became acquainted with the cuſtoms, manners, diſpoſitions, prejudices, &c. of the labouring part of the community, in various cities, towns, and villages; for years paſt, I have ſpent ſome of my leiſure hours among that claſs of people who are called opulent or genteel tradeſmen; nor have I been totally excluded from higher circles; but among all the ſchools where the knowledge of mankind is to be acquired, I know of none equal to that of a *bookſeller's ſhop*, eſpecially if the maſter is of an inquiſitive and communicative turn, and is in a conſiderable line of buſineſs; His ſhop will then be a place of reſort for men, women, and children, of various nations, and more of various capacities, diſpoſitions, &c.

To

To adduce a few inſtances by way of illuſtration:—Here you may find an old *bawd* inquiring for "The Counteſs of Huntingdon's Hymn-book; an old worn-out *rake*, for "Harris's Liſt of Covent-garden Ladies;" ſimple *Simon*, for "the Art of writing Love-letters;" and my lady's *maid*, for "Ovid's Art of Love;" a *doubting* Chriſtian, for "The Crumbs of Comfort;" and a practical *Antinomian*, for "Eton's Honeycomb of Free Juſtification;" the pious *Church-woman*, for "the Week's Preparation;" and the *Atheiſt*, for "Hammond's Letter to Dr. Prieſtley;" the *Mathematician*, for "Sanderſon's Fluxions;" and the *Beau*, for "The Toilet of Flora;" the *Courtier*, for "Machiavel's Prince," or "Burke on the Revolution in France;" and a *Republican*, for "Paine's Rights of Man;" the tap-room *Politician*, wants "The Hiſtory of Wat Tyler," or of "The Fiſherman of Naples;" and an old Chelſea *Penſioner*, calls for "The Hiſtory of the Wars of glorious Queen Anne;" the *Critic* calls for "Bayle's Hiſtorical Dictionary

—Blair's

—Blair's Lectures—Johnſon's Lives of the Poets, and the laſt month's reviews;" and my *Barber* wants "the Seſſions Paper," or "the Trial of John the Painter:" the *Free-Thinker* aſks for "Hume's Eſſays, and the young *Student*, for "Leland's View of Deiſtical writers;" the *Fortune-teller* wants "Salmon's Soul of Aſtrology," or "Sanderſon's Secrets of Palmiſtry;" and the *Sceptic* wants "Cornelius Agrippa's Vanity of the Arts and Sciences;" an *old hardened ſinner*, wants "Bunyan's Good News for the vileſt of men;" and a *moral Chriſtian* wants "The whole Duty of Man;" the *Roman Catholic* wants "The Lives of the Saints;" the *Proteſtant* wants "Fox's Book of Martyrs;" one aſks for "An Account of Animal Magnetiſm;" another for "The victorious Philoſopher's Stone diſcover'd; one wants "The Death of Abel;" another deſires to have "The Spaniſh Rogue;" one wants an "Eccleſiaſtical Hiſtory;" another, "The Tyburn Chronicle;" one wants "Johnſon's Lives

Lives of the Highwaymen;" another wants "Gibbons's Lives of pious Women;" Miſs *W*———h calls for "Euclid in *Greek*;" and a young *divine* for "Juliet Grenville, a novel;" whilſt the venerable *philoſopher*,

> "Drinks large draughts of the *Pyrenean* ſpring,
> "And likes a taſte of every THING."

But it would be an endleſs taſk to ſet down the various and oppoſite articles that are conſtantly called for in my ſhop. To talk to theſe different purſuers after happineſs, or amuſement, has given me much pleaſure, and afforded me ſome knowledge of mankind, and alſo of books: and to hear the debates that frequently occur between the different purchaſers is a fine amuſement; ſo that I have ſometimes compared my ſhop to a ſtage. And I aſſure you that a variety of characters, ſtrongly mark'd conſtantly made their appearance.

Would my health permit my conſtant attendance, I ſhould prefer it, to every thing in life (reading excepted) and you may recol-

lect

lect that for some years I sought no other amusement whatever.

Having been long habituated to make remarks on whatever I saw or heard, is another reason why I have succeeded so well in my business. I have for the last seven years successively told my acquaintances before the year began, how much money I should take in the course of it, without once failing of taking the sum mentioned. I formed my judgment by observing what kind of stock in trade I had in hand, and by considering how that stock was adapted to the different tastes and pursuits of the times; in doing this I was obliged to be pretty well informed of the state of politics in Europe, as I have always found that *bookselling* is much affected by the political state of affairs. For as mankind are in search of amusement, they often take the first that offers; so that if there is any thing in the news-papers of consequence, that draws many to the coffee-house, where they chat away the evenings, instead of visiting the shops of booksellers (*as they ought to do, no doubt*) or *reading* at home. The beſt time for bookſelling, is when there is no kind of news ſtirring; then many of thoſe who for months would have done nothing but talk of war or peace, revolutions, and counter-revolutions, &c. &c. for want of other amuſement will have recourſe to books; ſo that I have often experienced that the report of a war, or the tryal of a great man, or indeed any ſubject that attracts the public attention, has been ſome hundreds of pounds out of my pocket in a few weeks.

Before I conclude this letter, I cannot help obſerving, that the ſale of books in general has increaſed prodigiouſly within the laſt twenty years. According to the beſt eſtimation I have been able to make, I ſuppoſe that more than four times the number of books are ſold now than were ſold twenty years ſince. The poorer ſort of farmers, and even the poor country people in general, who before that period ſpent their winter evenings in relating ſtories of witches, ghoſts, hobgoblins, &c. now ſhorten the winter nights by hearing

their

their ſons and daughters read tales, romances, &c. and on entering their houſes, you may ſee Tom Jones, Roderick Random, and other entertaining books ſtuck up on their bacon racks, &c. If *John* goes to town with a load of hay, he is charged to be ſure not to forget to bring home "Peregrine Pickle's adventures;" and when *Dolly* is ſent to market to ſell her eggs, ſhe is commiſſioned to purchaſe "The hiſtory of Pamela Andrews." In ſhort all ranks and degrees now READ. But the moſt rapid increaſe of the ſale of books has been ſince the termination of the late war.

A number of book-clubs are alſo formed in every part of England, where each member ſubſcribes a certain ſum quarterly to purchaſe books; in ſome of theſe clubs the books after they have been read by all the ſubſcribers, are ſold among them to the higheſt bidders, and the money produced by ſuch ſale, is expended in freſh purchaſes, by which prudent and judicious mode, each member has it in his power to become poſſeſſed of the work of any particular author he may judge deſerving a ſuperior degree of attention; and the members at large enjoy the advantage of a continual ſucceſſion of different publications, inſtead of being reſtricted to a repeated peruſal of the ſame authors; which muſt have been the caſe with many if ſo rational a plan had not been adopted.

I am informed that when circulating libraries were firſt opened, the bookſellers were much alarmed, and their rapid increaſe added to their fears, and led them to think that the ſale of books would be much diminiſhed by ſuch libraries. But experience has proved that the ſale of books, ſo far from being diminiſhed by them, has been greatly promoted, as from thoſe repoſitories, many thouſand families have been cheaply ſupplied with books, by which the taſte for reading has become much more general, and thouſands of books are purchaſed every year, by ſuch as have firſt borrowed them at thoſe

libraries,

libraries, and after reading, approving of them, become purchafers.

The *Sunday-Schools* are fpreading very faft in moft parts of England, which will accelerate the diffuffion of knowledge among the lower claffes of the community, and in a very few years exceedingly increafe the fale of books.—Here permit me earneftly to call on every honeft bookfeller (I truft my call will not be in vain) as well as on every friend to the extenfion of knowledge, to unite (as *you* I am confident will) in a hearty AMEN.

Let fuch as doubt whether the enlightening of the underftandings of the lower orders of fociety, makes them happier, or be of any utility to a ftate, read the following lines (particularly the laft twelve) by Dr. Goldfmith, taken from his Traveller.

" Thefe are the charms to barren ftates affign'd,
" Their wants are few, their wifhes all confin'd;
" Yet let them only fhare the praifes due,
" If few their wants, their pleafures are but few;
" Since every want that ftimulates the breaft,
" Becomes a fource of pleafure when redreft.

" Hence from ſuch lands each pleaſing ſcience flies,
" That firſt excites deſires, and then ſupplies.
" Unknown to them, when ſenſual pleaſures cloy,
" To fill the languid pauſe with finer joy;
" Unknown thoſe powers that raiſe the ſoul to flame,
" Catch every nerve, and vibrates thro' the frame;
" Their level life is but a mould'ring fire,
" Nor quench'd by want, nor fann'd by ſtrong deſire;
" Unfit for raptures, or if raptures cheer,
" On ſome high feſtival of once a year,
" In wild exceſs the vulgar breaſt takes fire,
" 'Till buried in debauch, the bliſs expire.

" But not their joys alone thus coarſely flow,
" Their morals, like their pleaſures, are but low:
" Nor, as refinement ſtops, from ſire to ſon,
" Unalter'd, unimprov'd their manners run;
" And love's and friendſhip's finely pointed dart
" Fall blunted from each indurated heart;
" Some ſterner virtues o'er the mountain's breaſt,
" May ſit like falcons low'ring on the neſt,
" But all the gentler morals, ſuch as play
" Thro' life's more cultivated walks, and charm our way;
" Theſe far diſpers'd, on timorous pinions fly,
" To ſport and flutter in a kinder ſky."

It is worth remarking that the introducing hiſtories, romances, ſtories, poems, &c. into ſchools, has been a very great means of diffuſing a general taſte for reading among all ranks

ranks of people, while in ſchools, the children only read the bible (which was the caſe in many ſchools a few years ago) children then did not make ſo early a progreſs in reading as they have ſince, they have been pleaſed and entertained as well as inſtructed; and this reliſh for books, in many will laſt as long as life.

I am,

Dear Friend,

Yours.

LETTER XXXIX.

" Happy the man that has each fortune try'd,
" To whom ſhe much has given, much deny'd,
" With abſtinence all delicates he ſees,
" And can regale himſelf with toaſt and cheeſe."

* Art of Cookery.

" One ſolid diſh his week-day meals affords,
" And added Pudding conſecrates the Lord's."

DEAR FRIEND,

THE Public at large, and bookſellers in particular, have beheld my increaſing ſtock with the utmoſt aſtoniſhment, they being entirely at a loſs to conceive by what means I have been enabled to make good all my payments; and for ſeveral years, in the beginning of my buſineſs, ſome of the trade repeatedly aſſerted, that it was totally impoſſible that I could continue to pay for the large numbers of books that I continually purchaſed; and ten years ſince, being induced to take a journey into my own country, with a view to the reſtoration of my my health, which had been materially injured by intenſe application to catalogue-making, too much reading, &c. during the ſix weeks that I retired into the weſt, Mrs. Lackington was perpetually interrogated reſpecting the time that I was expected to return. This was done in ſuch a manner as evidently ſhewed that many thought I never intended to return at all. But how great was their ſurprize, when as a prelude to my return, I ſent home ſeveral waggon loads of books which I had purchaſed in the country.

As I never had any part of the *miſer* in my compoſition, I always proportioned my expences according to my profits; that is, I have for many years expended two thirds of the profits of my trade; which proportion of expenditure I never exceeded. If you will pleaſe to refer to Dr. Johnſon's "Idler" for "the progreſs of Ned Drugget," you will there ſee much of the progreſs of your humble ſervant depicted. Like Ned, in the beginning I opened and ſhut my own ſhop,

and

and welcomed a friend by a ſhake of the hand. About a year after, I beckoned acroſs the way for *a pot of good porter*. A few years after that, I ſometimes invited my friends to dinner, and provided them a roaſted *fillet of veal*; in a progreſſive courſe the *ham* was introduced, and a *pudding* was the next addition made to the feaſt. For ſome time a glaſs of *brandy and water* was a luxury; a glaſs of Mr. Beaufoy's *raiſin wine* ſucceeded; and as ſoon as *two thirds* of my profits enabled me to afford good *red port*, it immediately appeared: nor was ſherry long behind.

"Wine whets the wit, improves its native force,
"And gives a pleaſing flavour to diſcourſe,
"By making all our ſpirits debonair,
"Throws off the fears, the ſediment of care."

My country *lodging* by regular gradation was transformed into a country *houſe*; and the inconveniences attending a *ſtage coach* were remedied by a *chariot*. For four years, *Upper Holloway* was to me an *elyſium*; then *Surry* appeared unqueſtionably the moſt beautiful county

county in England, and *Merton* the moſt rural village in Surry. So now *Merton* is ſelected as the ſeat of occaſional philoſophical retirement.

" Here on a ſingle plank thrown ſafe aſhore,
" I hear the tumult of the diſtant throng,
" As that of ſeas remote or dying ſtorms.
" Here like a ſhepherd gazing from his hut,
" Touching his reed, or leaning on his ſtaff,
" Eager ambition's fiery chace I ſee;
" I ſee the circling hunt of noiſy men,
" Burſt law's incloſure, leap the mounds of right,
" Purſuing and purſu'd, each other's prey."

YOUNG.

But I aſſure you, my dear friend, that in every ſtep of my progreſs, envy and malevolence has purſued me cloſe.

When by the advice of that eminent phyſician, Dr. Lettſom, I purchaſed a horſe and ſaved my life by the exerciſe it afforded me, the old adage, " *Set a beggar on horſeback and he'll ride to the devil,*" was deemed fully verified; but when Mrs. Lackington mounted another, " they were very ſorry to ſee people ſo young in buſineſs run on at ſo

great

great a rate!" The occaſional relaxation which we enjoyed in the country was cenſured as an abominable piece of pride; but when the *carriage* and *ſervants* in *livery* appeared, "they would not be the firſt to hurt a fooliſh tradeſman's character; but if (as was but too probable) the *docket* was not already ſtruck, the gazette would ſoon ſettle that point."

> " Baſe Envy withers at another's joy,
> " And hates that excellence it cannot reach."
>
> THOMPSON.

But I have been lately informed that theſe *good natured* and *compaſſionate* people have for ſome time found it neceſſary to alter their ſtory. It ſeems that at laſt they have diſcovered the ſecret ſprings from whence I drew my wealth; however they do not quite agree in their accounts, for although ſome can tell you the very *number* of my fortunate lottery ticket, others are as poſitive that I found bank-notes in an old book, to the amount of many thouſand pounds, and if they pleaſe, can even tell you the title of the very for-

tunate

tunate old book that contained this treaſure. But you ſhall receive it from me, which you will deem authority to the full as unexceptionable, I aſſure you then upon my honour that I found the whole of what I am poſſeſſed of, in—SMALL PROFITS, *bound* by INDUSTRY, and *claſped* by OECONOMY.

Read this, ye covetous wretches, in all trades, who when you get a good cuſtomer are for making the moſt of him! But if you have neither honour nor honeſty, you ſhould at leaſt poſſeſs a little *common ſenſe*. Reflect on the many cuſtomers that your over-charges have already driven from your ſhops! do you think that you can find cuſtomers enough ſo deficient in penetration as not to diſcover your characters? no ſuch thing. Your exorbitant charges are a general ſubject of converſation and diſlike: you cannot with confidence look your own cuſtomers in the face, as you are conſcious of your meanneſs and impoſition, and your ſordid diſpoſition is evidently the reaſon, that ſome gentlemen are led to look with contempt and diſdain on tradeſmen.

But

But when men in trade are men of honour, they will in general be treated as ſuch; and were it otherwiſe,

"One ſelf-approving hour whole years outweighs,
"Of ſtupid ſtarers, and of loud huzzas:
"And more true joy Marcellus exil'd feels,
"Than Cæſar with a ſenate at his heels."

POPE.

I pity from my ſoul many poor wretches which I obſerve bartering away their conſtitutions, and what few liberal ſentiments they may poſſeſs; riſing early and ſitting up late, exerting all the powers of body and mind, to get what they call a competency, no matter by what means this is effected; thouſands actually deſtroy themſelves in accompliſhing their grand deſign: others, live to obtain the long-wiſhed for country retreat. But, alas! the promiſed happineſs is as far from them as ever, often farther. The buſy buſtling ſcene of buſineſs being over, a vacuity in the mind takes place, ſpleen and vapors ſucceed, which encreaſe bodily infirmities, death ſtares them in the face. The mean dirty ways by which much of their wealth has been obtained make

retroſpect

retrofpect reflections intolerable. Philofophy ftands aloof, nor ever deigns to vifit the fordid foul. Gardens and pleafure grounds become dreary deferts; the miferable poffeffors linger out a wretched exiftence, or put a period to it with a halter or piftol.

> "Were this not common would it not be ftrange?
> "That 'tis fo common, this is ftranger ftill."

The profits of my bufinefs the prefent year 1791, (as near as can be computed before the expiration of it) will amount to FOUR THOUSAND POUNDS. What it will increafe to I know not; but if my health will permit me to carry it on a few years longer, there is very great probability, confidering the rapid increafe which each fucceeding year has produced, that the profits will be double what they now are; for I here pledge my reputation as a tradefman, never to deviate from my old plan of giving as much for libraries as it is poffible for a tradefman to give, and felling them and *new* publications alfo, for the fame SMALL PROFITS that have been attended with fuch aftonifhing fuccefs for ſome years paſt. And I hope that my aſſiſtants will alſo perſevere in that attentive obliging mode of conduct which has ſo long diſtinguiſhed No. 46 and 47, Chiſwell-ſtreet, Moorfields; conſcious, that ſhould I ever be weak enough to adopt an oppoſite line of conduct, or permit thoſe who act under my direction ſo to do, I ſhould no longer meet with the very extraordinary encouragement and ſupport which I have hitherto experienced; neither ſhould I have the ſmalleſt claim to a continuance of it under ſuch circumſtances.

I am,

Dear Friend,

Yours.

LETTER

LETTER XL.

"But by your revenue measure your expence,
"And to your funds and acres join your sense."

YOUNG's Love of Fame.

"Learn what thou ow'st thy country and thy friend,
"What's requisite to spare, and what to spend."

DRYDEN's Persius.

DEAR FRIEND,

THE open manner of stating my profits will no doubt appear strange to many who are not acquainted with my singular conduct in that and other respects. But you, Sir, know that I have for fourteen years past kept a strict account of my profits. Every book in my possession, before it is offered to sale is marked with a private mark, what it cost me, and with a public mark of what it is to be sold for; and every article, whether the price is six-pence or sixty pounds, is entered in a day-book as it is sold, with the price it cost and the money it sold for: and each night the profits of the day are cast up by one of my ſhopmen, as every one of them underſtands my private marks. Every Saturday night the profits of the week are added together and mentioned before all my ſhopmen, &c. the week's profits, and alſo the expences of the week are then entered one oppoſite the other, in a book kept for the purpoſe: the whole ſum taken in the week is alſo ſet down, and the ſum that has been paid for books bought. Theſe accounts are kept publickly in my ſhop, and ever have been ſo, as I never ſaw any reaſon for concealing them, nor was ever jealous of any of my men's profiting by my example and taking away any of my buſineſs, as I always found that ſuch of them as did ſet up for themſelves came to my ſhop and purchaſed to the amount of ten times more than they hindered me from ſelling. By keeping an account of my profits, and alſo of my expences, I have always known how to regulate the latter by the former; and I have done that, without the trifling way of ſetting down a halfpenny-worth of matches, or a penny for a turnpike. I have one perſon in the ſhop whoſe conſtant employment it is to receive all the caſh, and diſcharge all bills that are brought for payment, and if Mrs. Lackington wants money for houſe-keeping, &c. or if I want money for *hobby-horſes*, &c. we take five or ten guineas, pocket it, and ſet down the ſum taken out of trade as expended; when that is gone we repeat our application, but never take the trouble of ſetting down the *items*. But ſuch of my ſervants as are entruſted to lay out money are always obliged to give in their accounts to ſhew how each ſum has been expended.

It may not be improper here to take a little notice of ſome very late inſinuations of my old envious *friends*. It has been ſuggeſted that I am now grown *immenſely rich*, and that having already more property than I can reaſonably expect to live to expend, and no young family to provide for, I for theſe reaſons ought to decline my buſineſs, and no longer engroſs trade to myſelf that ought to be divided into a number of channels, and thus ſupport many families. In anſwer to which I will obſerve, that ſome of theſe objectors were in trade before me, and when I firſt embarked in the profeſſion of a bookſeller, deſpiſed me for my mean beginning. When afterwards I adopted my plan of ſelling cheap, and for ready-money only, they made themſelves very merry at my expence, for expecting to ſucceed by ſo *ridiculous* a project, (as they in their conſummate wiſdom were pleaſed to term it) and predeſtined my ruin, ſo that no doubt I ought to comply with any thing they deſire, however unreaſonable it may appear to me.

To deny that I have a competence, would be unpardonable ingratitude to the public, to go no higher;

"I want but little; nor that little long."

But to inſinuate that I am getting money for no good purpoſe, is falſe and invidious. The great apoſtle St. Paul, who was an humble follower of CHRIST, thought that he might be permitted to boaſt of himſelf a little;

tle; after which I suppose it will not be thought very presumptuous in me, if I should state a few facts, merely to justify my conduct in carrying on my trade beyond the time that certain persons would prescribe to me.

It is now about five years since I began to entertain serious thoughts of going out of business on account of the bad state of health which both Mrs. Lackington and myself have laboured under; but it was then suggested by several of my friends, that as I had about fifty poor relations, a great number of whom are children, others are old and nearly helpless, and that all had justly formed some expectations from me: therefore to give up such a trade as I was in possession of, before I was absolutely obliged to do it, would be a kind of *injustice* to those whom by the ties of blood I was in some measure bound to relieve and protect. These and other considerations induced me to wave the thoughts of precipitating myself out of so extensive and lucrative a business; and in the mean time I apply a part of the profits of it to maintain my good old mother, who is alive at Wellington in Somerſetſhire, her native place. I have two aged men and one aged woman, whom I ſupport : and I have alſo four children to maintain and educate, three of theſe children have loſt their father, and alſo their mother, (who was my ſiſter) the other child has both his parents living, but they are poor ; many others of my relations are in the ſame circumſtances, and ſtand in need of my aſſiſtance.

" If e'er I've mourn'd my humble, lowly ſtate,
" If e'er I've bow'd my knee at fortune's ſhrine,
" If e'er a wiſh eſcap'd me to be great,
" The fervent prayer humanity was thine.
" Periſh the man who hears the piteous tale
" Unmov'd, to whom the heart-felt glow's unknown ;
" On whom the widow's plaints could ne'er prevail,
" Nor made the injur'd wretches cauſe his own.
" How little knows he the extatic joy,
" The thrilling bliſs of cheering wan deſpair!
" How little knows the pleaſing warm employ,
" That calls the grateful tribute of a tear.
" The ſplendid dome, the vaulted rock to rear,
" The glare of pride and pomp, be, grandeur, thine!
" To wipe from miſery's eye the wailing tear,
" And ſoothe the oppreſſed orphan's woe, be mine."

It

It has alſo been frequently ſaid, that by ſelling my books very cheap, I have materially injured other bookſellers both in town and country. But I ſtill deny the charge: and here I will firſt obſerve, that I have as juſt a reaſon to complain of them for giving credit, as they can have for my ſelling cheap and giving *no* credit; as it is well known that there are many thouſands of people every where to be found who will decline purchaſing at a ſhop where credit is denied, when they can find ſhopkeepers enough who will readily give it; and as I frequently loſe cuſtomers who having always been accuſtomed to have credit, will not take the trouble to pay for every article as ſent home; theſe of courſe deal at thoſe ſhops who follow the old mode of buſineſs; ſo that in ſuch caſes, I might ſay to the proprietors of theſe ſhops, 'You ought not to give any perſon credit: 'becauſe by ſo doing you are taking cuſ'tomers from me.' As to my *hurting the trade* by ſelling *cheap*, they are, upon the whole miſtaken; for although no doubt ſome inſtances will occur, in which they may obſerve that the preference is given to *my* ſhop, and the books purchaſed of me on account of their being cheap, they never conſider how many books they diſpoſe of on the very ſame account. As, however, this may appear rather paradoxical, I will explain my meaning farther:

I now ſell more than one hundred thouſand volumes annually; many who purchaſe part of theſe, do ſo ſolely on account of their cheapneſs; many thouſands of theſe books would have been deſtroyed, as I have before remarked, but for my ſelling them on thoſe very moderate terms; now when thouſands of theſe articles are ſold, they become known by being handed about in various circles of acquaintances, many of whom wiſhing to be poſſeſſed of the ſame books without enquiring the price of their friends, ſtep into the firſt bookſeller's ſhop, and give their orders for articles which they never would have heard of, had not I, by ſelling them cheap, been the original cauſe of their being diſperſed abroad;

abroad; ſo that by means of the plan purſued in my ſhop, whole editions of books are ſold off, and new editions printed of the works of authors, who but for that circumſtance would have been ſcarce noticed at all.

But (ſay they) you not only ſell ſuch books cheap, as are but little known, but you even ſell a great deal under price the very firſt-rate articles however well they may be known, or however highly they may be thought of by the literary world. I acknowledge the charge, and again repeat that as I do not give any credit, I really ought to do ſo, and I may add, that in ſome meaſure I am obliged to do it; for who would come out of their way to Chiſwell-ſtreet to pay me the ſame price in ready money, as they might purchaſe for at the firſt ſhop they came to, and have credit alſo.

And although firſt-rate authors are very well known, yet I well know that by ſelling them cheaper than others, many are purchaſed of me that never would have been purchaſed

purchaſed at the full price, and every book that is ſold tends to ſpread the fame of the author, and rapidly extends the ſale, and as I before remarked, ſends more cuſtomers to other ſhops as well as to my own.

I could relate much more on this ſubject, but will not unneceſſarily take up your time, as I truſt what is here advanced will convey full conviction to your mind, and as I believe it is univerſally known and allowed that no man ever promoted the ſale of books in an equal degree, with,

Dear Friend,

Yours.

LETTER

LETTER XLI.

" —This is a traveller, Sir; knows men and manners; and
" has plough'd up fea fo far, 'till both the poles have
" knock'd; has feen the fun take coach, and can diftinguifh
" the colour of his horfes, and their kinds, and had a Flan-
" ders mare leap'd there."

BEAUMONT and FLETCHER's Scornful Lady.

DEAR FRIEND,

AMONGST the variety of occurrences with which I have endeavoured to entertain you, perhaps not all equally interefting (and the moft material of them, I am duly fenfible, not entitling me to the claim of being efteemed a writer poffeffed of the very firft abilities this age or nation has produced,) I recollect my not yet having given you an account of my principal TRAVELS. Poffibly you might very readily pardon that omiffion, as from what has already appeared it muft be evident, the engagements which from time to time have fully engroffed my attention, have not furnifhed me with

with any opportunity of making the tour of Europe, or tracing the source of the river Nile; much less circumnavigating the globe. And even supposing I had been possessed both of the time and inclination for such extensive undertakings, the disadvantages which I labour under for want of having received a proper education, would have disqualified me from making such remarks and observations as naturally present themselves to those who have been fortunate enough to possess that advantage, and of course are qualified to present the world with a variety of subjects equally curious and instructive: 'though it is not without reluctance I think it necessary here to observe, that some of these gentlemen, not content with giving a true account of what actually occurred to them, and supposing that plain matter of fact would not be sufficiently interesting to excite that superior degree of attention and admiration which they were ambitious as authors to acquire, they have thought proper to intermix so much of the *marvellous* into their narrations,

as

as has been the occaſion of many perſons reading them with ſuch diffidence, as to doubt the truth of many relations, which though really ſtrictly conſiſtent with veracity, yet being novel and uncommon, they were unwilling to credit, leſt they ſhould incur the cenſure of being poſſeſſed of a ſuperior degree of weakneſs and credulity.) This I am alſo confident has induced many a modeſt author to omit paſſages, which though really true, he was cautious of publiſhing, from a fear of being ſubjected to the ſame ſevere animadverſions, or what is ſtill worſe, being ſuſpected of wilfully impoſing on his readers. Recent inſtances of which, were it neceſſary, I could adduce; but I ſhall proceed with cautioning you from being alarmed leſt I ſhould fall into either of theſe errors; nothing *very marvellous* will occur in what I mean to preſent you with; though I ſhall not be intimidated from relating *real facts*, from the apprehenſion of not being credited. As an additional recommendation, (no doubt) the hiſtory of my travels will be inter-

interſperſed with ſuch remarks on *men* and *manners* as have preſented themſelves to me during my peregrinations; and this I previouſly warn you, will be done in m·· "accuſtomed deſultory manner," from which as Mr. *Pennant* ſays in his——"*Of London,*" (there is a conciſe title-page for you) "I am too old to depart," that is, as Dr. *Johnſon* might poſſibly have explained it, "Sir, you are then too old to MEND." But you, my dear friend, are not ſo faſtidious a critic: although you may find the whole very *dull*, it ſhall not be very *long*; ſo that if it does not act as a cordial to enliven your ſpirits, it may (if read in the evening) prove a powerful *narcotic*, and afford you ſome pleaſing dreams, when

" Tir'd nature's ſweet reſtorer, balmy ſleep,
" His ready viſit pays."

I ſhall therefore not trouble you with a detail of bad roads, the impoſitions of innkeepers, what food I partook of, how many bottles of wine were drank, the height of ſteeples, &c. a ſufficiency of this, I truſt, has already ap-

peare

peared in different writers. Thus much by way of preparation for my journies. I now ſet out.

In *September*, Seventeen hundred and eighty-ſeven, I ſet off for Edinburgh; and in all the principal towns through which I paſſed, was led from a motive of curioſity, as well as with a view towards obtaining ſome valuable purchaſes, to examine the bookſellers ſhops for ſcarce and curious books; but although I went by the way of York, Newcaſtle-upon-Tyne, &c. and returned through Glaſgow, Carliſle, Leeds, Lancaſter, Preſton, Mancheſter, and other conſiderable places, I was much ſurpriſed, as well as diſappointed, at meeting with very few of the works of the moſt eſteemed authors; and thoſe few conſiſted in general of ordinary editions, beſides an aſſemblage of common trifling books, bound in ſheep, and that too in a very bad manner. It is true, at York and Leeds there were a few (and but very few) good books; but in all the other towns between London and Edinburgh nothing but traſh

was

was to be found: in the latter city indeed, a few capital articles are kept, but in no other part of Scotland.

In ſeventeen hundred and ninety, I repeated my journey, and was much mortified to be under a neceſſity of confirming my former obſervations. This remarkable deficiency in the article of books, is however not peculiar to the northern parts of England; as I have repeatedly travelled into the weſtern parts, and found abundant cauſe for diſſatisfaction on the ſame account, ſo that I may venture without fear of contradiction to aſſert, that London, as in all other articles of commerce, is likewiſe the grand emporium of Great Britain for books, engroſſing nearly the whole of what is valuable in that very extenſive, beneficial, and I may add lucrative branch of trade. As to Ireland, I ſhall only obſerve, that if the bookſellers in that part of the empire do not ſhine in the poſſeſſion of valuable books, they muſt certainly be allowed to poſſeſs ſuperior induſtry in reprinting the works of every Engliſh author

thor of merit, as ſoon as publiſhed, and *very liberally* endeavouring to diſſeminate them, in a ſurreptitious manner through every part of our iſland, though the attempts now generally proves abortive, to the great loſs and injury of the ingenious projectors.

At Newcaſtle, I paſſed a day or two in the year 1787, where I was much delighted with viewing a ſingular phœnomenon in natural hiſtory, namely the celebrated *crows neſt* affixed above the weather cock, on the upper extremity of the ſteeple, in the market-place. In the year 1783, as I was well informed, the crows firſt built this curious neſt, and ſucceeded in hatching and rearing their young. In the following year they attempted to rebuild it: but a conteſt enſuing among ſome of the ſable fraternity, after a fierce engagement they were obliged to relinquiſh it, and the neſt was demoliſhed by the victorious party before it was finiſhed. This bad ſucceſs, however, did not deter the original builders and poſſeſſors from returning in the year 1785, when they took quiet poſſeſſion of their freehold, rebuilt the premiſes, and reared another family. This they repeated the three following years with equal ſucceſs, and when I was there in the year 1790, much of the neſt remained, but the crows had forſaken it. The above occurrence, though to many it may appear incredible, is an undoubted fact. That *crows* ſhould come into the center of a populous town to build their neſts, is of itſelf remarkable; but much more ſo, that they ſhould prefer a weathercock to any other ſituation, where the whole family, and their habitation turned round with every puff of wind, though they were perfectly ſecured from falling, by the ſpike of iron which roſe above the fane, around which the whole made their revolutions; and as on one ſide the neſt was higher than on the other, that part being always to windward, by this ingenious contrivance of the feathered architects, the inſide of the neſt was conſtantly kept in a proper degree of warmth. I never recollect theſe

various

various circumſtances, without being loſt in admiration at the extraordinary ſagacity of theſe birds.

In this town however, I met with a greater curioſity, as well as a more amiable ſubject of it than a crows neſt, to excite my aſtoniſhment.

In my firſt journey, Mr. *Fiſher* the bookſeller introduced me to his daughter, a charming young lady, who being unfortunately born deaf, was conſequently dumb, till a gentleman a few years ſince taught her to underſtand what was ſaid to her by the motion of the lips. I had the pleaſure of converſing with her ſeveral times, and found that ſhe had much of the Scotch accent, which as Mr. Fiſher informed me, ſhe acquired of the gentleman who taught her not only to underſtand the converſation of others but to *ſpeak*, he being a native of that country; he remarked alſo, that ſhe never had ſpoken the Newcaſtle dialect. This young lady, I was alſo informed, dances exceedingly well, keeping exact time with the music, whether it is played slow or quick. When it is considered what an intense application must have been used, both on the part of the teacher and his fair pupil, to produce such a happy effect, it surely reflects great credit on each of the parties.

In the year 1790, when I again visited Newcastle with Mrs. Lackington, this young lady became the first object of inquiry, and we were both introduced to her.

I have lately been informed of a lady now in London, who although she is deaf, takes great *delight in music*, and when asked how she is affected by it, she answers that she feels it at her *breast* and at *the bottom of her feet.*

Being on the subject of *Curiosities*, and having just related the pleasure I experienced on account of a lady acquiring the use of speech, permit me now to present you with another *rarity* indeed !—somewhat connected with the former, no doubt, but intended as an effectual remedy (temporary, at least) for

an

an oppoſite complaint of the ſame organs, viz. too great a *volubility of ſpeech*, with which, (as it is ſaid) many females are ſo infected, as ſometimes to lead them to exceed the bounds of due moderation and female decorum, and even diſplay itſelf in the utterance of ſuch harſh (though frequently inarticulate) terms, as tend too much to diſgrace the unhappy patient, and violently affect the auditory nerves of all perſons within a conſiderable diſtance.—To quit metaphor.

At the town-hall I was ſhewn a piece of antiquity called a *brank*. It conſiſts of a combination of iron fillets, and is faſtened to the head by a lock fixed to the back part of it; a thin plate of iron goes into the mouth, ſufficiently ſtrong however, to confine the tongue, and thus prevent the wearer from making any uſe of that reſtleſs member. The uſe of this piece of machinery is to puniſh notorious *ſcolds*. I am pleaſed to find that it is now conſidered merely as a matter of curioſity, the females of that town happily having not the ſmalleſt occaſion for the application of ſo harſh an inſtrument: whether it is that all females apprehenſive of being included in *that* deſcription, have travelled ſouthward, to avoid the danger of ſo degrading an exhibition, or whatever other reaſon is aſſigned, I forgot to enquire. It however affords me pleaſure to reflect, that the ladies of Newcaſtle are left at liberty to adopt a head-dreſs of their own chooſing, confident that they poſſeſs a more refined taſte than to fix upon one by no means calculated to diſplay their lovely countenances to advantage, as I am perſuaded the *brank* would caſt ſuch a gloom on the faireſt of them, as would tend much to diminiſh the influence of their charms, and give pain to every beholder. It may be prudent, notwithſtanding, ſtill to preſerve it *in terrorem*, as who knows what future times may produce? As I eſteem it a very ingenious contrivance, and as there may be parts of the country ſtill to be found, where the application of ſuch a machine may be uſeful in ſome chriſtian families (I will not ſay in *all*, having ſufficient grounds for

aſſerting

aſſerting the contrary) I here preſent you with an accurate ſketch of it,

together with the manner of its application: that if any ingenious artiſt ſhould be applied to, he may not be at a loſs how it is to be made. I would, however, adviſe ſuch a one to be cautious in offering them to public ſale, and by no means to advertiſe them (eſpecially if a married man, or having any views towards matrimony).

I am, dear Friend,

Yours.

LETTER XLII.

"O, land of cakes! how oft my eyes
"Defire to fee thy mountains rife;
"How Fancy loves thy fteeps to climb,
"So wild, fo folemn, fo fublime."

"All the ftage-coaches that travel fo faft,
"Muft get now and then an unfortunate caft."

DEAR FRIEND,

IN my firft journey to Scotland I fometimes travelled poft, but often entered the different, ftage-coaches, &c. for a ftage or two, when I happened to fee any fetting out fo as to fuit my time and inclination: but at laft I had pretty nearly paid dear for it, as the driver of the diligence from Darlington to Durham happened to be much inebriated and before his quitting Darlington had almoft overfet us; not obferving the man was drunk, we attributed the fault to the horfes, we were however very fpeedily undeceived in that refpect by many concurrent circumftances, fo that

that we were one minute nearly in the ditch on the right hand, and the next but juſt eſcaping that on the left; at other times we experienced *ſtriking proofs* of the inability of our conductor againſt the numbers of one-horſe *coal-carts*, not to mention their frequently running foul of us for being on the wrong ſide of the road; (for drivers of coaches and carts can be to the full as ſavage towards each other in the country, as in London): however notwithſtanding all theſe "hair-breadth eſcapes," we retained our ſeats, till we arrived within three quarters of a mile of Durham, when at lengh the ſpecific gravity of the driver's head preponderating over all the other parts of his frame united, precipitated him with violence from the elevated ſtation he had, till then (though with difficulty) poſſeſſed to his parent earth. There were three unfortunate paſſengers in the carriage, left to the diſcretion of the horſes, viz. a gentleman, an innkeeper's wife, and your humble ſervant: the lady in ſtrict compliance with the practice of her ſex in ſimilar ſitua-

tions,

tions, on ſeeing the rapid deſcent of our charioteer, immediately honoured us with a loud and ſhrill ſhriek; the *quadrupeds*, not accuſtomed to this pretty female note ſo much as the ſonorous voice of a coachman, miſtook for a ſignal to mend their pace, and they, habituated to pay all due obedience to the commands of their ſuperiors of the biped creation, when underſtood by them, and finding no check, inſtantly proceeded to a full gallop; and we, however reluctantly, followed them down a gentle deſcent, not at a *gentle* rate, but with prodigious velocity. As I was quite calm and collected, I coolly reconnoitred the road before us, and obſerving that it was perfectly clear, as for half a mile not a coal-cart was to be ſeen, although we had lately paſſed ſeveral ſcore, I began to reaſon with my companions, and they ſpeedily became calm enough to aſſiſt in holding a council what was beſt to be done in our critical ſituation. Our debates were quickly ended, as we were unanimous in opinion that if we once entered the city of Durham, the

carriage

carriage muſt inevitably be torn to pieces, owing to the variety of turnings and obſtructions we ſhould have to encounter, we therefore entered into an immediate reſolution, *nem. con.* that to open the doors, and exhibit our agility by leaping out, was, of "two evils, chooſing the leaſt:" this we inſtantly did, in as careful a manner as poſſible; we firſt alighted on our feet, and next complimented the ground with our noſes, without receiving much injury. Our female companion indeed, by being rather too precipitate, alighted in a manner which on any other occaſion would not have appeared ſtrictly decent, of which ſhe, poor lady! was ſo ſenſible, that ſhe immediately "hoped *as how* we were both *married* gentlemen;" which was quickly replied to by both in the affirmative; and thus we ſaved our fair one the trouble of exerting herſelf in another ſcream, and ourſelves the puniſhment of hearing it.

Being

Being no longer parties concerned in the danger, it afforded us ſome entertainment to obſerve the progreſs of our vehicle now conſiderably lightened by our eſcape from it, and becoming every moment ſtill lighter by the excluſion of ſmall trunks, boxes, parcels, great coats, &c. they, in imitation of our example making leaps, ſome from the inſide of the carriage, and others from the boot; whether occaſioned by the *repulſion* of the carriage and its appendages, or the *attraction* of the earth, I am not ſufficiently verſed in philoſophy to decide. Poſterity when they peruſe my labours, no doubt will determine this *weighty* point, and tranſmit it to the remoteſt period of time, properly dignified by *F. R. S.* in *Phil. Tranſ.*

The horſes finding themſelves leſs incumbered and urged on by the noiſe of the door, continually flapping, increaſed their ſpeed: happily however the carriage was ſtopped before it entered the city, and no damage was ſuſtained either by the horſes or the carriage.

Before we left the inn, our careful *son of the whip* arrived, not in the least injured, but rather benefited by his disaster, being suddenly transformed into a state of perfect sobriety; after him followed two countrymen laden with the several articles which had been so violently ejected. As I reflected that this unguarded man might not always be equally successful, either to himself or his passengers, as in the present instance, I obtained a promise from the innkeeper never to permit him to drive any carriage in future, in the management of which he had any concern.

It is astonishing what a number of fatal accidents continually happen from carelessness and the want of sobriety in this thoughtless race of beings. I was informed that only two days previous to my arrival at Durham, a coachman quitting his box to step into an adjacent house, in his absence the horses began to move gently, and a lady in the carriage giving a loud scream, the noise occasioned

ſioned the horſes to ſet off full gallop, in conſequence of which a lady of Durham, happening unfortunately at that inſtant to be croſſing the way, was thrown down, and the wheels paſſing over her, ſhe died on the ſpot. —One of the many melancholy effects reſulting from the ridiculous practice of ſcreaming. But I crave pardon of the ladies; when I begin paſſing cenſure on them, it is high time to cloſe my epiſtle (which if not very long will perhaps be deemed ſufficiently impertinent) with,

I am,

Dear Friend,

Yours.

LETTER

LETTER XLIII.

"O that the too cenſorious world would learn
"This wholeſome rule, and with each other bear!
"But man, as if a foe to his own ſpecies,
"Takes pleaſure to report his neighbour's faults,
"Judging with rigour ev'ry ſmall offence,
"And prides *himſelf* in ſcandal."

HAYWOOD's D. of Brunſwick.

"A nation fam'd for ſong, and beauty's charms;
"Zealous, yet modeſt, innocent, though free:
"Patient of toil; ſincere amidſt alarms;
"Inflexible in faith: invincible in arms."

BEATTIE's Minſtrel.

DEAR FRIEND,

IT is reported of a very eminent author, that he never blotted a line of what he had once written: on which it has been remarked, that it was a pity he had not blotted a thouſand. Now though my extreme modeſty will not permit me to put myſelf on a level with that great man as an author, whatever the impartial world may think of our comparative merits, I muſt confeſs

confeſs I do not like to blot what I have once written, fearful leſt when I begin, (another proof of my modeſty,) I ſhould deface the major part of my manuſcripts, and thus deprive the public of the great advantages which may reſult from them. What I allude to, is an unfortunate ſlip of the pen in my laſt; however, as "confeſſion of a fault makes ſome amends," and I immediately checked myſelf, craved pardon, abruptly cloſed my letter, and threw the offending pen from me with ſome degree of anger, I hope thoſe lovely fair ones, who might think I meant to affront them, will with their accuſtomed benignity forgive, and indulge me with a ſmile on my future labours; and as a convincing proof how ſenſible I am of their kind condeſcenſion, I here engage never more to expreſs my diſlike of their *ſcreaming*, except they ſhould omit purchaſing books of me, which I am ſure every candid fair (and what *fair* one is not candid?) will think ſufficiently provoking.

But

But in order to remind them that every great character does not always conduct himself with equal politeness towards the ladies, I beg permission to introduce a *very* great man to them: no less a personage than Doctor JOHNSON. Of whom indeed so much hath already been sung and said, that the subject may be supposed to be nearly exhausted; which is, however, so far from being the case, that notwithstanding two quarto volumes of his life by Mr. Boswell are just published, we are taught to expect another life by a different hand. Indeed until some other great man makes his exit (myself out of the question) we are likely to be entertained with fresh anecdotes of him; but when that period once arrives, then farewel *Johnson!*

The Doctor, whose extreme fondness for that agreeable beverage *tea*, is well known, was once in company with a number of ladies assembled to partake with him of the same refreshment. The lady of the house happened to be one of those particularly attentive to punctilio, and had exhibited her fineſt ſet of china for the entertainment of her gueſts; the Doctor, who drank large quantities, and with conſiderable expedition, could not always wait with becoming patience ceremoniouſly to aſk for and receive in due form the addition of a lump of ſugar when neceſſary; he therefore without permiſſion put his finger and thumb into the ſugar-diſh, tumbling the contents over, till he met with a piece of the proper ſize; the lady kept her eye fixed on him the whole time, and deeming his conduct a great breach of decorum, reſolved to make him ſenſible of it, by immediately ordering the ſervant to change the ſugar-diſh. The Doctor, tho' apparently attentive only to his tea, noticed it, and as ſoon as he had emptied the cup, put it together with the ſaucer under the fire-place, with due care, however, not to break them. This was too ſevere a trial for the poor lady, who, apprehenſive for the fate of her dear china, after a decent ſcream, with warmth demanded the reaſon of his

treating

treating her in ſo rude a manner. "Why, "my dear madam, (replied he) I was "alarmed with the idea that whatever I "touched was thereby contaminated, and "impreſſed with anxious deſire to contri-"bute towards your felicity, I removed the "object ſo defiled from your preſence with "all poſſible expedition." This reply, tho' it extorted a ſmile from all the company preſent, did not ſatisfy the lady to whom it was addreſſed, who notwithſtanding ſhe exerted herſelf to appear in good humour, was too much offended to forget the affront.— This anecdote has been related to me with ſome *addenda* which heighten the ſtory, though more to the diſadvantage of the Doctor; but I believe as here related, it may be depended on as the real fact.

During my continuance in Scotland, which was about three weeks the firſt time, and about a month the laſt, I often reflected with pain on the illiberal, not to ſay brutal treatment the inhabitants received from the Doctor. At Edinburgh I heard various anecdotes related of him, which were perfectly novel to me, and in all probability will be so to you. I shall therefore give you a specimen.

Being one day at a gentleman's house in Edinburgh, several ladies and gentlemen came in to pay their respects to him; and among others the then Lord Provost went up to the Doctor, bowing repeatedly, and expressing the highest respect for him; to all which the Doctor paid not the least attention. Exceedingly hurt at so flagrant a mark of disrespect, he turned round, and put a shilling into the hand of the gentleman of the house. On being asked what the shilling was intended for, he replied, "Have not I seen your *bear?*"

The Doctor being drinking tea at another gentleman's house, the lady asked him if he did not choose another cup: It seems she had forgot her having before asked him the same question; and on her repeating it he replied, "Woman, have I not already told you

you that I had done?" On which the lady anſwered him in his own gruff manner. During his continuance in her houſe ſhe always talked to him without ceremony, and it was remarked that ſhe had more influence with him than any other perſon in Scotland.

I was much pleaſed with the politeneſs of the gentleman who related to me this ſtory of the Doctor, as he appeared anxious to excuſe him for his want of due decorum, and thus to palliate a moſt obvious blemiſh in the character of one of the moſt eminent of my countrymen. I could wiſh the compilers of the biographical department of that truly great and uſeful work, the "*Encyclopoedia Britannica*" would obſerve the ſame politeneſs and impartiality. And I hope that this hint will alſo induce them in ſome ſubſequent edition, when I am gone to

"That Bourne from whence no traveller returns,"

to do juſtice to my *great and aſtoniſhing merits*, by way of compenſation for having fallen ſhort in ſpeaking of other *great men*; and ſhould I happen to be *out of print* by the time the editors of the *Biographia Britannica* arrive at letter *L.* (which ſeems extremely probable, according to the very deliberate progreſs of that work,) I hope they will not ſlightly paſs *me* over. If they ſhould, let them take the conſequence; as I here give them fair and timely notice, and they have not to plead as an excuſe, the want of materials.

I will give you one anecdote more of the great Doctor, becauſe it relates to a Scotchman very eminent in the literary world. I had it from Mr. Samuel, who was one of the party.

Dr. Johnſon being one afternoon at the houſe of Mr. Samuel's uncle, (whoſe name I have forgot) who lived in one of the ſtreets that leads from the Strand to the Thames, a number of gentlemen being preſent, they agreed to croſs the water and make a little excurſion on the other ſide; in ſtepping into

the

the boat one of the company ſaid, Mr. Hume, give me your hand. As ſoon as they were ſeated, our Doctor aſked Mr. Samuel if that was Hume the Deiſt. Mr. Samuel replied, that it was the great Mr. Hume, the deep metaphyſician and famous hiſtorian. Had I known that (ſaid the Doctor) I would not have put a foot in the boat with him. In the evening they had all agreed to ſup together at a houſe near St. Clement's Church in the Strand, and Doctor Johnſon coming in after the reſt of the company had ſometime been met, he walked up to Mr. Hume, and taking him by the hand, ſaid, "Mr. Hume, I am very glad to ſee you," and ſeemed well pleaſed to find him there; and it appeared to Mr. Samuel, that the Doctor had thus choſe to atone for his haſty expreſſion before related.

As I do not recollect any thing being recorded reſpecting the Doctor's *pugiliſtri* abilities, (excepting his knocking down Oſborn the bookſeller, be conſidered as ſuch) I ſhall beg leave to relate another anecdote which I received from the gentleman who favoured me with the preceding one.

Dr. Johnſon being at the water ſide when ſome ladies had juſt quitted a boat and were endeavouring to ſettle the fare with the waterman, this ſon of the Thames, like too many of his brethren, inſiſted on much more than his due, accompanying his demand in the uſual ſtile of eloquence, with abuſive language, the Doctor kindly interfering, furniſhed the ladies with the opportunity of retreating, and transferred the whole abuſe to himſelf, who finding that argument had made no impreſſion on the waterman, tried what he could effect by the ſtrength of his arm, and gave the refractory fellow a hearty drubbing, which had the deſired effect.

One word more concerning our great Lexicographer. It muſt be allowed by every candid and impartial perſon, that the extreme contempt and prejudice he entertained towards our friends of *North* Britain, reflected

a very

a very ſtrong ſhade on his character, which his warmeſt admirers cannot juſtify.

Were I, as a South Briton, called upon to give my fair and unprejudiced opinion reſpecting the national character of the natives of Scotland and thoſe of England, and I flatter myſelf I have had ample opportunities of obſerving the peculiar traits of both countries, I would ſay, that if we in England excel them in ſome virtues, they no leſs ſhine in others; and if the North-Britons poſſeſs ſome peculiar frailties and prejudices, we of the South are not intirely free from ours; ſo that were the virtues and vices of a certain number of each country placed in an hydroſtatical balance (it muſt however be a pretty large one,) I believe it very difficult to prognoſticate which of the two would preponderate. It is true, I have met with one very great villain in Scotland, in Mr. S. which only tends to prove there are probably *ſcoundrels* to be found every where, and that without taking the trouble which Diogenes did, in ſearch of an *honeſt man*; and I am much afraid,

afraid, were I to enquire of ſome North Britons, they could without any great difficulty point out to me ſome of my own countrymen as bad.

I deteſt all national prejudices, as I think it betrays great weakneſs in the parties who are influenced by them. Every nation of the habitable globe, nay each particular province of thoſe countries has certainly ſome peculiar traits belonging to it which diſtinguiſhes it from its neighbours. But if we are diſpoſed to view one another with the ſeverity of criticiſm, how eaſy, nay how frequent it is to diſcover ſuperior virtues (as we think) as well as abilities in that particular ſpot which gave birth to ourſelves, and equally diveſted of that ſtrict impartiality which alone can enable us to judge properly, diſcover proportionable blemiſhes in the natives of other countries.

" But travellers who want the *will*
" To mark the ſhapes of good and ill,
" With vacant ſtare thro' Europe range,
" And deem all bad, becauſe 'tis ſtrange,

" Thro'

"Thro' varying modes of life, we trace
"The finer trait, the latent grace,
"Quite free from ſpleen's incumb'ring load,
"At little evils on the road;
"So while the path of life I tread,
"A path to me with briars ſpread;
"Let me its tangled mazes ſpy,
"Like you, with gay, good humour eye,
"And be my ſpirit light as air,
"Call life a jeſt, and laugh at care."

In ſaying thus much, I do not mean to infer, that we ought not to be inſpired with a laudable ambition to excel, not thoſe of other countries only, but even thoſe with whom we are more intimately connected: but that ſhould be done without drawing invidious compariſons of the merits or demerits of others. In ſhort, let it be the earneſt endeavour of each country, and every individual of that country in particular, united under our amiable monarch, to ſtrive which ſhall have a ſuperior claim to the title of being GOOD MEN, uſeful members of ſociety, friends to the whole human race, and peaceable ſubjects of a government, which though not abſolutely in a ſtate of *perfection*—(and can

can that man be really deemed *wiſe* who expects to meet with perfection in any human eſtabliſhment ?) is ſtill happily ſuperior to every other in the known world, not forgetting our neighbours the French, our *natural enemies*, according to the long adopted language of national prejudice : but I hope that narrow minded diſpoſition will henceforth ceaſe ; certainly nature never deſigned us as enemies, it has placed our ſtations near to each other, and ſurely there is not ſo great a diſſimilarity in our national traits of character, as to occaſion us to be in perpetual enmity ! The contraſt now is leſs than ever. Like Britons, they have caught the ſpark of freedom, and nobly emancipated themſelves from a ſtate of abject and degrading ſlavery, to a diſtinguiſhed and honourable rank among nations. Long as time ſhall laſt, may they, with us, enjoy the bleſſing ſo glorioully obtained, with that due moderation which always properly diſtinguiſhes between *liberty* and *licentiouſneſs* ! The friends of *liberty* merit

rit the full enjoyment of every advantage attending it; thoſe of *licentiouſneſs* are unworthy the ſmalleſt ſhare of it.

But whither am I *travelling?* I am imperceptibly got into the road of politics. Coachman! turn off immediately into another road. —'Tis done, and happy am I to get out of ſo dangerous a track unhurt, which has broke the necks of numbers of clever fellows, and deprived many a bright genius of that ſuperior part of HIM from whence all his bright effuſions for the good of his country were emitted. For *patriotiſm* (as you know) is *always* the motive which impels thoſe worthies to ſuch hazardous expeditions as have ſo frequently in the event proved fatal to them. For proofs we need not conſult hiſtory; inſtances are, alas! freſh in our memories: witneſs London, 1780, and Birmingham, 1791.

At all events, it is certainly too rugged a road for a bookſeller to travel, it being already

ready crowded with many much abler adventurers. And whilst Mr. Burke, of the "Monarchy" (late of the "Fox") Inn, and Mr. Paine, at the sign of "the RIGHTS of MAN" provide rich and ample entertainment for "men and cattle," let the public take their choice, or if they please (which indeed appears to be the most rational mode) try them both, as some constitutions find one kind of food more easy of *digestion*, some the other; and I remain fully satisfied with the subordinate character of continuing an humble distributor of the viands provided by those and other very able caterers, and that upon easier terms than the admirers of such food will meet with elsewhere, according to the elegance or plainness of the *dishes* they are *served up* in. Some preferring *rich foreign china, elegantly gilt*; others, good substantial *English porcelain*; others, again being pleased with *Queen's ware*; and many more content with a *Welch dish*, or common *earthen ware*.

I am now suddenly conveyed again to Edinburgh. The old town, so called, has not

not much to boaſt of; but the new town is by far the moſt compleat and elegant I ever ſaw. In various towns of England and Scotland, I have indeed ſeen ſome good ſtreets, and many good houſes, but in this the whole is uniformly fine; not one houſe, much leſs a whole ſtreet that can be termed indifferent in the whole town.

And here let me do juſtice to North-Britiſh hoſpitality, and their very polite attention to ſuch Engliſhmen who happen to travel to the "land of cakes." I can truly ſay, that the polite and friendly behaviour of the inhabitants towards Mrs. Lackington and myſelf, claims our warmeſt gratitude and ſincereſt thanks. This the more civilized part of my countrymen will readily believe; and as to thoſe of another deſcription (happily but a comparatively ſmall number, I truſt) are welcome to treat my aſſertion with that contempt uſually attendant on prejudice, which is the reſult of ignorance.

The

The ſubject I now mean to enter into being a delicate one, permit me here to cloſe my letter; thus affording you a ſhort reſpite, and myſelf a little time for conſideration on the propriety of ſubmitting my ideas (as you ſeem determined all thoſe I ſend you ſhall be) to public notice.

I am,

Dear Friend,

Yours.

LETTER XLIV.

" Set *woman* in his eye, and in his walk,
" Among daughters of men the faireſt found,
" Many are in each region paſſing fair
" As the noon ſky, more like to goddeſſes
" Than mortal creatures; graceful and diſcreet,
" Expert in amorous arts, inchanting tongues:
" Perſuaſive, virgin majeſty, with mild
" And ſweet allay'd, yet terrible to approach;
" Skill'd to retire, and in retiring, draw
" Hearts after them, tangl'd in amorous nets;
" Such objects have the power to ſoften and tame
" Severeſt temper, ſmooth the rugged'ſt brow,
" Enerve and with voluptuous hope diſſolve;
" Draw out with credulous deſire,
" At will, the manlieſt reſoluteſt breaſt."

MILTON's Samſon Agoniſtes.

DEAR FRIEND,

IN my laſt I expreſſed ſome diffidence reſpecting the propriety of committing to paper my thoughts on a particular ſubject; I have ſince weighed it with due caution, and the conſideration of my having during the long courſe of my epiſtolary cor-

 reſpondence

respondence always declared my sentiments freely on every subject, soon determined me not to degrade myself by shrinking back, now it is so near drawing to a conclusion.

The subject then is—that bright lovely part of the creation, WOMAN!—the source of all our joys, the assuagers of all our griefs; deprived of whose powerful and attractive charms, man would be a wretch indeed. But alas! the utmost efforts of my abilities are far inadequate to do justice to their merits; happily that pleasing theme has engaged the attention of the ablest and worthiest of men, from the remotest period down to the present time; and I trust ever will, nay must, so long as a spark of virtue remains to dwell in the human breast. And when I reflect, that

"They are not only FAIR, but JUST as fair,"

I have nought to fear.

I therefore proceed with cheerfulness to say, that in Edinburgh, Glasgow, Stirling,

ling, &c. there are more really fine women to be found than in any place I ever visited. I do not mean to infer, we have not as many handsome women in England; but the idea I wish to convey is, that we have not so many *in proportion:* that is, Go to any public place where a number of ladies are assembled, in either of the above towns, and then go to any place in England where an equal number are met, and you will notice a greater number of fine women among the former, than among the latter. It must be obvious that in making this declaration, I allude to the genteeler part; for among the lower classes of women in Scotland, by being more exposed to the inclemency of the weather, the majority are very homely, and the want of the advantages of apparel, (which those in a higher sphere can avail themselves of, and know how to apply) together with their sluttish and negligent appearance, does not tend in the least to heighten their charms.

Having both read and heard much related of the manner of waſhing their linen, which I muſt confeſs I would not credit without having ocular demonſtration, during my continuance at Glaſgow, curioſity led me to the mead by the river ſide. For the poor women here, inſtead of the water coming to them, as in London, are obliged to travel loaded with their linen to the water; where you may daily ſee great numbers waſhing, in *their* way; which if ſeen by ſome of our London prudes, would incline them to form very unjuſt and uncharitable ideas of the modeſty of theſe Scottiſh laſſes. Many of them give a trifle to be accommodated with the uſe of a large waſh-houſe near the water, where about a hundred may be furniſhed with every convenience for their purpoſe. But by far the greateſt part make fires, and heat the water in the open air, and as they finiſh their linen, they ſpread it on the graſs to dry; which is the univerſal mode of drying throughout Scotland. Here the

"Maidens bleach their ſummer ſmocks."

I had

I had walked to and fro ſeveral times, and began to conclude that the cuſtom of getting into the tubs and treading on the linen, either never had been practiſed, or was come into diſuſe; but I had not waited more than half an hour, when many of them jumped into the tubs, without ſhoes or ſtockings, with their ſhifts and petticoats drawn up far above the knees, and ſtamped away with great compoſure in their countenances, and with all their ſtrength, no Scotchman taking the leaſt notice, or even looking towards them, conſtant habit having rendered the ſcene perfectly familiar.

On converſing with ſome gentlemen of Glaſgow on this curious ſubject, they aſſured me that theſe ſingular laundreſſes (as they appeared to me) were ſtrictly modeſt women, who only did what others of unblemiſhed reputation had been accuſtomed to for a long ſeries of years; and added, that at any other time a purſe of gold would not tempt them to draw the curtain ſo high. By way of contraſt, let me obſerve that many of our

London ſervant-*maids*, though not always ſo nice in other reſpects, would not be ſeen thus habited *in public* on any terms, leſt their precious characters ſhould be called in queſtion. A ſtriking inſtance of the powerful influence of habit! Pomfret ſays;

> "Cuſtom's the world's great idol we adore,
> "And knowing that we ſeek to know no more."

Moſt of the female ſervants in Edinburgh, Glaſgow, &c. do all their work, and run about the town the fore part of the day without ſtays, ſhoes or ſtockings; and on Sundays I ſaw the country-women going to Ward's Kirk, in the ſame manner (ſtays excepted;) however they do not go into kirk, till they have dreſſed their legs and feet; for that purpoſe they ſeat themſelves on the graſs, ſomewhere near, put on their ſhoes and ſtockings, and garter up very deliberately,

> "Nor heed the paſſenger who looks that way."

Moſt of theſe poor young country-women go without any caps or hats; they have in general

general fine heads of hair, many plait it, others let it hang loose down their backs; and I assure you, my friend, they look very agreeable.

I returned each time through Buxton, where staying a week or two, I visited Castleton, and spent several hours in exploring that stupendous cavern, called The Devil's A— in the Peak. I also surveyed Poole's Hole, near Buxton, and purchased a great variety of petrifactions. In our way home I saw the great marble manufactory at Aston, in the water, spent some days at Matlock, the most romantic village that I ever saw, but the sight of it cost me dear; as we were conveyed there in an old crazy post-chaise, in which I caught a violent cold, the lining being very damp.

I am,

Dear Friend,

Yours.

LETTER XLV.

"Good ſeen expected, evil unforeſeen,
"Appear by turns as fortune ſhifts the ſcene:
"Some rais'd aloft come tumbling down amain,
"Then fall ſo hard, they bound and riſe again."

DRYDEN's Virgil.

"New turns and changes every day
"Are of inconſtant chance the conſtant arts;
"Soon fortune gives, ſoon takes away,
"She comes, embraces, nauſeates you, and parts.
"But if ſhe ſtays or if ſhe goes,
"The wiſe man little joy or little ſorrow knows;
"For over all there hangs a doubtful fate,
"And few there be who're always fortunate.
"One gains by what another is bereft:
"The frugal deſtinies have only left
"A common bank of happineſs below,
"Maintain'd, like nature, by an ebb and flow."

How's Indian Emp.

DEAR FRIEND,

I Did not intend to trouble you or the public with an account of any more of my *wonderful travels*, but being now at Lyme, for want of other amuſements this rainy

rainy morning, I thought that a ſhort account of this journey might afford you ſome entertainment.

My ſtate of health being but indifferent, and Mrs. Lackington's ſtill worſe, I was induced to try what effect a journey would produce; it being immaterial what part I travelled to; and as I had not for a long time ſeen my native place, and perhaps might not be furniſhed with another opportunity, we reſolved to viſit it.

"And many a year elaps'd, return to view
"Where once the cottage ſtood, the hawthorn grew,
"Rememberance wakes with all her buſy train,
"Swells at my breaſt————————
—— —— —— —— —— ——
"I ſtill had hopes, for pride attends us ſtill,
"Amidſt the ſwains to ſhew my book-learn'd ſkill,
"Yes, let the rich deride, with proud diſdain
"The ſimple bleſſings of the lowly train,
"To me more dear, congenial to my heart,
"One native charm, than all the gloſs of art;
"Spontaneous joys, where nature has its play,
"The ſoul adopts, and owns their firſt-born ſway:
"Lightly they frolic o'er the vacant mind,
"Unenvy'd, unmoleſted, unconfin'd."

GOLDSMITH.

Accordingly

Accordingly in July laſt, 1791, we ſet out from Merton, which I now make my chief reſidence, taking Bath, Briſtol, &c. in our way to my native place Wellington.

In Briſtol, Exbridge, Bridgewater, Taunton, Wellington, and other places, I amuſed myſelf in calling on ſome of my maſters, with whom I had about twenty years before worked as a journeyman ſhoemaker. I addreſſed each with, "*Pray Sir, have you got any occaſion?*" which is the term made uſe of by journeymen in that uſeful occupation, when ſeeking employment. Moſt of thoſe honeſt men had quite forgot my perſon, as many of them had not ſeen me ſince I worked for them: ſo that it is not eaſy for you to conceive with what ſurprize and aſtoniſhment they gazed on me. For you muſt know that I had the vanity (I call it *humour*) to do this in my chariot, attended by my ſervants; and on telling them who I was, all appeared to be very happy to ſee me, And I aſſure you, my friend, it afforded me much real pleaſure to ſee ſo many of my old

acquaintances

acquaintances alive and well, and tolerable happy. The following lines often occurred to my mind:

> " Far from the madding crowd's ignoble ſtriſe,
> " Their ſober wiſhes never learn'd to ſtray:
> " Along the cool ſequeſter'd vale of life
> " They keep the noiſeleſs tenor of their way."

At Taunton and Wellington it ſeemed to be the unanimous determination of all the poorer ſort, that I ſhould by no means be deficient in *old acquaintance*. Some poor ſouls declared that they had known me for *fifty* years (that is, years before I was born;) others had danced me in their arms a thouſand times; nay, better ſtill, ſome knew my grandmother; but, beſt of all, one old man claimed acquaintance with me, for having ſeen me many times on the top of a ſix-and-twenty round ladder, balanced on the chin of a merry Andrew! The old man was however egregiouſly miſtaken, as I never was ſo precariouſly exalted, my ambition, as you well know, taking a very different turn. But that was of no conſequence: all the old fellow

fellow wanted was *a ſhilling*—and I gave it him. No matter (as Sterne ſays) from what motive. I never examine into theſe things. This I obſerved, that none of them were common beggars, but poor uſeful labouring people. Giving to common ſtrollers is but encouraging idleneſs and every other vice. *And as ſmall matters made many happy*, I was ſupremely ſo, to be the means of contributing to their comfort. And indeed who would heſitate at being the means of diffuſing happineſs on ſuch eaſy terms, and with ſo little trouble?

The bells rang merrily all the day of my arrival. I was alſo honoured with the attention of many of the moſt reſpectable people in and near Wellington and other parts: Some of whom were pleaſed to inform me, that the reaſon of their paying a particular attention to me was their having heard, and now having themſelves an opportunity of obſerving, that I did not ſo far forget myſelf, as many proud upſtarts had done; that the notice I took of my poor relations and

old

old acquaintance merited the reſpect and approbation of every real gentleman. They were alſo pleaſed to expreſs a wiſh, that as ſoon as I could diſpoſe of my buſineſs, I would come down and ſpend the remainder of my days among them. This reception was the more pleaſing, as I have ſometimes obſerved a contrary conduct practiſed by ſome, who have been pleaſed to ſtile themſelves gentlemen, and on that ſcore think that they have a right to treat men of buſineſs (however reſpectable they may be) as by much their inferiors; and it too often happens that one of thoſe petty gentry who poſſeſſes but a hundred or two per annum, will behave in a haughty manner to a man in buſineſs who ſpends as many thouſands; but ſuch ſhould be told, that a real gentleman in any company will never either by word or action, attempt to make the meaneſt perſon feel his inferiority, but on the contrary.

They ſhould be informed alſo how highly impolitic and unjuſt it is to attempt to fix a ſtigma a ſtigma on trade and commerce, the very things that have cauſed England to riſe ſo high in the political ſcale of Europe.

'Tis true that even in England you may ſee great numbers of very opulent tradeſmen who have not an idea but what they have acquired behind the counter; but you may alſo find many thouſands of the ſame claſs of life who are poſſeſſed of very liberal ideas, and who would not commit an action that would diſgrace a title. For my part, I will endeavour to adhere to the advice given by Perſius as it is tranſlated:

"Study thyſelf what rank, or what degree
"The wiſe Creator has ordain'd for thee:
"And all the offices of that ſtate
"Perform! and with thy prudence guide thy fate."

William Jones, Eſq. of Foxdowne, near Wellington, informed me of a remarkable *prognoſtication* in my favour; he told me that when I was a boy, about twelve years of age, Mr. Paul, then a very conſiderable wholeſale linen-draper, in Friday-ſtreet, London, (I believe

believe ſtill living) paſſing by my father's houſe one day, ſtopped at the door and aſked various queſtions about ſome guinea-pigs which I had in a box. My anſwers it ſeems pleaſed and ſurprized him, and turning towards Mr. Jones, ſaid, "*Depend upon it, ſir, that boy will one day riſe far above the ſituation that his preſent mean circumſtances ſeem to promiſe.*" So who knows what a great man I may yet be?—perhaps

"A double pica in the book of fame."

Give me leave to introduce another prediction, though not altogether ſo pleaſing as that juſt related. An Italian gentleman, and if we may judge by appearance, a perſon of rank, was ſome years ſince looking at ſome books of *palmiſtry* in my ſhop, and at the ſame time endeavoured to convince me of the reality of that ſcience. In the midſt of his diſcourſe, he ſuddenly ſeized my right-hand, and looking for ſome time with great attention on the various lines, he informed me that I had twice been in danger of loſing my my life, once by water, and once by a wound in my head. He was certainly right, but I believe by chance, as I have many other times been in very great danger. He added, that I had much of the goddeſs *Venus* in me, but much more of *Mars*; and aſſured me that I ſhould go to the wars, and arrive at great honour. He likewiſe informed me, that I ſhould die by *fire-arms* pointed *over a wall*.—How far the former part of this gentleman's prediction may be relied on, I will not pretend to decide, but the laſt part of it was lately very near coming to ſuch a deciſion as would have proved the fallibility of that part of his prognoſtication, though even in that caſe he might have pleaded his being pretty near the matter of fact, only ſubſtituting *gunpowder* inſtead of *fire-arms*, and I ſhould not have had it in my power to contend the point with him. I will endeavour to render this intelligible: On Tueſday the fifth of July, 1791, I very nearly eſcaped being blown up with the powder-mills belonging to Mr. Bridges, at Ewell, near Mer-

ton

ton in Surry. A quarter of an hour before that event took place, I was riding out within one mile of the mills, and having enquired of Mr. Rofe, at Coom-Houfe, for the way that leads round by the mills, I actually rode part of the way, with an intent of vifiting them. But fomehow or other, I fcarce knew why, I turned my horfe about, and a few minutes after I had done fo, I faw the fatal cataftrophe; which happening by day, refembled a large cloud of fmoke, of a very light colour, and the report reached my ears immediately after. I inftantly concluded, it could be nothing lefs than the powder-mills blown up; and on my return to my houfe at Merton, I foon learnt that it was the identical powder-mills that in all probability I fhould have been in, or clofe by, at the time of the explofion. By this accident it feems four men were killed, fome of whom had large families. The bodies were fo much mangled by the explofion, that they could not be diftinguifhed

 from

from each other, and the head of one of them was thrown to a great diſtance.

But to proceed with my journey. I eſteem myſelf peculiarly happy, on one account in particular, that I undertook it; and have only to regret it did not take place ſooner, as it tended to undeceive me in a matter in which I had long been in an error. The caſe was this: I had for ſeven years paſt ſuppoſed that the parents of my firſt wife were dead; and on enquiring after them of Mr. Caſh at Bridgewater, he confirmed the report. However, as we paſſed through South Petherton, being but a mile from the place where they formerly lived, I could not help ſtopping to find out the time when they died, and what other particulars I could learn relative to them, but to my very great ſurpriſe, I was informed that they were both living at Newton, two miles diſtant. On this information I gave the coachman orders to drive us there, but ſtill could ſcarcely credit that they really were alive.—But, O my dear Friend,

Friend, it is utterly impoſſible for me to deſcribe the ſenſations of Mrs. Lackington and myſelf, on entering

> ———————— "The cobweb'd cottage,
> "With ragged wall of mold'ring mud,"

which contained them!

> "Then Poverty, grim ſpectre, roſe,
> "And horror o'er the proſpect threw."
>
> AMWELL.

There we found—two

> "Poor human ruins, tottering o'er the grave!"

The dim light on our entrance ſeemed a little to flaſh in the ſocket, and every moment threatened to diſappear for ever! while their "pale wither'd hands were ſtretched out towards me, trembling at once with eagerneſs and age." Never before did I feel the full force of Shakeſpear's deſcription,

> "———— Laſt ſcene of all
> "That ends this ſtrange eventful hiſtory,
> "Is ſecond childiſhneſs; and mere oblivion:
> "Sans teeth, ſans eyes, ſans taſte: ſans every thing."

 From

From ſuch a ſtate of poverty and wretchedneſs, Good God, deliver every worthy character.

The old man is ninety years of age, and the good old woman eighty. The old man's intellects are much impaired; he for a moment knew me, and then his recollection forſook him. The old woman retained her ſenſes and knowledge during the whole of the time we were with them. On inquiry I found, that what little property they had poſſeſſed had been all expended for ſome years.

> "How many once in Fortune's lap high fed,
> "Solicit the cold hand of Charity!
> "To ſhock us more—ſolicit it in vain!"
>
> Dr. Young.

Amidſt this dreary ſcene, it was ſome alleviation to learn that their pious ſon had given them weekly as much as he could afford from his own little family, and I have added enough to render them as comfortable as their great age can poſſibly admit of. But for your ſake and my own, I will drop this gloomy

gloomy ſubject; which to me proved one of the moſt affecting ſcenes that ever I experienced in the whole courſe of my life.

During our continuance at Wellington, I one morning rode over to Black Down, on purpoſe to inſpect an immenſe heap of ſtones on the top of the hill, ſtrait before the town, which I remembered to have ſeen when a boy. The diſtance from Wellington is about two miles. Thoſe ſtones cover about an acre of ground, and riſe to a great height. The country people informed me with great gravity, that "the Devil brought them there in one night in his *leathern apron.*" But the name of it, as well as the form, prove what it was. It is called Symmon's *Borough* or *Barrow*; which, you know, ſignifies a burial-place. I ſhould not have taken any notice of it here, had I ever ſeen any Barrow of *ſtones* beſides this, and five other ſmaller Barrows, about half a mile from the large one. The country people informed me that the *devil* brought the five

 heaps

heaps in his *glove.* I alſo obſerved the remains of a large camp near the ſpot. Camden has taken notice of a large camp at Roach Caſtle, three or four miles from hence; it is ſtrange that neither he nor Gough ſhould take any notice of ſo ſingular a Barrow as this certainly is.

I remain,

Dear Friend,

Yours.

LETTER

LETTER XLVI.

" Ye who amid this feverifh world would wear
" A body free of pain, of cares the mind,
" Fly the rank city : fhun its turbid air :
" Breathe not the chaos of eternal fmoke
" And volatile corruption from the dead.
" The dying, fickening, and the living world
" Exhal'd : To fully Heaven's tranfparent dome
" With dim mortality. It is not air
" That from a thoufand lungs reeks back to thine,
" Sated with exhalations, rank and fell,
" The fpoil of dunghills, and the putrid thaw
" Of Nature : when from fhape and texture fhe
" Relapfed into fighting Elements ;
" It is not air, but floats a naufeous mafs
" Of all obfcene, corrupt, offenfive things,
" Much moifture hurts : here a fordid bath,
" With daily rancour fraught, relaxes more
" The folids than fimple moifture can."

ARMSTRONG's Art of Health.

Lyme, Sep. 4, 1791.

DEAR FRIEND,

BEING now at one of thofe places ufually called *watering-places*, that is, a place where invalids refort in great numbers for the real or pretended purpofe of drinking the waters for which each particular ſituation is in repute, and bathing in them with a view to the reſtoration of their health; I ſhall trouble you with a few obſervations which have occurred to me on the ſubject. I cannot entertain a doubt but that many by this practice have been highly benefited; but at the ſame time I muſt obſerve that ſuch relief is only to be reaſonably expected where the parties poſſeſs a ſufficient ſhare of prudence to conform to thoſe rules which are laid down to them by thoſe who are beſt acquainted with the nature of the ſeveral complaints, the ſtrength, or weakneſs of their conſtitutions, and the different virtues thoſe ſeveral waters poſſeſs, ſo as properly to adapt them to each particular caſe, by drinking the waters at proper ſtated periods, as well as in proper doſes; beſides conforming to ſuch a regimen as ſhall co-operate with them in producing the deſired effect. But where invalids neglect all, or indeed any of thoſe rules, is it not rather an abſurdity to expect relief?—I will endeavour to explain myſelf:

Thoſe waters either poſſeſs powerful virtues, or they do not. If they do, is it not obvious that ſome judgment and caution is neceſſary in the uſe of them? which muſt either produce good or bad effects, according to the prudence with which they are applied. If on the other hand, they are of ſo inſignificant a nature, that they may be uſed at any time, and in any proportion without injury; and that too in diſorders and conſtitutions very much varying from each other, then ſurely the inference muſt be, that no dependance is to be placed on them, and conſequently it matters not if they are never uſed at all. For what purpoſe then do ſuch numbers put themſelves to the inconvenience, expence, and trouble of travelling (frequently from diſtant parts of the kingdom) and that too when many of them are in ſo debilitated a ſtate, that their very removal is attended with extreme danger, and ſometimes proves fatal? But that thoſe waters are not inactive, I am well convinced, having ſeen the bad effects ariſing from the im-

prudent

prudent uſe of them, in many inſtances, as well as the happy conſequences attending their being uſed with due caution.

I was firſt led into theſe reflections by having been highly diverted, when I viſited Buxton ſeveral ſummers, with the prepoſterous and abſurd conduct of ſome of the company who reſorted thither for the purpoſe of reſtoring their health. I remember ſix or ſeven gentlemen informing me, that they were violently afflicted with the gout and rheumatiſm, and had undertaken this journey in hopes of receiving benefit by the waters. Theſe gentlemen often rode or walked about the cold dreary hills, in very damp wet mornings, and afterwards drank claret from three o'clock in the afternoon to three the next morning: But I did not continue there long enough to be a witneſs of the happy effects which muſt inevitably be produced by a perſeverance in ſuch a judicious regimen.

I alſo viſited Freeſtone, near Boſton in Lincolnſhire: to which place a number of

tradeſmen

tradeſmen and farmers reſorted with their wives, in hopes of receiving benefit from the uſe of the ſalt water, in a variety of complaints; which they had been adviſed to do by the faculty, for a month, with particular directions to bathe every other day, and on the intermediate days to drink half a pint of the water in the courſe of that day. But theſe wiſe people on duly conſidering the matter, were fully convinced that this would detain them from their families and buſineſs longer than was altogether convenient; and alſo (which they ſuppoſed their medical friends never thought of) that they could bathe the full number of times, and drink the preſcribed quantity of the water, in a week or a fortnight at fartheſt, and thus not only expedite the cure, but likewiſe enable them to return to their families and buſineſs ſo much earlier, as well as ſave the neceſſary expences attending their continuing for ſuch a length of time at the watering place. Theſe united conſiderations appeared to them ſo conſiſtent with prudence and oeconomy,

that

that they reſolved to put them into immediate practice. I remonſtrated with ſeveral of theſe good people on the impropriety of their conduct; but whether they concluded I was a party intereſted in detaining them on the ſpot, or whether they deemed my judgement inferior to their own, I know not; but I obſerved that ſome of them bathed ſeveral times in a day, and drank ſalt water by the quart, the conſequence of which was, that they left the place when the time expired which *they* had preſcribed to themſelves, much worſe than they came. Some indeed were ſo very weak, that I am perſuaded they could with difficulty reach their homes alive. And in theſe caſes the want of ſucceſs, inſtead of being attributed to the *folly* of the patients, is generally transferred to the *waters*, and to the want of judgment in thoſe who adviſed the uſe of them.

I aſſure you, my dear friend, this is pretty much the caſe at Lyme. My rooms commanding a view of the ſea, I have this and ſeveral other days noticed many decent look-

ing

ing men going down the beach three or four times in as many hours, and drinking a pint of water each time. I have made the ſame obſervation at *Seaton*, *Charmouth* and other places, ſo that the obſervation of Crabſhaw's nurſe in "the adventures of Sir Lancelot Greaves" has frequently occurred to me: "Bleſſed be G— (ſaid ſhe) my patient is in a fair way! his apozem has had a bleſſed effect! five and twenty ſtools ſince three o'clock in the morning!"

Relating theſe particulars to a medical friend, he informed me that ſuch ſpecimens of ignorance and obſtinacy were by no means confined to the watering places; as he had in the courſe of his practice met with repeated inſtances, where patients with a view of haſtening the cure, and *getting out of the doctor's hands* (whom the vulgar *charitably* ſuppoſe wiſh to retain them there as long as poſſible) have ſwallowed a half pint mixture intended for ſeveral doſes at once, and a whole box of pills in the ſame manner. The conſequences of which have been, that from the

the violence of the operations they have remained *in his hands* a considerable time, some so long as life (thus foolishly trifled with) lasted.

But here are many of another class; some of whom, though not *all*, came on purpose to bathe, but during the whole of their continuance here, never found time to bathe once. Some hasten to the billiard-room as soon as they are out of their beds in the morning, and there they continue until bed-time again. A few of these are indeed much benefited, being cured of *consumptions in their purses*, while others become proportionably as much emaciated. And a great number, both of ladies and gentlemen devote the whole of their time to dressing, eating, and playing at whist. Charming *exercise* it must be! as they frequently sit still in their chairs, for eight or ten hours together.

Here are others again, who, like the gentlemen at Buxton, sit drinking until three or four in the morning; making a delightful noise,

noiſe, to *compoſe* thoſe in the ſame houſe who are real *invalids*, and who deſirous of obtaining reſt, retire early, though frequently to very little purpoſe.

I have alſo obſerved, that all the above places are as healthy for *horſes*, as they are for their maſters. For as the innkeepers depend almoſt entirely on the ſeaſon, they take great care, and do all they can to make theſe places comfortable. So that if gentlemen have fat, lazy, prancing horſes, and want to reduce them in ſize and temper, they may be ſure to have it done in ſome of the inns and ſtables at the various watering places: Where ſuch *hay* is procured as muſt infallibly anſwer the purpoſe even though they be allowed a double portion of corn.

There is yet another very great advantage (which I had like to have forgot) reſulting from attending the watering places. Such gentlemen who happen to have ſervants too honeſt, too induſtrious, too attentive, too cleanly, too humble, too ſober, &c. by taking

ing them to any of theſe places, where they have ſo much leiſure time, and where theſe party-coloured gentry meet together ſo often, and in ſuch numbers, no one can go away unimproved, except he is a very dull fellow indeed.—This is not merely my own obſervation: for ſeveral gentlemen of my acquaintance aſſured me that they had always found their ſervants improved prodigiouſly after each of theſe excurſions.

We purpoſe ſetting out for Weymouth in a day or two: but as I intend that this ſhall be my laſt epiſtle, I will not conclude it until I arrive at Merton.

"If into diſtant parts I vainly roam,
"And novelty from varied objects try,
"My buſy thoughts reſeek their wonted home,
"And ſicken at the vain variety."

Merton, Sept. 15th. We arrived here ſafe laſt night, being my birth-day. At Weymouth we had the honour of walking ſeveral evenings on the Eſplanade, with their majeſties and the four princeſſes. His majeſty

ſeems

ſeems in perfect health and ſpirits, and diffuſes life and ſpirits to all around him. Long, very long may he continue to enjoy the ſame degree of health and happineſs! But I could not help pitying Mr. Hughes, the manager of the Theatre there; as the company in general ſeem to pay but very little attention to plays, while they can partake of the pleaſure of walking and breathing the ſea air with ſo many of the royal family. But his majeſty, whoſe humanity is by no means the leaſt of his many virtues, will no doubt conſider Mr. Hughes, who is induſtrious to an extreme, as he is ſcarce a moment idle. For beſides managing his company, performing himſelf ſix, ſometimes eight characters in a week, he paints all his own ſcenes, and attends to many other ſubjects; and although he has had a large expenſive family (nine children,) the theatre there, and that alſo at Exeter is his own. Weymouth theatre he rebuilt about four years ſince; every thing is very neat; his ſcenes are fine, and his company a very good one. I ſaw them perform four pieces with a deal of pleaſure; notwithſtanding I had often ſeen the ſame in London, I remarked here as I had long before done at Bath, that the parts were more equally ſupported than they often are at Drury-lane and Covent-garden; for although at thoſe places we have many firſt-rate actors and actreſſes, yet ſometimes parts are given to ſuch wretched performers as would diſgrace a barn, which I never ſaw done at Bath or Weymouth.

In our road home, within half a mile of Dorcheſter, we ſtopt and ſpent half an hour in looking round the famous Roman Amphitheatre. It is cloſe to the road, on the right hand ſide, and covers about an acre of ground. It is judged that ten thouſand people might without interruption have beheld ſuch exerciſes as were exhibited in this ſchool of the ancients; it is called Mambury, and is ſuppoſed to be the compleateſt antiquity of the kind in England.

I alſo amuſed myſelf, as I travelled through Dorſetſhire and Wiltſhire, in ſurveying many of the numerous camps, fortifications,

tifications, and barrows; which laſting monuments of antiquity are to be ſeen in abundance in theſe counties, a great number of them remain in a perfect ſtate.

Nor could I any longer omit the opportunity of ſeeing that ſtupendous piece of antiquity on Saliſbury Plain, the famous *Stonehenge*, two miles from Ameſbury. We ſpent near two hours there in aſtoniſhment; and had not night came on, we ſhould not have been able to have parted from it ſo ſoon. We found a very good inn at Ameſbury, which proves very convenient to ſuch whom curioſity may detain on this wonderful ſpot until it is late. It is remarkable, that although ſo many able antiquaries have devoted their time and attention to the inveſtigation of Stonehenge, it remains ſtill a matter undecided when and for what purpoſe this amazing pile was formed; nor is there leſs cauſe of admiration, how ſtones of ſuch magnitude were brought hither! I ſhall not preſume, either to decide on this curious point, or offer any conjectures of my own.

I have now, ſir, not only given you the moſt material circumſtances of my life, but have alſo ſuper-added a ſhort ſketch of ſome of my *travels.* And ſhould the fine air of Merton preſerve the ſtock of health and ſpirits which I have acquired in this laſt excurſion, I intend during the ſummer to ſpend a few hours in the middle of three or four days in every week in Chiſwell-ſtreet, devoting the mornings and evenings to my rural retreat,

"Where cheerfulneſs triumphant fair,
"Diſpels the painful cloud of care,
"O, ſweet of language, mild of mien,
"O, Virtue's friend, and pleaſure's queen!
"By thee our board with flow'rs is crown'd,
"By thee with ſongs our walks reſound;
"By thee the ſprightly mornings ſhine,
"And ev'ning hours in peace decline."

During the winter I purpoſe ſpending moſt of my time in town; where I hope again to enjoy the company of you, ſir, and ſome others of our old philoſophical friends. In the mean time, I am,

Dear friend, yours.

P. S.

P. S. I ſhould deem myſelf deficient in point of juſtice to the ingenious artiſt who painted the portrait from whence the engraving affixed as a frontiſpiece to this volume is taken, if I did not embrace this opportunity of acknowledging the approbation it has been honoured with by all who have ſeen it, as a ſtriking likeneſs.

The following circumſtance, though to many it may appear in a ludicrous point of view, yet as it is a fact which does not depend ſolely on my aſſertion, I ſhall not heſitate to mention it.

Before the portrait was finiſhed, Mrs. Lackington, accompanied by another lady, called on the painter to view it. Being introduced into a room filled with portraits, her little dog (the faithful *Argus*) being with her, immediately ran to that particular portrait, paying it the ſame attention as he is always accuſtomed to do the original; which made it neceſſary to remove him from it, leſt he ſhould damage it; though this was not accompliſhed without expreſſions of diſſatisfaction on the part of poor Argus.

Thoſe

Thoſe who are converſant in hiſtory will not doubt the fact; ſeveral ſimilar inſtances being recorded of the ſagacity and nice diſcrimination of theſe animals.

A PRAYER.

" O may my work for ever live!
" (Dear friend, this ſelfiſh zeal forgive;)
" May no vile miſcreant ſaucy cook
" Preſume to tear my learned book,
" To ſinge his fowl for nicer gueſt,
" Or pin it on the turkey's breaſt.
" Keep it from paſtry bak'd, or buying,
" From broiling ſteak, and fritters frying;
" From lighting pipe or wrapping ſnuff.
" Or caſing up a feather muff;
" From all the ſeveral ways the grocer
" (Who to the learned world's a foe, Sir,)
" Has found in twiſting, folding, packing,
" His brain and ours at once a racking:
" And may it never curl the head
" Of either living block, or dead.
" Thus when all dangers they have paſt,
" My leaves like leaves of braſs ſhall laſt.
" No blaſt ſhall from a critic's breath,
" By vile infection cauſe their death,
" 'Till they in flames at laſt expire,
" And help to ſet the world on fire."

AMEN.

FINIS.

www.ingramcontent.com/pod-product-compliance
Lightning Source LLC
Chambersburg PA
CBHW052331110726
47901CB00005B/1196
* 9 7 8 3 3 3 7 0 9 4 9 3 5 *